JUNK ON THE HILL

JUNK ON THE HILL

A MYSTERY BY

JEREMY PIKSER

Carroll & Graf Publishers, inc.
New York

Published by arrangement with Pluto Press

"Lush Life" reproduced by kind permission of
Tempo Music, 750 Park Avenue, New York, NY 10021

First Carroll & Graf edition 1985

Carroll & Graf Publishers, Inc.
260 Fifth Avenue
New York, NY 10001

Library of Congress Cataloging in Publication Data

Pikser, Jeremy.
  Junk on the hill.

  (Pluto crime)
  I. Title. II. Series.
PS3566.I47J8   1985   813'.54   85-3761
ISBN 0-81884-134-X

Manufactured in the United States of America

For Luise

1. Melody Gold

Joe Posner folded his *Bergen Record* and lobbed it onto the corner of his desk. He took a gulp of his now cold coffee and screwed up his face in exaggerated displeasure. The late afternoon sun was that waited-for-it-all-winter warm, and he leaned back into it gratefully, putting his feet up on the desk, letting one hand dangle at his side and slowly kneading his prematurely balding head with the other.

Business was slow.

A cowboy actor was President; a power-hungry general was Secretary of State; the Knicks couldn't beat the good teams; and business was slow.

Joe Posner wondered why. When the economy is bad it's supposed to be good for the divorce business. And like it or not, Joe Posner was in the divorce business. All five-seven, one sixty pounds of him. He hadn't expected to do divorce work when he'd quit Customs and applied for his private investigator's licence. The detectives on T.V. never did divorce work. But they didn't work in the suburbs, either. The first six months had been rough for Joe Posner: one missing person whom he hadn't found, two accident witnesses whom he had, half a dozen errands for the county court. Then he'd dropped a slice of pizza on an assistant prosecutor, the court jobs stopped, and Joe Posner started doing divorce work. The next six months had been better. Not great, but the rent was usually paid on time. Until this month. Lately, even the divorce business had slowed down. The economy must be *so* bad, he figured, that though people were getting more divorces, they were economizing by doing the snooping themselves. If so, it would indicate a new trend in the surburban American lifestyle that would spell disaster for struggling detectives everywhere.

He might have to call his father's cousin Sid and ask for more free-lance indexing work on *The Bibliography of Tibetan*

Studies (Sid's tax write-off). The thought made him shudder.

Posner was beginning to reach his grim-reality saturation point, and almost ready to pull out his office twelve-inch to check out an afternoon hospital soap, when he was startled by the unfamiliar sound of his front door buzzer. A client? Probably a salesman. He pressed the door release button anyway.

After an unusually light and rapid flurry of footsteps, a young girl presented herself between the faded green curtains at the top of the stairs. Posner guessed her to be sixteen, give or take a year. Her hair was a luxuriant mass of pure black that fell freely almost to her waist. Her face wasn't especially pretty, but had that smooth tan that only rich people have in April. She was small, about five feet, and if her body wasn't precociously developed, it was dressed so it would look like it was, in a green leotard, an expensive red belt with a turquoise and gold buckle, and a tight denim skirt, slit deeply enough to show Joe Posner more sixteen-year-old thigh than he was ready for. She stood in the doorway, head back, tanned arms floating a few inches from her sides. She was used to scoring points with her looks.

'Don't tell me you want a divorce,' Posner said without getting up.

'Don't be stupid.' Her voice had an unpleasant, almost whiney edge, that Posner didn't think she knew about. 'Can I sit down?'

'If I can watch – I mean please do. What can I do for you, Miss . . . '

'Gold.' She sat down, crossing her legs as she did so. Either she didn't get his joke or was seeing it and raising it. 'Call me Melody.' She looked up at him coquettishly, after lowering her head for the purpose. 'Somebody stole something from me, and I want you to get it back.'

'I see. Well, Melody, I don't normally do work for minors . . . May I ask how you happen to come to me?'

'My friend Dessie Levine said you spied on her mother when her parents were splitting up, and you were cute.' She stared flatly into his green eyes, her silence implying no disagreement with the verdict. 'I'll give you a thousand dollars to start and two hundred dollars a day for every day after tomorrow.' She looked around the sub-Spartan office. 'It looks like you could use it.'

There was no arguing that point, and it kicked the hell out of all the other points that might have ended the conversation before it started. 'Well, *if* I take your case, I'm going to have to know a little more about it.' The girl rolled her eyes, taking his facetiousness for genuine stupidity. 'For instance, what was taken, when, and why don't you ask your parents to go to the police about it?'

She closed her eyes and shook her head, like a five-year-old playing exasperated parent with a doll. 'You *are* cute; but maybe a little dumb? I hope you can handle this.'

Joe Posner just took that one.

'O.K. One: What was taken is a little antique amethyst and amber box,' she lectured. 'Two: it was stolen Friday night. Three: My father's out of the country, my mother's a total pig, and I don't like cops. By the way, I'll pay a lot to whoever has it to get it back.'

'Natch.' Posner saw no way to play this scene but deadpan. His own high school experience was clearly going to be of no help. 'You realized it was gone on Friday?'

'I had a party Friday night. It was the last night before Easter vacation. Everybody from school was there. Anyone could of gotten into my room and taken it. It was in my bottom dresser drawer.' She paused to gather some extra sincerity. 'Listen, I really don't want my parents to know about this, you know? My father gave it to me as a really special present. O.K.? A secret. My mother doesn't know about it.' She stiffened visibly on the word 'mother', the way a moral majority preacher might say 'abortionist.' While she spoke, she ran the fingers of her right hand slowly back and forth along the smooth, perfect skin of her left arm.

'What school do you go to, Melody?' Joe Posner took out a pad and started to take notes, more because he wanted something businesslike to do, than because he'd decided to take the case.

'The Human Learning Space.'

'Excuse me?'

3

'It's an alternative school over on Ramapo Street. Where the Jewish Community Center used to be.'

'Oh yeah. I've been by there. Sort of a hippy place, right?'

Melody Gold didn't try very hard to conceal the ridicule in her smile. 'Oh, wow, groovy vibes, mahn.'

Posner took that one, too. A paragon of self-control, Posner was. All he allowed himself was a brief reflection on how unattractive parody could be in the wrong hands. 'What is it exactly that you think I can do that you can't do yourself? I mean, you know these kids, and if you put up a sign at school offering a thousand bucks for the return of the box, no questions asked, don't you think you'd get it?' Posner made a mental note, as he spoke, to kick himself hard for trying to talk himself out of several months' rent.

'Do I have to tell you everything? First, like I already told you, school is on vacation, and I really can't wait two whole weeks. Second, I'm going out of town in a few days, so I really won't have time to talk to everyone one by one, like you could. And I want it found by the time I get back, or the whole deal's off – except for the thousand up front, of course. Third . : . '

'Wait. I'm starting to get the picture.' Jesus, Posner thought, this girl likes to make lists.

'Third, this could get really heavy. Do you have a gun?'

'A gun? Well, no, actually, I don't . . . '

'Well get one. I do.'

'You *do*?'

'Nowadays? Believe it. Fourth, a lot of people might lie to me who'd be scared of you . . . '

That seemed unlikely. 'Wait. Please. Melody. What do you mean, this could get really heavy?'

'Oh, God. Look, I've gotta go. I'm late for another appointment. I'll explain it more tomorrow.'

'Just one thing. Can you get me a list of the kids at the party?'

'Sure. I'll bring you a student list from school. Like I said, practically everybody was there. I'll get you a staff list, too.'

'A staff list?'

'Sure. The teachers come to all the parties. All the really good ones. And my parties are excellent. You should really

4

come to one.' She got up from the chair, fished an envelope from her bag, dropped it on the desk and started for the door.

'There's your grand.'

'Hold on, Melody. I think I'm going to need your signature on an agreement before I take any money. And do you mind my asking where you got all this money from?'

She paused in the doorway leading to the stairs and looked over her shoulder. 'Yes, I do mind, Joe. And I'll sign your agreement tomorrow. I'm a very agreeable person.' She gave Joe Posner a knowing look to make sure he got it. 'You keep the money till then. It'll make me feel better just to know you're on the case. Be good.' She ran down the steps as lightly as she'd come up them, and banged through the front door.

Joe Posner dropped the envelope in his desk drawer and locked it. He knew an agreement signed by a minor wasn't valid. He knew Melody Gold looked and sounded like pure trouble. He knew her story added up like a senator's taxes. He knew all about that. Like he knew not to lie down in front of a bus. Like he knew he needed a thousand bucks.

He'd have to think about it.

Through his office window he saw Melody Gold bounce into a shiny black Pontiac Firebird Trans Am and plunge into traffic without a second's hesitation. Past the Porsche-Audi dealer, past the windowless, white brick factory outlet shoe store, past the Discount Variety Store, through a red light, and out of sight.

He'd have to think about it, alright.

2. On the Park Road

At ten o'clock that night Joe Posner knew he had to make up his mind. Chicken Too Good would only be open another half hour. It would take time, energy, half a gallon of gas, and ninety cents to push his face into one of their succulent, peppery chicken breasts. And maybe four hundred calories. He didn't need it. He wasn't really hungry. The spaghetti and tomatoes – no oil – he'd cooked three hours earlier had filled his belly. He was nervous. And there was nothing on T.V. even worth sneering at. He wanted to eat something. His kitchen cabinet, he knew, held nothing but a can of La Seur baby peas and an extended family of cockroaches. What kind of life was this? He leaned forward in the secondhand armchair that was one of three pieces of furniture in his living room and put his face in his hands. I should move back into the city, he thought. This is crazy. Living above a family of born-again Christians on some nowhere street nowhere between two nowhere towns. Two years is enough. He had thought the fresh air and quiet would be worth it. He had thought wrong. But could he make it as a detective in New York? So, he reminded himself, was he making it in Jersey? He stood up suddenly, put on his old leather jacket, and headed for the stairway down to his separate entrance. Chicken Too Good. The only cultural center of worth in the area.

The warmth of the afternoon was all gone, and the evening air had chilled his ageing Dodge Dart. It stalled twice before he could get it onto the road. As he turned the ignition and revved the engine, Joe Posner tried to sort out Melody Gold and her thousand bucks. He drove down roads lined with old, heavy trees. Behind the trees were old, heavy houses. Big, rambling wooden houses that moderately rich people lived in. Richer people lived in bigger houses further up the hill. Houses surrounded by more trees, bigger trees, heavier trees. He sure could use that money. The job would be worth at least sixteen hundred. But could he take sixteen hundred from a teenager to find a naughty playmate? And deep down inside, or maybe not so deep down inside, he was worried how much his recent stretch of celibacy was affecting his attitude toward the all too young Miss Gold. Sure, he could rationalize that there are worse depravities in this world than a horny thirty-year-old male having a simple affair with a precocious and willing sixteen-year-old female. But, thought Joe Posner, a good detective hates rationalization. A good detective deals in facts.

A good detective.

The brutal truth was that helping a teenager find a naughty playmate was as close to a real case as Joe Posner had gotten in his eighteen months as a private eye.

Up ahead, off to the right, the trees throbbed with a red glow. As he rounded the bend, Posner saw an ambulance and a cluster of police cars docked beside the wooden fence that surrounded the cleared section of the municipal park. They were parked at the skewed angles he knew cops like to use to denote dynamic response to emergency. Hi-tech multiple cherrytop systems flashed wildly, further ensuring the sense of pandemonium. Joe Posner eased his Dart onto the soft shoulder behind one of the squad cars and got out, leaving his door open.

He stepped deliberately but modestly, over the soft, almost muddy ground toward the ambulance. Two paramedics were loading a stretcher into the back. 'What's going . . . ' Joe Posner stopped in mid-sentence, recognizing first the black hair, then the young face of Melody Gold on the stretcher. With growing anxiety, he scanned the assembled constabulary for a familiar face, found one, and walked quickly up to it.

'Webster. Hi. What's happened?'

'Posner.' He pronounced it with a short 'o', the way Joe Posner hated. 'What you doing here?' Sgt. Doug Webster was one of three town cops Joe Posner knew by name. He'd always seemed like an alright enough guy, for a cop, except for being an anti-semite bastard. Not that he'd ever done anything in particular to make Posner feel that way. Just little things. Like mispronouncing his name. Of course, the black shirt and leather chest strap that the town cops wore did nothing to allay the feeling. Neither did Webster's college boy blond hair and smooth, pink face.

'Just passing by. What's the story?'

'Fuckin' nice night, huh?'

'Yeah. What's going on?'

'Not much. Yanks look good this year, huh?'

'Will you fucking tell me what the fuck happened, Webster?' Joe Posner was having some difficulty keeping himself together.

'Drug overdose. What's eatin' *you*?'

'Pills?'

'Heroin.'

'Heroin?' It didn't seem to fit. 'How far gone is she?'

'All the way. That's one dead little girl.'

Posner's neck twitched deeply one time. The blood drained from his face. His knee trembled. It seemed all wrong.

'How do you know it was heroin?' he heard himself ask.

'Needle still in arm when found.'

'How *did* you find her?'

'Phone call. Anonymous. Female.'

'Jesus, Webster, talk in sentences, will ya? When did you get the call?'

'About twenty-five minutes ago. Told us where to find her on the benches over there. Crazy, huh? White kids doing junk.'

'Let me take a look, Webster.'

'What the fuck do you want to do that for?'

'I just want a quick look.'

'What're you, queer for dead teenagers or something?' Webster chuckled, then, thinking he'd said something really funny, laughed a little harder.

By sheer concentration of will, Joe Posner managed to smile, 'Just a quick look, Webster.'

'Not possible.'

'Why not?'

'You're not authorized, that's why not.'

'*Auth*orized? Fuck that, Webster. Gimme a break.'

'Not *pos*sible.'

'Fuck *that*.'

'Not *pos*sible.' This was a fun game for Sgt. Doug Webster – just the kind of meatheaded junior varsity jocularity he loved. Football and Lowenbrau. Circle jerks and Jew-baiting.

'Fuck *you*,' Posner sulked.

Webster's eyes brightened with the opportunity to cap their repartee with his ace bon mot: 'Suck shit, scumbag.'

Posner had had enough and walked back towards the Dart without attempting a topper. As he passed the ambulance, he looked back, caught Webster looking the other way, and turned to the paramedic standing like a fire plug next to the ambulance doors. 'Webster told me to take a look.' The paramedic almost

8

moved his eyes enough to look at Posner, but apparently didn't want to strain himself. Posner climbed in wondering why he'd bothered with Webster in the first place.

Joe Posner sat looking at the white corpse of Melody Gold. The tan was a sour shade of green now, and there was a lurid purple bruise on the right side of her chin. He was oddly unaffected sitting so close to her. It was too impossible, too horrible to take in. He looked at her left arm. It wasn't so perfect anymore. An ugly puncture; bigger, Posner thought, than necessary for a hypodermic needle. The bruised discoloration around it stood out on her pale, bloodless skin. Next to the big puncture, was another, smaller one. The belt he had seen that afternoon was gone.

He climbed out of the ambulance and wobbled back to Webster. 'Webster. Why two holes?'

'Huh?'

'She's got two holes in her arm.'

'I thought I told you to stay the fuck out of there.'

'I forgot.'

Sergeant Webster didn't think that was too funny. 'I ought to bust you, asshole.'

' "Unauthorized looking at dead girls!" I could get twenty to life.'

'You could get your fucking licence pulled, smuck.'

Smuck? Posner marveled. A young girl who was possibly my client is dead, and I have to play games with a poster boy for the SS who says 'smuck'. 'Webster, she's got two holes in her arm. And a bruise on her chin. How come?'

'Look, Posner,' he mispronounced it softly, as if he were trying to be patient, 'it's got nothing to do with me. I'm not in charge, I just work here. I don't give a good goddamn if she's got two assholes. Get it? Now go play junior G-man somewhere else, and get the fuck out of my face: I'm busy.'

Jos Posner didn't bother to thank Sgt. Webster for his help. The flashing red lights were starting to get to him. He wanted to cry. Or vomit. He wasn't sure.

Back at his car, he sat with his head on the wheel for a few minutes before starting the engine. On the way home his mind was running all over the place – looking for somewhere to hide. But it couldn't. It kept bumping into things. Things like Melody Gold's perfect arms. Arms he didn't believe she would puncture with a needle. Arms that definitely hadn't been punctured with any regularity. And the bruised chin she hadn't had at his office. And the belt that she had. He thought about the thousand bucks in his desk and the big case he wasn't going to have. And the affair he wasn't going to have, either. And it made him ashamed to think about these things. He tried to separate not wanting to believe she was dead from actually not believing she'd died of an overdose.

As he climbed the steps to his apartment, he accepted that he wasn't going to figure it out that night. Not in the shape he was in. For the moment there was nothing to do but seek unconsciousness. Fast. He got two Seconal from the bathroom and a large slug of scotch from the kitchen. He threw the poisons down his throat, went into his bedroom, dropped his clothes on the floor, lay face down on the bed, and waited for morning.

3. The Morning After

The sign on Ramapo Street said 'Human Learning Space', stylishly lettered in dark gray on a light gray background. It stood in front of the squat, yellow brick fifties building that used to be the Jewish Community Center. The parking lot was in front, and off to the left of it was a three-vehicle garage that was covered with psychedelic drawings in bright colors. A drycleaner and a tuxedo rental shop sat across the street, looking like somebody had dumped them there temporarily and forgotten to pick them up again.

Joe Posner's Dodge joined a white VW Beetle and an orange Datsun in the otherwise empty lot. The Seconal and scotch had kept him out till almost ten, and his head still felt a bit like cement. He got out of the car and stood for a minute, with eyes closed, absorbing the warm late-morning sunshine. The brightness burned through his eyelids, but felt therapeutic. The soft air smelled sweetly of young things growing and Posner sucked up enough of it to tickle the bottoms of his lungs, before heading up the steps.

Not stopping to look at the drawings, photos, and crudely lettered announcements haphazardly stuck up around the walls of the corridor, he followed the scent of coffee and the one institutional-looking sign that pointed to the office. The halls resounded with the emptiness of a school on vacation.

The office door was open, and he saw a plump, cheery young woman, her hair in a bun, cursing at her IBM Selectric, both hands held up beside her head, long cherry-painted nails spread wide. The second she saw him her frustration vanished, and a wide, warm smile lit her face.

'Oh, hi! How are you?'

Posner was caught completely off guard by the seemingly sincere concern of her question. 'Uh, O.K., thanks.' He wondered whether he knew her from some place.

'My name's Norma. What's yours?'

Posner was starting to feel like he'd stumbled upon some isolated tribe whose customs and rituals were still unsullied by civilized guile.

'Joe Posner.'

'Hi. Joe.'

'Hi. I . . . uh . . .'

'What can I do you for?'

'I was hoping you could give me the address of Melody Gold's family.'

'Oh, gee,' she grimaced with disappointment. 'I don't think I can do that. What's it in reference re?'

'Well, Melody gave me something, and I have to return it to her folks as soon as possible, and there are so many Golds in the phone book . . .'

'I'd love to help you, Joe, but you'd have to get Les to O.K. that.'

'Les?'

'The principal. But he's not in just now.'

'I see.' He couldn't believe there was no way around her.

'Do you want to leave it with me, and I'll see Melody gets it?'

Posner's stomach knotted. 'Melody's dead, Norma.' He paused to let it sink in a little. 'So you see it's very important.'

Norma's face paled and her wide eyes widened further. 'Oh my God. What are you talking about?'

'She died last night. It's terrible, I know.'

'Oh my *GOD*! Oh my *GOD*!' She put her hand over her mouth and sat still.

'So please,' Posner pressed on, 'can I have the address?'

'How?'

'An accident. I don't know the details.'

'Oh my *GOD*!'

'I know how you feel. Can I have the address?'

'Oh my God,' Norma stared into space.

'Norma?'

'Uh huh?'

'Can I have the address, please?'

She snapped into action. 'I'll tell you what, Joe: I better try calling Les at home. He'll want to know about Melody anyway.' She reached for the phone and started punching numbers.

'Thanks, Norma.' Just on general principles, he tried to catch the number, but Norma's push-button touch was the lightning flurry of a champion. While she listened to the rings, she muttered a few different combinations of 'Oh my God' and 'I can't believe it,' then put the phone back down and shook her head. 'He's not home, Joe. And I just can't give out that kind of information to anybody. I'm sorry.'

Posner rubbed his eyes and temples. 'Maybe he's on his way in?'

'I don't know. Maybe. You want to sit down? Pour yourself some coffee.' She shuddered and shook her head. 'I've got to get back to work.' She held her face in her hands, while Posner eagerly poured some coffee from the Mr. Coffee machine into a styrofoam cup and added some fake milk powder. It tasted awful, but it was almost hot. He slouched into a chair to wait, and watched Norma shake her head a few more times, repeating something that sounded like 'You make your own reality' to herself, and then start typing.

12

Joe Posner slouched deeper into his chair, took another gulp, and thought it all over again. He didn't really *want* to return the money. But he knew he had to. It wasn't exactly a moral consideration. He was afraid something bad would happen to him if he kept it. That he might get into trouble. He didn't know where the money was from. He didn't have an agreement. Rationally, the safest and happiest thing he could do was to spend the money quickly. It was almost certainly untraceable. He had felt that it was cash through the envelope. But he was never rational about these things. Like the time he'd registered his car at his aunt's house in Maryland to save seventy bucks on the insurance premium: constant *spilchis* until he'd changed it. And this: a dead teenager. Drugs. A thousand bucks. He had to get rid of it. This way he was clean. His story was true. He'd received the money just before closing the night before; he was returning it first thing the next morning. They could check the bills for his fingerprints, even. He hadn't opened the envelope, even. Clean.

The clacking of Norma's Selectric wasn't helping his head any. Then, on top of it, he heard a low rolling thunder coming down the hallway. It kept getting closer, apparently unnoticed by Norma, until a tiny boy, about eight years old, swerved into the office on a skateboard, did a complete turn on the back wheels, flipped the board into the air with his toe, and caught it only a foot or two from Norma's head. A large golden retriever padded in behind him.

Without looking up from her typing, Norma intoned, 'No skateboarding in the halls, David.'

Seeing no hope of appreciation from Norma, the kid turned to Posner and smiled at his own feat. His brown hair was kinky and down to his shoulders. His nose was freckled and looked like it weighed as much as the rest of his body. He wore dungarees and a sky-blue T-shirt which read '69 – Try it, You'll like it.' Posner smiled back.

'I need Allyson's number, Norma.'

Norma typed on. 'I'm busy, David.'

'C'mon. I *need* it.'

Norma finally looked at him, flashing all the anger Posner

guessed she owned, which wasn't a lot. Without looking, she reached to the bulletin board behind her, snatched a yellow mimeographed list from it and handed it to the kid. 'Bring it back when you're finished,' she said with devotional seriousness, and went back to her typing.

David remounted the board and skated back into the hall.

'No skateboarding in the hall,' Norma called after him.

'C'mon, Trog,' was his only response.

Posner made his move quickly. 'Mind if I use the men's room, Norma?' he asked.

'Of course not, Joe,' Norma smiled down at her keys. 'Turn right out of the office, and it's on your left.'

'Thanks.' He slipped into the hall, wondering how Norma would do at the CIA. He caught up to the kid and his dog at the payphone. The dog went right for his crotch and started sniffing.

'Hey, David, mind if I look at that list for a second?'

'Who are you?' he squeaked, in a tone that was suspicious and not a little snide for such a little kid.

'Joe Posner.'

'Oh. O.K.' A name seemed to be enough. 'Let me just dial this number first.' He stretched up on his toes to insert his dime and dialed from the list. Then he banged the phone down. 'Fuckin' busy. Here.' He handed Posner the list.

Posner started to scan it, then, for no particular reason he'd admit to, asked, 'O.K. if I keep this? You can copy down Allyson's number for later.'

'I've gotta give it back to Norma.'

'C'mon. What d'ya want for it?'

'Got any reefer?'

'How 'bout a buck?'

'How 'bout five?'

'Forget it.'

'What'll I tell Norma?'

'Tell her your dog ate it,' Posner shrugged and pulled a single from his pocket.

The kid's eyes narrowed in serious consideration. 'That's excellent. *Ex*cellent.' He grabbed the buck and skated toward the exit. 'You can keep Allyson's number. I'll call her from home.'

Joe Posner chuckled on his way back to the office, slipping the list into his back pocket. He stuck his head in the door. 'I've gotta get going, Norma. Thanks anyway.'

'O.K., Joe. I still can't believe it about Melody. Sorry I couldn't help you. Try back this afternoon. Bye now.'

Posner started back towards the entrance, but something that sounded like sobbing stopped him halfway down the hall.

4. Wet Sandals

The sound was coming from an open door a few feet to his right. He followed it through the doorway and found a tall, thin woman, her back to him, hunched over an open drawer of a filing cabinet. Drab, brown hair lay tangled and knotted like day-old spaghetti over her shoulders and back. Next to her, on one of four long tables that were scattered around the room, was a cardboard box almost filled with papers and files. He had been right about the sobbing.

Posner looked around the room. A small blackboard on the far wall had what appeared to be several generations of writings overlaying one another. In one corner he saw 'love=loving =caring.' On another part he read 'Are you a Cadillac or a Volkswagon?' In the middle of the board, in the center of an erased area, the names 'Kierkegaard' and 'Brautigan' were scrawled. Several Escher prints were stuck up on the pastel pink walls. Blackout curtains had been closed against the spring sun, and the light in the room was a sickly blue coming from a fluorescent ceiling fixture. Joe Posner closed the door behind him, hoping the sound would get the woman's attention. It did. She jumped like a deer at a rifle shot and spun to face him, holding her hands behind her. Her face was young, boney, and pale. She wore a dull, white blouse with a Peter Pan collar and a circular brooch. The blouse might have been prim if it had ever

15

been ironed. An incongruous skirt of faded denim fell shapelessly to just above her ankles, where the tops of her white tube socks almost met the bottoms of her waffle-quilted longjohns. On her feet she sported a pair of expensive rubber hunting boots.

'Who are you?' she asked, still choking slightly on her tears.

'Joe Posner.'

The answer perplexed her. Bloodshot was the only color in her eyes; and staring out at Posner they looked as empty as a Monday morning movie.

'Is that your first name or your last name?' It was the flat, nasal voice of someone who took things literally.

'What?'

'Joposner.'

'No. Joe's my first name. Posner's my last name.'

'But you said it like one name.' She was showing signs of irritation now, as if she felt deceived.

'Yeah,' he apologized, 'I just like to say it like that.'

'Oh. I'm Alice.' She moved closer to him.

'Alice what?' The question seemed to hurt her feelings a bit.

'Les says last names are really about our parents, not us.'

'Les who?' Posner asked, deadpan.

'Les Coniff.' Alice frowned, then added, 'Cabot.'

'Les Coniff Cabot?'

'No. Les Coniff. Alice Cabot.'

'Ah ha. You teach here?'

She nodded her head a few times, not wanting to speak more then necessary.

'What do you teach?'

She took a deep breath and exhaled her answer.

'Philosophy.'

'Really?' Posner was surprised. 'Is there a large need for a philosophy teacher at such a small school?'

Alice Cabot hung her head in shame. 'I was a philosophy major in college. I only taught one philosophy course this term: The Philosophical Roots of Richard Brautigan. I also teach Intimacy Workshop and Mexican Cooking. Or I used to. I'm not teaching here anymore.' She gestured towards the box. 'I'm packing.'

This last confession turned her tears back on like she was a sprinkler system. She jumped at Joe Posner and wrapped her arms tightly around him. 'Please. Just hold me for a minute.' She turned them both around and pushed him back into the filing cabinet, closing it with his back. She smelled faintly of wet sandals and aged perspiration. Posner remained motionless as he felt the inexplicable, but undeniable friction of her crotch against his leg.

As promised, after a minute, she released him. The crying had stopped with a good fifteen seconds to go. Somewhere, perhaps Intimacy Workshop, Posner speculated, she'd learned the measure of her hysteria. 'Thank you,' Alice said with eyes closed. 'I hope that wasn't too terrible for you.'

'Uh, no. No. It was, uh, fine. No problem.' Joe Posner searched his pockets for a handkerchief, although he knew he didn't have one. He didn't even own one. Alice Cabot pulled one out of a knapsack lying on the floor. Posner could see that the handkerchief had been used a lot and washed a little. While she wiped her eyes and blew her nose into the gray cloth, Posner noticed that the brooch on her collar looked expensive. 'That's a lovely brooch.'

'Thank you.'

'Is it an antique?'

'Uh huh.'

He moved toward her – with some trepidation – to get a closer look. 'What are those stones?'

'Amethyst and amber.' She was still wiping her eyes.

'Really. It's gorgeous. May I ask where you got it?'

'Alice Cabot's eyes widened over the handkerchief. 'It was a gift.'

'From an admirer, no doubt.'

Alice ignored the comment and went back to loading manila files into her cardboard box.

'I just mean, it looks expensive, so I figured it must be from somebody pretty special. I didn't mean to get too personal.'

Alice tried to smile and not to snap, but only half-succeeded at each. 'Well, you did, I guess.'

'I'm sorry.' Posner tried to sound like he meant it, and didn't do much better.

'That's O.K. What are you doing here, anyway? Are you looking for someone?'

'Oh, it's sort of a long story. I was trying to get Melody Gold's address.' Alice's face looked like a retired fighter trying to prove he could still take a punch to the belly. 'She wanted me to help her find a missing box of hers.'

'Oh, really,' Pale lids fluttered on her vacant eyes. 'That's interesting. Will you excuse me?' She tilted her head to the side, and said through the teeth of a slightly nauseous smile, 'I've got to move my bowels now. It's been nice talking to you.' She moved to the door like a zombie with a hangover. She didn't seem to hear Joe Posner's 'I'll wait for you here.'

Joe Posner knew he was poking his nose where it didn't belong, but the coincidence of the brooch was just too damn interesting to ignore. And Alice's reaction had been as Kosher as a canned ham. If she knew Melody was dead, she was pretending not to. And if she didn't, she was pretending about something else.

He browsed around the room a bit. He opened the manila folder on the top of a pile and looked at a stack of mimeoed sheets titled 'Modern Philosophy Take Home Final.' He supposed it was from an earlier term. It read:

Answer any one of the following seven questions. Write for at LEAST five (5) minutes.
(1) My main reality is:
(2) I am/am not scared of dying because:
(3) My main feelings about people are:
(4) I like phenomenology over positivism because: (or vice-versa)
(5) To me, the importance of out-of-body experiences is:
(6) What did John really mean in 'I am the Walrus?' Be specific.
(7) Which do you think is more important – parents or attitudes? Why?
Papers are due Thursday. SEE YOU AT GRADUATION!!

18

Posner nosed around some more, but didn't find much. Just out of curiosity he thought it might be interesting to look at a class register to see if Melody had been in any of Alice's classes and how she'd done, but he didn't find one. After fifteen minutes, Posner figured that Alice had had enough time to move her bowels, as she had so quaintly put it, to Schenectady and back. He padded down the hallway to the door marked 'Toilet' and tried it. It was locked.

'*Occupado*,' Alice sang a bit nervously.

'Alice? Are you O.K.?'

There was no answer.

'Alice, it's Joe.'

'I know.'

'Are you O.K.?'

'Yes. May I have some privacy, please?'

'Will you be out soon?'

'I don't think so. I think you should go away.'

'Uh huh. O.K. Sure. Sorry if I bothered you.' Whatever Alice Cabot knew, he wasn't going to find it out by banging down a toilet door. And, interesting or not, it still wasn't any of his business. Not really. 'Well, I guess I'll be going, Alice. Nice to have met you.'

'You, too, Joe,' she said through the door. 'Bye.'

'Bye.' He walked slowly toward the door, until he got to a bulletin board covered with a couple of dozen eight-by-ten photos and paused to give them a look.

They appeared to be photos of a camping trip: campfires, swimming, down vests and flannel shirts, guitar playing, water fights, cooking. Posner was impressed, both by the quality of the photos and the good spirit and camaraderie they had captured. Then, near the bottom, one photo stopped him cold.

It was Melody Gold, seemingly caught by surprise and smiling. Smiling like a sixteen year old: with all the young, wide-open heart she'd hidden in his office. Smiling behind a split lip. Smiling behind a closed, black eye. Smiling behind a swollen jaw. It must have hurt to smile with a face like that, Joe Posner thought. It must have hurt like hell.

5. Gold Antiques

The house was ordinary enough, for the neighborhood: huge, square, made of pink bricks, with white wooden trim and cedar shingle roofing rather half-heartedly aspiring to a gingerbread effect. It could have been pretentious, but it didn't seem to know what it was pretending to be.

The door was opened by a thin, middle-aged black woman with bored yellow eyes. She made no response to Posner's request to see Mr. or Mrs. Gold except to walk away from the door and wave her hand vaguely in the direction of the living room.

Posner passed through the black and white tiled foyer with its rococo pedestals and statuary. The living room was cluttered with expensive-looking antiques, none of which complemented the others. It wasn't so much in bad taste, as apparently uninformed by an identifiable taste at all. It was what his mother would have called *ungepatchke*. Off to one side of the room, a door was open and Posner could hear a cigarette-coarsened woman's voice. He lowered himself tentatively onto a chair that looked like a French Louis the something sort of thing and didn't stop himself from listening.

'Don't tell me I can't have cocktail franks at a funeral. Whose funeral is it? What d'ya want, I should have some goddamn sponge cake? You think we're some kind of Hassids here? I want cocktail franks. Yeah. Hold on a minute.' Buttons clicked. 'Mother. Yes, dear. I'm back. Please, mother, try to stop being so hysterical, will you? No, we don't *know* how. *Don't* come here. God, Mother, I'm already going crazy here. Please. No, he's not. Cape Town. Where else? Later. The company plane's flying him in this afternoon. Is he ever here when I need him? Yes. Wonderful. Wonderful. You're a sweetheart. Love to Daddy. Be good.' More buttons clicked. 'George. Sorry to keep you waiting, sweetheart. It's a madhouse here. Yes. Only

four? I thought it was four *Chipp*endales and *five* of the creden-
zas. Uh-huh. What the fuck. O.K. Whatever, darling. I told
you I didn't want to do any business today. I can't. Really.
Yeah. You take care of it. Love you. Be good.'

More buttons clicked, and Posner made the connection.
Gold. Gold Antiques. There had been a series of robberies that
winter from a warehouse owned by Gold Antiques, a large
importing and wholesaling operation. He'd read about it in the
paper. These must be the people.

Mrs. Gold ploughed on. 'Oscar. Listen. Do whatever the hell
you want. Just don't give me one of those dreary old country
deals. O.K., honey? Thanks.' She banged the receiver down,
exhaling a 'Holy Moses,' before sweeping into the living room
in a shiny pink and turquoise caftan. It wasn't hard to see that
she was Melody's mother. The arms – tanned to leather and
jangling half a dozen bracelets each – were held out from the
body much as Melody had held hers, only tighter, with more
effort, but less intention. The head was held back at the same
angle, the jet black hair lacquered back into ram's horns. She
didn't notice Joe Posner at first, and when she did, she turned
on him. 'Who're you? You look like one of the teachers. A lot
of nerve one of your bunch coming here now.'

'No, ma'am,' Posner answered coolly. 'I'm not. My name's
Joe Posner.'

'Oh,' she sagged into a Victorian-looking armchair.

'I hope this isn't business,' she sighed sadly. 'We've had a
terrible loss here.'

'Yes, ma'am. I know. If I could explain . . .' Posner took the
envelope out of his jacket pocket.

Phyllis Gold put her forehead into her hand. 'Go ahead.'

'I'm a private investigator . . . '

Mrs. Gold lifted her head enough for a look. 'You're kidding.'

'No, ma'am. I am. Melody tried to hire me yesterday.'

Mrs. Gold screwed up her eyebrows in puzzlement and her
eyes opened widely in what looked like it could have been
worry.

'She left me some money – against my wishes – and I thought

21

I should return it to you right away. I'm very sorry about what happened.'

Mrs. Gold stared at him blankly. Her face was lightly oiled, but otherwise had no make up. A well-shaped, straight nose and largish green eyes suggested that the face had been attractive once. But too many suntans, too many forced smiles, and too much aggravation had left a look of corrosion and moral fatigue. Posner guessed she wasn't even forty-five. She looked not only older than that, but fading fast. She held her stare through a few flutters of her eyelids, then said, 'Why would Melody hire a private investigator?'

'I'm afraid I can't go into that.' Posner forced himself to meet the woman's steady gaze.

'Oh, I see. You can't go into that.' She smoothed her bright caftan over her knees with fingers rigid with tension. 'I'm not sure I understand what you're trying to say, Mr . . . what did you say your name was?'

'Posner. Joe Posner. Really, all I wanted . . .'

'Let me finish,' she smiled sourly. 'Now, I don't know what you're up to or what you take us for, but let me explain one thing to you. I'm not someone who grovels in the misery of the past.' She turned her head sharply away and bit her upper lip. 'Melody's death is in the past. Nothing can bring her back. Nothing.' She turned her face to Posner. Her eyes were dry. 'We don't want anyone stirring things up, or sniffing around, or picking at things.'

Joe Posner didn't much like being considered a picker, a sniffer, or a stirrer. In fact, he'd always been considered a good eater by his family. More to the point, he wondered why his refusal to answer had brought on this morbid floor show. 'Please believe me, Mrs. Gold. I'm not interested in any of that. I just came to return the money.' He held the envelope for her to take.

After eyeing it suspiciously for a few seconds, she accepted it, gingerly, as if she might want to change her mind and drop it. Then she opened it, looked in and shot her eyes back at Posner, who was already trying to come up with an exit line.

'What's your game, Mr. Posner?' she smiled demurely.

22

'None. Really. In fact, I really should be going . . . '

'Why don't you just lay your cards on the table. O.K.?'

'I don't *have* any cards. All I wanted to . . . '

Phyllis Gold sighed heavily. 'Mr Posner, Mr. Posner.' The eyes closed. The voice was low. 'Melody was everything to me. The jewel in my crown, the money in my bank . . . '

The metaphors were more telling than she realized, but they were still awful. Posner couldn't take anymore. 'Mrs. Gold, why don't you just tell me what you want me to say?'

She smiled again, as humble, sweet, and steady as a granite daffodil. 'I want you to tell me why you're here, why Melody hired you, and . . . what is on your mind.'

'Look, Mrs. Gold. I have no racket. I have no cards. I don't even have a ping pong paddle. All I came here for was to return that money. But to tell you the truth, I wish I knew why everyone is so damn anxious for me not to find out anything about your daughter.'

'Perhaps it's because it isn't any of your damn business. Did you ever think of that?'

'Every thirty seconds, Mrs. Gold. Every thirty seconds. Now, if I may, I'd like to go.' Joe Posner stood slowly.

'Do I have your assurance that you're going to stay out of our private affairs?' The question was unhistrionic, direct, business-like. For just a moment, Joe Posner saw Mrs. Gold's face turn into Melody's, beaten but sneering, 'My mother's a total pig . . . ' He had no words and turned for the door.

Mrs. Gold called after him. 'Go play private eye with somebody else's daughter, you bastard. Wait till my husband gets back . . . ' Posner slammed the heavy door behind him.

6. Business

Joe Posner paced around the office, sat down, stood up, and sat down again. He switched on 'Ryan's Hope,' and switched it off again. If something interested you, it seemed, if there was something that you wanted to do, if there was something that seemed *right* to do, nobody would pay you to do it. You got paid for doing boring things, stupid things, useless things. No one had taught him this at the small liberal arts college he'd attended. He'd figured it out himself. Later. He called the Human Learning Space.

'Hello, Space.'

'Hi, Norma. This is Joe Posner. Did Les get there yet?'

'Uh-uh, Joe. I'm sorry. Do you want to leave your number?'

'O.K. Sure. It's 769–5850. Can you give me his home number, so I can try him there?'

'I'm sorry, Joe,' – again the sincere disappointment – 'I can't. But I'll see he gets your message.'

'O.K. I'll look it up myself.'

'It's not listed, Joe.'

'Oh . . . Well, O.K., Norma. Ask him to call me.'

'I will, Joe. Bye, now.'

Joe Posner tapped his foot, bit the end of a pen and scowled out his window at the empty liquor store parking lot and the green garbage tip at its back. He grabbed the phone again and dialed. The police operator answered, and he asked for Webster.

'Webster, Hi, it's Joe Posner.'

'Posner,' as always, he mispronounced it. 'I could still be pissed, but I'll forget it.'

'Thanks. Say, what's the latest on that girl?'

'Still dead.'

'Very funny. Did they do a blood test?'

'Sure. No surprises. Just a little too much junk. Somebody bigger would of just had a long nap.'

'What about the second puncture? And the bruise on her chin?'

'What's the matter, Posner, you trying to make trouble?'

'You know me better than that.'

'I don't know nothin'. I'm a cop, remember?'

'I'm just curious. Didn't anybody wonder?'

'Well, as a matter of fact, Sherlock, I asked the coroner about it myself.'

'Yeah? What'd he say?'

'He said "So what?" is what he said. Satisfied?'

'What the hell does "So what" mean?'

'It means it coulda been a lotta things. His guess was she might of changed her mind about takin' the shot a few times. She didn't have tracks, so she wasn't a regular user. *But* it coulda been a lotta things.'

'Was there anything around for tying her arm?'

'You don't have to tie your arm. It just makes it easier to get a vein and better for the rush.'

'Webster, she was wearing . . . '

'Look, Posner, I'm busy. We're busy. I'm sorry if the girl was a friend of yours or something, but it's over. Case closed, as they say. The only thing that's different is that she's white and she's rich. It happens to a nigger kid every day. We don't think it's weird. The mother don't think it's weird. It ain't weird. O.K.?'

'I think it's weird.'

'You would. *You're* weird.'

'What about the bruise on her chin?'

'The mother explained that. When she came down to identify the body. Seems the girl hit her chin on the edge of the swimming pool.'

'Webster, it's fucking *April*.'

'What's the matter, poor boy, never heard of heated pools? C'mon. What's this all about?'

'She wanted to hire me. Yesterday. She told me to get a gun.'

'What?'

'Melody Gold. She came to my office, gave me a thousand bucks, told me to get a gun, and ran off before I could open my mouth. I gave the money back to the mother just now. Unopened.'

'April Fool's day was two weeks ago, Posner.'

'For real, Webster.'

'Well, fuck me. What did she want you to do?'

'Somebody stole an antique box of hers. I know it doesn't add up, but that's what she said. Also that she didn't want her folks to know anything.'

'And she told you to get a gun?'

'I thought it was strange, too. And let me tell you something else strange: she was wearing a belt she didn't have on in the ambulance, but she wasn't wearing the bruise. This was after four o'clock. You still think there's nothing weird?'

'The lieutenant tells me what to think. I'll have to tell him about this. He may want to talk to you.'

'That's what I was afraid of.'

In a uncharacteristic display of imagination, the policeman affected a Jack Webb voice. 'If you're innocent, ma'am, you have nothing to be afraid of.'

'That's great, Webster. I always had a hunch that cops watched that show. Let me know what the lieutenant says as soon as you hear, O.K.?'

'Sure. So long, asshole.'

'So long, handsome.' Posner dropped the phone on the hook. Shaking his head, he reminded himself of the rule: Never underestimate the stupidity, venality, brutality, or laziness of the police. So Melody knocked her chin on the edge of the swimming pool. And the Russians stole her belt. And above all, nothing was weird. They ought to talk to Alice Cabot for five minutes.

He looked down the student list he'd bought from the kid at the school and found Dessie Levine. '557 Homestead Ave., Teaneck. Parents: Harold (212-977-8830) and Ethel. 568-4408.' Harold and Ethel. Harold had thought Ethel was cheating on him; or hoped so, thinking it might get him a better alimony deal. Posner had watched her for a week and told Harold he was crazy, she should be so lucky. While he dialed the number, Posner wondered how Dessie, the elder daughter, had known he'd been on the case, and cringed at the thought he'd blown his cover, without realizing it.

'Hello?' It was the voice of a little girl, maybe seven or eight years old.

'Hi. Is Dessie there?'

'Uh-uh. She's up at Kinnehonka.'

'Kinnehonka? What's that?'

'It's a camp, dummy. In Harriman. She's on ASE.'

Posner saw no choice but to let himself in for more abuse.

'ASE?'

It's a school thing. Her and mom are both up there. They left this morning.'

'Oh. Is this Rosalind?'

'Yeah. Who're you?'

'My name's Joe Posner.'

'Oh! You're the guy who spied on us!'

'Uh, yeah,' Posner winced, 'sort of.'

'What d'ya want Dessie for?'

'I wanted to ask her some questions about Melody Gold.'

'Melody's dead y'know,' she said plainly.

'I know. That's what I . . . '

'I know 'cause Pam Concannon told me. Dessie doesn't even know yet. Melody was here last night, too.'

'She *was*?'

'Yeah. She almost stayed for dinner, but mom kicked her out.'

'When did she get there, Rosalind? Do you remember?'

'Yeah. It was during Uncle Floyd. She wouldn't shut up, the jerk.'

'And do you know when she left?'

'We were just gonna start dinner. Carol Burnett was on. It was a mess. Mom got mad and Dessie got mad and then Dessie and Melody left. Mom almost wouldn't let Dessie go on ASE.'

'Dessie and Melody left together?'

'Yeah.'

'Do you know where they went?'

'Uh-uh.'

'When did Dessie come home?'

'I don't know. I had to go to bed after "Happy Days," and she wasn't back yet.'

'What was the fight about?'

'I don't know. Mom and Melody hate each other. They always fight.'

'Listen, Rosalind, when are they supposed to get back from Kinnahonka?'

'Two days. My Aunt Effie is staying with me till then.'

'That's very nice. Thanks a lot. It's been nice talking to you,

Rosalind.'

'O.K.,' she said and hung up.

Joe Posner squeezed his mouth together with his hand and twisted it till it almost hurt. Harriman State Park was an hour – and a quarter of a tank of gas – into the mountains. He looked back out the window at downtown Bergentown, that two-story oasis of brick and concrete in the desert of nature rejuvenate, and reminded himself again that it wasn't any of his business. Then he set his answering machine, grabbed his jacket, and split.

7. Advanced Survival Experience

The Palisades Parkway was practically empty, and Joe Posner pushed the Dart past its fifty-five miles-an-hour shimmy point and cruised at sixty. The first half-hour's worth of scenery was pretty dull. Even though everything was green, the brightness of the mid-afternoon sun had flattened all the different shades to one uninteresting grayish tone. Once he got up into the mountains, though, the red branches of the still-budded trees gave a glowing, almost rose cast to the hillsides. Getting out of Bergentown had been a good idea.

The radio in the Dart hadn't worked for four or five months, so Posner sang himself a few Ellington tunes, until he got eight bars into 'In a Sentimental Mood,' where he always lost the melody. After that he just watched the scenery.

He took the Seven Lakes Parkway exit and followed it around to a traffic circle, where he spotted a Park Policeman sitting in a parked police car, and pulled up alongside him. 'Excuse me,' he called out, 'Can you tell me where Kinnehonka is?'

The cop, who had been looking at his lap or something on it, snapped into action, whipping his head around to Posner. His face had been terribly scarred by burns, and what with his mirror sunglasses, cowboy-style ranger hat, and severely cropped moustache, he was as terrifying as he was hideous. 'Kinne-honka's reserved for group camping, buddy.' His tone seemed intended to make it clear that any unauthorized use of Kinne-honka would result in severe penalties.

'Yeah. I'm looking for someone in a school group that's using it.'

The cop stared at him expressionlessly for a few seconds, then sneered, 'Pull over to the side of the road, buddy,' and got out of his car.

Holy Shit, Posner wailed to himself, he can't bust me for asking directions, can he? He pulled over and got out of the Dart, cursing fate and telling himself never to ask a cop for anything again. No matter what.

When he got to the police car, he realized with relief that the cop had unfolded a map of the park on his hood.

'You're here,' the cop pointed at a spot on the map. 'Go down here to this circle, go three corters way round, then take the secin turn off on the left. K–42. That's it.'

'Thanks a lot.' Posner started back to the Dart, but the cop wasn't finished. Joe Posner would have to pay for the help he'd gotten.

'Hold up a secin, buddy. You think that was a very safe thing you just did?'

'Thing I just did?'

'Stopping your vehicle right out in the middle of the artery there?'

'Uh, gee. I'm sorry . . . There wasn't any other traffic . . . '

'I really oughtta give you a citation,' he paused for sadistic effect. It was obvious, but successful. 'But I'm lettin ya go this time. Nex time you wanna ask d'rections, you pull over.'

'I will. I will. That's very kind of you. I won't do it again.' It was times like this that gave Joe Posner a lot of sympathy for cop killers.

He followed the cop's directions and found himself driving down an axle-bending dirt and rock road. About a quarter of a mile down, he came to a clearing where he found a minibus marked Human Learning Space and parked next to it. 'Advanced Survivel Experiance' was lettered on a piece of cardboard stuck on the inside of the windshield.

Marveling at the luminescent greens and yellows of the thick forest, he continued down the road on foot. Off to his right, from higher up on the hill, he heard the crashing of twigs and leaves. The sound got louder. Something or somebody was running down the hill in his direction. The sound kept getting louder, until a boy and a dog crashed through the trees into the road. The dog was an Irish Setter, large, but not old. Its ears and tongue flapped around its head as it gamboled onto the path. The boy wore jeans and no shirt, and ran bent from the waist, his arms hanging towards the ground. His shoulder-length blond hair flapped like the dog's ears and his tongue, too, stuck out. All in all, they looked more like brothers than master and pet.

Posner called out, and they both stopped, turned and smiled mutely. The boy had a cut in the middle of his forehead that bled freely, but it didn't seem to bother him. Around his face and shoulders, half a dozen scars large enough to be visible from where Posner was standing, suggested that he was used to such injuries.

'You from the Space?' Posner asked.

The boy and the dog looked at each other. 'Yeah,' the boy finally said. 'We're from there.'

'I'm looking for Dessie Levine.'

'Jake'll find her for you.' The boy started to run again, but the dog stayed.

'Wait!' Posner yelled. 'How do I find Jake?'

The boy stopped and turned. 'Oh, yeah. Go on down the road till you see a blue-colored tent. That's Jake's.'

'Thanks.' The boy and the dog were already running again. Posner did not consider himself an expert in survival techniques, but such activity seemed to him somewhat counterproductive.

A few yards down the road, Joe Posner could hear music. It was the Rolling Stones doing a recent song that Posner had heard, but didn't know. A few yards further along, and Jake's blue 'tent' came into view. The music pounded from inside it. The tent was a dome, about ten feet in diameter and five feet high, made of blue nylon stretched across arched poles. A doorway, an arched projection, opened onto a stunning view of wide, still Lake Kinnehonka.

When he got up to Jake's blue igloo, the music was quite loud. Realizing the futility of knocking on nylon, Posner called out a 'hello.'

'Yeah. C'mon in,' was the answer. Posner stooped and, as he waddled through the opening, he was hit by the powerful smell of chocolate.

Inside, a young man, about twenty five, with a perfectly proportioned, dramatically muscled body, was rubbing cocoa butter into his perfectly golden tan. Stretched out across a foam floor, which was covered in Indian bedspreads, he wore only gold shorts and matching running shoes. His hair was done up in beaded cornrows that fell to his shoulders. On the floor next to him was an enormous Sony tape machine, a bottle of Bordeaux with a chateau label, and a cut crystal glass half-filled with maroon wine. A survival specialist if Posner had ever seen one.

'Jake?' Posner asked.

Jake was startled and half sat up. 'Yeah. Who're you?'

'My name's Joe Posner. I'm looking for Dessie Levine.'

'What for?' He seemed more nervous than truculant.

'I just want to talk to her.'

'You a cop?'

'Me? Hell no.'

'How do I know? You could be a unmarked cop.'

'I'm not a cop. I promise.'

'Well,' he tried to pull himself up to a pose of responsibility, 'I'm not sure about my comfortability on this . . .'

A holler came from down near the lake. It sounded like someone was calling Jake. Jake ignored it. 'How do you . . .'

Posner interrupted, 'I think somebody's calling you.'

Jake concentrated his eyes almost to the crossing point. 'I know. How do you know Dessie? Why do you want to talk to her?'

The hollering got closer, and Posner thought he detected some urgency in it. 'Jake! Jake!' Posner stuck his head out the opening of the dome and saw Ethel Levine huffing up the slope from the lake. She wore a denim pants suit over her sagging, but not fat body. As she ran and shouted, she waved her arms over her head, extending them out from her sides occasionally to keep her balance.

'Jake! May I have a word with you?' Her voice was singsongy, but not quite a whine. Posner looked back at Jake. Jake did not move. The woman got on her hands and knees to crawl through the opening, and Posner backed further into the tent to give her room. 'Hello,' she said to Posner, without recognition. She was trying to be cordial, but was either too timid or not interested enough to introduce herself. Her mouth was full and might have been sexy twenty years earlier. Now her lips hung loosely from her puffy face and yellow teeth. Deep lines of worry and disappointment fell from fearful eyes. She raised her head from her doggie position to face Jake.

'Jake, I wonder if you could talk to Desdemona for a minute.'

'If she wants to talk to me she could come here.'

'Well . . . you know how I hate to intervene when she's having fun. Her adventurousness is so much of what makes her who she is, really . . . ' Jake was not listening. He was lovingly working the cocoa butter into the left side of his rib cage with the fingers of his right hand. 'It's just that in this particular situation, I honestly think she's involved in a situation that may be somewhat over her head. I think it's our responsibility as adults to intervene in this situation.' Jake still wasn't listening. 'She's climbed a tree, and . . . well, I know she's climbed trees before, but this one seems particularly dangerous, and . . . of course she won't listen to me, and . . . she was with Jeannie and Davida . . . on the island?' She looked out of the corner of her eye at Posner as if 'island' had been a code that Jake would know. 'And those Rangers were around before, and it could jeopardize our permit, and that's not fair to the others. Also, Jake, I think she's . . . on something.' After a fearful pause, she added. 'The tree's down by that wood foundation.'

Jake rolled languidly onto his back and took a deep breath. 'O.K., Ethel.' In one fluid motion, he went through a crouch, out the opening, and into a run. Posner waddled out to watch.

Jake ran effortlessly with enormous, smooth strides, his beaded cornrows flapping on his shoulders.

Ethel started after him, then stopped. She looked at Posner and shrugged her shoulders. 'I . . . I . . . ' Shaking her head against the tears welling in her eyes, she lit a Kent and took a drag so deep that it consumed almost a quarter of its length. Posner set off to follow Jake.

About a hundred yards or so around the lake, next to a wooden tent foundation, Jake stood at the base of a tree, looking up. Lolling around the ground at its base were two girls and a boy. The girls were naked, the boy had cut-off blue jeans. Their eyes were as red and glazed as maraschino cherries. They didn't speak. Sitting on a branch, Dessie – except for the dandelions and leaves stuck in her frizzy dark hair – was also naked, and dangling her legs around a branch fifteen or twenty feet from the ground. Joe Posner didn't know what to do with his eyes. Jake, who didn't seem affected by the nudity, was speaking to Dessie softly, but in the same nervous tone he'd used with Posner.

'C'mon, Dessie. This is stupid. I know you can get down.'

'I caaan't, Jake,' she insisted, then switched into a clumsy self-parody. 'I'm too 'luded up, mahn,' and went into a giggle.

'If you don't come down now, I'm gonna climb up there and break your fucking arm.' Jake's voice never varied from its low, nervous monotone.

'Oh, ho,' she mocked, 'a big tough mucho macho,' and wagged her head from side to side. 'Hey, Davida, Jake's Mr. Mucho Macho!'

None of the kids on the ground moved a muscle.

'Look, Dessie, Ethel's on my back. It's not fair to me.'

Dessie giggled on.

'I'll give you a joint of my Thai stick if you come down.'

'You *will*?' she was interested. 'Groovy, man,' she said in her parody voice and stood up on the limb. Posner put his hands over his eyes, but looked through his fingers. Then, with a considerable wobble, but without hesitation, Dessie ran along the limb and shimmied down the trunk, raised her hands like a gymnast finishing a turn, and sang 'Ta dum,' as her knee buckled, and she fell to the ground giggling. Jake was unamused. The kids on the ground were unaware. Posner really didn't know what to think.

Jake grabbed Dessie's arm and yanked her to her feet. 'On account of you, I hadda leave my concentration on what I was occupied on, Dessie. And you laugh? What is that? How does that say about your awareness of me?'

Dessie was humiliated by this stinging rebuke. 'Fuck off, Jake,' she said in a hurt and defensive tone, and started to walk away from him. 'Where's my Thai stick?'

'Sure,' Jake countered sarcastically, 'All you care about is what you take out from it. But not what went into it. All the worry that was . . . went along . . . in it. For instance Ethel.'

'Fuck Ethel. I told her not to go here. She follows me around like a cockroach or something.'

Posner was astounded by the conversation. Whatever primitiveness Advanced Survival Experience lacked in equipment they made up for in language. This was real stone age stuff.

Jake turned his back on Dessie and started back to his tent. 'I'll give you the joint later,' he called over his shoulder.

'Fuck you,' Dessie called back guiltily as she walked away from the tree and the kids around it.

Posner ambled over to her. The uneven forest floor and his discomfort over her nakedness made it a bumpy journey. 'Hi,' he said, as casually as possible. He looked straight into her eyes to avoid the rest of her. They were large and brown and very glassy, with dark shadows under them.

'Hi,' she sulked.

'Can I talk to you a minute?'

'I don't need another bossy lecture.'

'I don't care about that stuff.'

'You don't?' she asked warmly, desperate for an ally.

'Hell, no,' Posner assured her. 'What's the big deal in climbing a tree?'

'*Real*ly,' She swept the air with her arm, her eyes became confused, and she fell on the ground again, landing in a cross-legged, sitting position. 'Oh, wow,' she said, a little disappointed at her dizziness.

34

Joe Posner knelt in the leaves and brought his face as close as his modesty would allow. 'Listen, Dessie . . . '

Dessie squinted her cloudy eyes. 'Wait a minute. I know you. You're Joe Posner, private eye,' then opened her eyes wide and rolled them around, Jerry Mahoney style.

'Yeah. Listen . . . '

Dessie placed a hand, fingers spread, between her breasts and stretched her neck. 'Y'know it was me who told Melody about you.'

'Yeah. Thanks a lot,' Posner grunted.

'How come you're *here*?'

Joe Posner knew he couldn't break the news of Melody's death to Dessie; at least not now, the way she was. 'Do you know why Melody came to me?'

'Totally. I'm like her best friend. She tells me everything. It was cause of the box, right? *I* know who took it,' she frowned poutily.

'You *do*. Who?'

'Tony.'

'Tony?'

'Tony Bagliano. Her so-called boyfriend. Mr. Puke-o-rama. I told her I knew, too.'

'If you told her that, why'd she come to me?'

'How should *I* know?' She threw her arms up, uncrossed her legs, and fell onto her back, wriggling her rear end into the fallen leaves.

'Wait. Dessie. How do you know Tony took it?'

'I saw him, the creep.'

'When did you tell Melody?'

'The next day. When she told me it was gone.'

'Why'd you wait till then?'

'Huh?'

'Why'd you wait till then?'

'Dessie closed her eyes slowly and smiled, as she piled leaves and dirt onto her belly. 'I don't get you.'

'If you saw him take it, why didn't you tell her right away?' Posner insisted.

Dessie didn't want him to. 'Oh, shut *up*!'

Posner took the load off his knees and shins, and sat back into the leaves. 'Dessie . . . there are a few things I'd really like to know. Will you help me?'

'What do you *want*?' she whined.

'First, tell me about Melody and drugs.'

'What d'ya mean?'

'Like, what does she use?'

'Hey! Forget it! Ask her.'

'How about heroin?'

'Heroin? Oh, God, don't be stupid. Nobody does heroin.'

'Nobody you know?'

'Uh-*uh*. We have too much respect for our bodies.'

'Sorry, I should have realized that. Something else: Rosalind told me you and Melody left together last night. Where'd you go?'

'Rosalind, my fucking sister? That total little fuck. I'm gonna kill her.' She pounded the ground with clenched fists. 'I hate when she talks about me.'

'Where'd you go?'

'Nowhere much. She just gave me a lift over to Salt's.'

'What's that?'

'What's what?'

'Salt's.'

'Dawn Salt's house. I was just gonna hang out. Melody was going to see Tony for a while. Hey, why are you asking me all this stuff? Why not ask Melody?' She rolled over on her stomach and lay her face on the ground. Posner ignored the question, and she was too far gone to notice.

'She was meeting Tony at his house?'

'Uh-uh. Maybe at Les's.'

'Les's house?'

'Yeah.'

'Why there?'

'*I* don't know. I'm not psychic, y'know.'

'Where does he live, Dessie?'

'Who?'

'Les!'

'Oh. Yeah. Near Cresskill.'

'Do you know the address or phone number?'

'Uh-uh. I know where it is, but I can't remember addresses.'

'Did Melody and Tony meet there other times?'

Dessie's face went quiet for a second. '*I* don't know if they went there. I know she was going to Fort Lee afterwards. She wanted me to meet her at the Fort Lee Diner at 10.30. I had like a big fight with Ethel about it. Auggh. Goddamn Ethel! I told her not to come here. But noooo. Just cause she teaches one crummy French class she thinks she can come on ASE. I swear she tries to totally ruin everything I do, y'know?'

'What was she doing in Fort Lee?' Posner persisted.

'When?'

'Last night.'

'Ethel wasn't in Fort Lee last night.'

'No, *Mel*ody. What was Melody doing in Fort Lee?'

'*I* don't know. She said she had this heavy date, but I think she was bullshitting. She kept saying it was with some "excellent dude". I mean she was so pseudo about it, I took it like a goof, y'know? But like she wouldn't like tell me what she was really doing, y'know? She just like kept saying it: "heavy date". "Excellent dude". I got totally sick of it.'

'Did you meet her afterward?'

'*No*. I *told* you. Ethel wouldn't let me. She was gonna stop me from coming on ASE if I went.'

'So you haven't talked to Melody since she dropped you at the Salts's?'

'Uh-uh.'

'Dessie,' Posner put as much honey in his voice as he could. 'I saw a picture at the school of Melody all beaten up. Who did that?'

Dessie's red eyes looked out dryly from under heavy lids. 'Ask Melody. She told me she fell down the steps, but I think Tony did it. I've seen him hit her. Will you carry me to my tent?'

Posner had to smile. 'Try walking. I've gotta go. Let me just get this straight: As far as you know, Melody didn't plan to go home from the time she got to your house till 10.30, when she said she'd be finishing a heavy date with an excellent dude. And after she dropped you off at the Salts's, she was planning to see Tony, maybe at Les's.' As he finished his summary, he realized that Dessie hadn't been listening. She rolled onto her back.

'Nobody ever carries me anymore.'

'Yeah,' Posner agreed, 'I know what you mean.' And he headed back toward the Dart.

8. Al B.Lopes

By the time Joe Posner made the Bergentown exit, the Palisades Parkway was jammed with commuters going the other way, and he smiled at his good luck at not being one of them. A few seconds later, stopped ten cars back from a red light, he realized that the exit would release him into the same sort of jam. There was a lesson in that somewhere, but Posner didn't want to think about it. By the time he got back to his office, it was growing dark.

His answering machine was flashing, and he rewound it, anxiously hoping he'd heard from Les, Webster, or maybe even a client who'd pay him for something. It wasn't any of them. It was Al B.Lopes, private investigator un-*extraordinaire*.

'Posnuh. Gimma a call at the office, pronto. If ya fuhgot, it's 568–2331.'

Posner almost groaned. If there was anything worse than not getting the messages he wanted, it was getting one from Al B.Lopes. He dialed the number.

'Lopes Investigations. Al B.Lopes speaking.'

'Lopes. Posner.'

'Posnuh, I gotta talk to you.'

'So, what's stopping you?'

'Don't be funny. I got something you want. Maybe exactly what you want.'

'You mean a medium rare porterhouse with madeira and anchovy sauce?'

'What the fuck are you talking about? This is serious

business.'

'So tell me what it is, already.'

'Not on the phone. Can you meet me?'

'Lopes. Is this for real?'

'You want this, Posnuh. Believe me.'

'O.K. Where?'

'Fort Lee. Meet me at the diner, third booth on the right – no, that's no good. Someone might be in it. I'll tell you what: I'll be wearing a trench coat with a red carnation so you'll know me. Got it?'

'Lopes,' Posner was touched by his own patience, 'I *do* know you. But maybe we should agree on a time?'

'I was gettin' to that, wiseguy. Let's see, it's five-fifteen now. How about six?'

'O.K. Six. See ya.'

'Posnuh . . .'

'Yeah?'

'Keep this eyes only, O.K.?'

'You mean, ears only, don't you?'

'Huh?'

'Never mind. See you at six.'

'Yeah.'

Posner put down the phone and rubbed his eyes. In the blue light of dusk, his office felt very empty and overtime tired. He called the Human Learning Space again, hoping he'd catch Norma.

'Hello, Space.'

'Norma. Hi. It's Joe Posner again.'

'Oh, Joe Posner. Joe Posner. Hi, Joe. Hi.'

'Hi.' Posner rubbed his eyes some more. 'I suppose Les never got there, huh.'

'Les? no. I mean, he was here, but he's gone now. He's not here. I gave him your message, though, and I'm sure he'll get in touch. Just be patient, OK?'

'Do you think he might call me tonight?'

'Do I think he might call you tonight? Uhm, No. No. I doubt it. He . . . Yes, he said he'd be out and be busy tonight. All night.'

'O.K., Norma. Great. Thanks. Bye, now.'

'Bye, Joe.'

Joe Posner put the phone down slowly. His office was almost completely dark now, but he didn't put on the light. He decided to wait till morning to try to get a hold of Tony Bagliano, and reached for his office T.V., then thought better of it. He reset the answering machine and headed over to the Human Learning Space to see if he could catch Les Coniff. If Norma was going to be that transparent, he ought to take advantage of it. This Les guy might not be so easy to catch up with.

The streets of Bergentown were now fully engorged by homeward bound commuters, and it took him nearly fifteen minutes to make the mile and a half to the school. While stopped at a red light two blocks from the school, he spotted an old, cream colored Mercedes convertible sedan tear out of the Space parking lot and head north. By the time his light had changed, it was out of sight. When he got to the lot, he saw Norma's car was gone, too, so he made a left at the next corner and headed for Fort Lee.

Despite the traffic, he got to the diner at a quarter to six. To make things as easy as possible for Al B.Lopes, Posner took the third booth on the right, sat on the side facing the door, and opened a menu. The Fort Lee Diner wasn't a great diner, but it was a good diner, and the menu was breaking Joe Posner's heart. Though he hadn't eaten all day, he'd blown at least ten bucks' worth of gas on the trip to Kinnehonka, and even the corned beef hash with poached egg was $3.95 plus tax. Plus tip. He'd order a cup of coffee and get some eggs and cheese on the way home for an omlette. The idea aroused no enthusiasm. The diner smelled like everyone in it was eating hash, but Posner just told himself to play it tough.

At five to six Posner saw Al B.Lopes enter the glass vestibule of the diner, reach into his trench coat, pull out a pack of Larks, light one, look around him in all directions, and walk into the diner. On his coat lapel was a white carnation.

He walked up to Posner's table without looking at him and squeezed his round torso behind the table. He was about forty-five, but had a smooth, fat, baby face with the downy moustache of a teenager. His greasy hair looked like it had been cut with a dull hacksaw.

'Hi, Lopes. What happened to the red carnation?'

Lopes still hadn't looked at him, as if he were pretending they weren't at the same table. 'They were out of them.'

'Lucky I recognized you.'

Finally, Lopes looked at him, and it was a plenty dirty look. 'You want this or not?'

'What is it?'

Lopes took a deep drag on his Lark and exhaled the smoke diffusely through nose and lips. 'I hear you're working on a case in regard with a young girl who snuffed it last night at Davis Park.'

'Where'd you hear that?'

'I'm not on liberty to disclose that.'

'O.K. You heard wrong. I'm not working on anything at the moment. But if I were?'

'If you were . . . I'd have something for you.'

'And am I supposed to pay you for this? 'Cause if that's it, we can forget it right now.'

'Nah. This is free.' Lopes reached out and grabbed a passing waitress by the wrist, and she turned to him in astonishment.

'Lissen, honey, get me two pizzaburgers, a large order of onion rings, and a large Diet Pepsi. O.K.?'

'O.K., O.K.,' she answered. 'Just keep you hands to yourself, O.K.?'

Lopes thought there was something funny in her reply, and he mugged broadly to Posner, winking two or three times, until they could both hear the waitress's stagewhispered, 'Big fat asshole.'

'Free, huh?' Posner couldn't stand the thought of Lopes's two pizzaburgers. 'Who's paying you?'

'Do I look like the kind of slob who'd give out a client's identity?' Lopes grinned, pulled at his cigarette, and dug some wax out of his ear.

'Exactly.'

'Oh, you're the fuckin' funnyman tonight, Posnuh. Do you want this or not?'

'You better hurry and tell me before we're both retired.'

Lopes laid his arms on the table and leaned forward. 'Be at the Lan-more Luncheonette in Edgewater tonight at exactly between twelve-thirty and a quarter to one, and someone's gonna give you what you're looking for. Got it? And don't be late. That's top priority.'

'What kind of a luncheonette is open after midnight, Lopes?'

'It'll be open, buddy.' Lopes sucked at something stuck between his teeth. 'Just be on time.'

'Lan-more, huh? It's on the main drag there, by the docks?'

'That's it.' He stubbed out his cigarette.

'And how am I supposed to know this person?'

'He'll know you. I don't know nothin else. That's all I got.'

'Thanks, Lopes. If I was working on this, I might be interested.' Posner got up. He wanted to be well away before Lopes's food came. 'Since somebody's paying you, pick up the coffee. O.K.?'

'Hey, wait a minute . . . '

'So long, Lopes.' Posner hustled himself into the parking lot and headed grimly for his omlette.

9. Close Misses

Jos Posner schlepped up the steps to his apartment, dropped his bag of groceries on the kitchenette bar-counter, pulled the evening *Record* from the bag, and switched on the T.V.

Warner Wolf was popping his buttons over the Knicks' first round elimination from the playoffs. Posner dropped his newspaper on the wooden floor; then, in front of it, lay on his stomach on the oversized bathmat he used as an area rug. He rested his chin on the backs of his hands and started to read. More advisors to El Salvador. He was glad he was too old to be drafted. Unless they raised the age, of course. With no surprise, he noticed that there was no mention of Melody Gold's death and figured Mrs. Gold was happy about that. Whether it was by pure coincidence or not he didn't know, but there was a feature story about heroin use in the area high schools. 'Epidemic' is what they called it. Kids take heroin when they think they have no future. That's what Joe Posner thought about it. Warner Wolf thought Kingman could hit thirty-five homers that season. As Joe Posner fell asleep on his paper, he could just hear Warner's lunatic cackle, 'Boom! F'rget abaht it! It's outta there!'

When the ringing of the phone woke him, Posner found his nose in a small pool of saliva on the newspaper. He jumped to his feet and made his way to the phone, still more asleep than awake. He wiped his wet cheek on his sleeve.

'Hello?'

'Joposner?'

'Alice?'

'Yes. How did you know it was me?' She sounded astonished.

'Never mind. What is it?' He reeled with sleepy, irritable confusion as Warner Wolf hollered the same exact inanities he'd heard before falling asleep. He looked at the clock and realized he'd slept from the 6.45 Warner to the 11.20 edition. Almost five hours. He must be depressed, he thought, or maybe just not used to working. Either way it was late for Alice to be calling.

'I need to talk to you. Now. Can you come over?'

'Sure.' His heart quickened. She was ready to spill. He struggled to clear his head. 'I'll be right there.' He hung up the phone and grabbed his jacket. The phone rang again. 'Hello?'

'Do you know my address?'

'Oh. Jesus. No. What is it?' She gave him a Fort Lee address and he rushed to the Dart.

On the way over he tried to remember as much as he could about their strange encounter of that afternoon. The amethyst and amber brooch and the photograph were two things he would certainly want her to talk about. But how to handle it? She obviously would scare easily. But would she talk or clam up if he scared her? No. Comfort was the ticket. Sympathy. Understanding. Patience. Then it hit him that she probably had heard about Melody's death, if she hadn't before. Maybe that's what had set her off. Then something else hit him: fucking Lopes's tip!

He'd forgotten all about it. What to do? Posner figured he had to go. Edgwater was just down the hill from Fort Lee. He could spend forty-five minutes with Alice and still be able to make it by 12.30. It smelled as fishy as a cannery town in August, but what did he have to lose? Lopes was greasy, but harmless. He wasn't likely to be involved in anything too heavy. Then he saw Melody; alive, tan legs crossed. 'Get a gun. This could get really heavy.' He went over the people who knew he was interested in the case: the mother, maybe the principal, Norma, Alice. That was it. At least that was all he knew about. He didn't know whom Melody had told. Dessie knew, but she was in the woods. Busy surviving. Fuck it. He'd check it out.

Alice's house was one of half a dozen or so still standing in a five-block area that was otherwise cleared. Another new high-rise in the offing, Posner figured. It was very small, practically a bungalow, and with cheap shingle siding in serious disrepair. Shutters were unhinged. Half of the screening in the screen door was torn loose. The concrete of the front steps was badly crumbled. What had once been a small lawn was now just dirt. Light shone through Indian bedspreads hung across the windows. The white VW he had seen in the school parking lot was parked in front. Next to it was a battered Saab with New Hampshire plates.

Posner padded up the walkway and steps to the front door. Voices from inside sounded like an argument. One of them was Alice Cabot's. The other also sounded like a woman's but its deep alto could have been that of a boy or a light-voiced man. The doorbell button had been ripped out. He had to shake the screen door to unstick it and get it open. At the sound of the shaking door, the voices stopped abruptly. Joe Posner knocked but got no answer. He knocked again.

'Hello.' The voice of Alice Cabot was cold.

'Alice, it's Joe.'

'Joe.' There was a pause. 'Joe. I'm sorry I called you over. Something's come up. Can you come back first thing in the morning?'

44

'Open the door, Alice. Let's just talk a minute.'

'No, Joe. It's not possible. Come back in the morning. Nine o'clock.'

Posner couldn't believe his big break was disappearing like this, so quickly. He figured he had no choice but to continue playing it cool. 'Whatever you say. I'll see you in the morning.'

'Good night, Joe. I'm sorry.'

'Alice, have you got Les's address or phone number?'

Alice didn't answer right away. 'No. I don't know. Sorry. I'm sorry. About everything.'

'Don't worry about it. Good night, see you tomorrow.' Being stoic was one of the things Joe Posner liked best about being a detective. Also being sly. He stayed on the stoop, after closing the screen door, and waited for the voices to resume. They didn't. He figured they were waiting for the sound of his engine, and decided there was no point in keeping them waiting.

Now he had at least half an hour to kill. The Fort Lee Diner was only two blocks away. He thought again about their corned beef hash with poached egg: gooey and salty and attractively served with toast made of the softest, squarest, whitest bread. He'd slept through dinner. He was starving. It would still cost him nearly five bucks, but what the hell. It would be after one by the time he got home. He hopped in the Dart and drove to the diner a happy man. He was still glowing when he left the Dart in the parking lot, but halfway up the steps he stopped.

Why not be really clever, he thought. Why not take another crack at it? He covered the two blocks back to Alice Cabot's house at a full trot. Posner felt excited and surprisingly limber as his good sneakers carried him smoothly over the asphalt. Off to his left, the lights from the George Washington Bridge bleached the night sky. Fumes from the bridge traffic and the brackish salt smell of the Hudson at high tide alternated in his nostrils.

By the time he got to the sidewalk in front of the house, he was winded. The Saab and the VW were still parked there. The lights were out. He waited till his breathing was normal before he got closer. Then, stepping slowly and lightly, he got back to the front door. He couldn't hear anything. Posner made a slow, silent creep around the house. He stopped next to a rear window. It was open a crack, but the curtain was drawn. He could hear a light snore. That was fast, he thought. From argument to sleep in less than fifteen minutes. He walked over to the Saab and looked in. There was nothing to see.

Joe Posner headed back to the diner, walking this time, and speculated on the situation. The house was too small for more than one bedroom. But then there was probably a couch. He wished he had a better idea of the age and gender of the second voice. Of course Alice could be alone now. Whoever belonged to the Saab could have left on foot, or been picked up by someone else. Maybe the other person didn't have anything to do with the Saab. Not likely. He'd bet they were both still in there. Remembering Alice's crotch on his leg, he guessed they were together. Tomorrow morning at nine o'clock would tell. Maybe. For the next twenty minutes Joe Posner would concentrate on corned beef hash. With a poached egg.

The road down the hill from Fort Lee to Edgewater was dark, and, since the first budget crunches of the seventies, full of pot holes. Joe Posner didn't like driving down it as fast as he was, but he was already late. Wolfing his food at the diner had proven futile, since it had taken eight minutes to get the check. Now it was already 12.45.

Halfway down the hill all the buildings started looking like Alice Cabot's house. Nobody, it seemed, wanted to tear down Edgewater and put up high rises. Not yet, anyway. Except for the heavy-industrial quality of the junk – boilers, heavy-duty plumbing and heating fixtures, gears, turbine parts – that lay rusting in the vacant lots, it could have been Appalachia. Sagging, unpainted porches, Texaco signs washed out by rain, screens ripped from their frames and clogged with soot, tall grass growing from cracks wherever there was concrete. Mud everywhere else.

At the bottom of the hill, just past where the road flattened, a small, chocolate brick town house development hugged the river edge. It was new and looked like it would stay new-looking for at least another six months. On the right, under the

Palisades, was downtown Edgewater, which looked not a hell of a lot different from downtown Bergentown, except smaller, more depressed, and in worse repair. Craning his neck, Posner could see the flotilla of Fort Lee high rises along the crown of the Palisades above. It was like a thirty-year time warp from bottom to top, but Posner knew it was really only a real estate warp, a money warp, a class warp.

A couple of blocks further down, two policecars were parked nose-to-nose, flashing blue lights – Edgewater police had blue lights. It seemed like stumbling onto late-night police maneuvers was getting to be a habit with Posner, and it wasn't one he much liked. A crowd had gathered. Posner slowed down to rubberneck and caught the old painted green and white Coke sign of the place where they'd stopped: Lan-more. He parked in front of a No Parking sign and ran over to the place. An ambulance sped around a corner, cackling electronic bleeps.

Posner didn't know any Edgewater cops, but, remembering how much good knowing Webster had done him, he decided to see what he could find out anyway. He wriggled his way to the front of the crowd – teenagers, mostly – holding beer cans and chatting loosely, as much in celebration as curiosity. In front, he pushed in next to a short, wiry old woman dressed in a red hunting jacket and a plastic rain kerchief, and got the attention of the cop holding back the line.

'What's going on?' Posner asked the cop. Three medics hustled into the luncheonette.

The cop was big and wore mirror sunglasses – a bad sign, Posner thought, at one in the morning. 'Police business,' the cop snorted.

'I was supposed to meet somebody in there five minutes ago. Can I find out if he's alright?'

The cop's face stayed frozen. 'If he was in there, he ain't alright – he's dead.'

Posner's heart started to race. 'What d'you mean?'

The cop ignored him. The old woman had turned to Posner and watched him during the interchange with the cop, nodding her head, wart-covered chin thrust forward, as if she had something to say. 'Do you know what he means?' Posner asked her.

She smiled and nodded her head. 'Dey kilt 'em awl.' Her smile broadened in gleeful excitement. 'Dey come for Santangelino, but dey kilt 'em awl. Ev'ybody in de whole friggin' place. I got here ahead of de cops, y'know. Whew! What a hit. No witnesses. Not that's alive, anyhow. What a hit!'

Posner looked around in all directions, unzipped his coat, scratched his head, pulled his nose. 'They killed everybody who was in the place?'

She laughed. 'Even de cockaroaches!'

The corned beef hash in Posner's stomach turned to lava. 'Who were they? Who's Santangelino?'

The old woman looked up at him out of the corner of her eye, and shook her head. 'You don't know much, do ya? Santangelino was de head of de family operation aroun' heah. "Dey" was, in my guess, probly de Forlinos. It's been comin', but what a hit!'

'Santangelino's a drug boss?' Posner didn't know why she should know, except that she seemed to know everything else.

'Nah. Numbers. I'd bet my welfare check on that dere wasn't no drugs in dis hit. Nah. Eh-eh. Numbers.'

'Who else was in there?'

'Just de guy at the countah, his brudduh, and Santangelino's body guards. Didn't even get dere pieces outta dere pockets,' she laughed, 'I'll tell you, buddy, dat was one beeyootiful set-up. One beeyootiful set-up.'

10. Connections

The second morning after Melody Gold's death a cold rain was falling. Joe Posner stood by his bedroom window and watched the rain saturate the recently thawed earth around the house. The window was old and loose-fitting, and the heavy chill draft from it told him that winter would be back for the day. The night had been mostly sleepless. Two large scotches hadn't kept away the dozens of anxious dreams that he was still rattled by, but couldn't remember. He found a pair of khakis that were almost clean and not too wrinkled and a fresh wool shirt he'd hoped he wouldn't need again till the next fall. A trace of heartburn still lingered from the hash, so he decided to go over to Alice Cabot's without coffee.

Joe Posner took the steps gently. He opened the door a crack and looked at the street before going out. When he checked under the Dart's hood for a bomb, he wasn't certain whether he was being melodramatic for looking or foolishly reckless for not catching the next plane to another continent.

The streets of Fort Lee were clogged with Manhattan-bound commuters looking to avoid the more severely clogged major approaches to the bridge. Steam rose from the hood of Posner's Dodge while it stood in a long single file, seven or eight cars back from the light. Small neon signs, specks of color in the dark morning wet, shone from small businesses: stationery, bagels, sporting goods, factory second linens. Plywood sheets boarded up the rest. Signs of the times. Anxious adrenalin coursed through Posner's arteries, riding bareback on the blood cells. Every twenty seconds or so, he checked his rearview mirror for black sedans filled with gangsters, but saw none. He looked at his watch. Even with traffic he'd be there by nine.

It was five-to when he parked in front of Alice Cabot's house. The Saab and the Volks were both gone. That made him even more nervous, and he ran up the sidewalk and banged on the door. Every two or three seconds a large glob of cold water dropped from the roof and hit him on the head, making him wince. He banged on the door again; harder this time. He tried the door. It was open.

There were two bare, single mattresses on the floor, arranged in an L, like two sofas. On the other side of the room there was an empty bookcase about two and a half feet tall, leaning heavily to the right. A pile of old copies of the *New York Times* sat on top. A few sections were scattered around the floor. Otherwise the front room was empty. The Indian bedspreads that had covered the windows were gone. Posner walked into the bedroom, fairly certain of what he'd find. He found it. Nothing. Another mattress. This one was a double, but just as thin, just as crummy, just as bare as the two in the front room. No clothes. No dresser. Nothing in the bathroom. He found a cheap bridge table in the kitchen with a stack of greasy pots and pans. They were old and hadn't been good when they were new. He guessed they had been stacked up to be taken and then deemed not worth it. There wasn't anything in the place anybody was going to come back for.

He made a dash through the rain and pulled himself into the driver's seat of the Dart. He started the engine to get the heater going and sat thinking. All of a sudden things were getting scary. He decided to try the school again, and picked up a paper on the way.

The paper store had a stack of *Post* Metro editions by the cash register. The front page was the predictable 'MOB RUBOUT IN NJ!' in white on black. He dropped his quarter on the counter and picked one up. The young man with thick glasses who worked the register smiled. 'Local stuff – sellin' like hot shit.'

'Great,' Posner grunted. Seeing it in the paper – even a Rupert Murdoch paper – made it all seem more real, and right away he started wishing he hadn't looked. The *Post* version was pretty close to that of the Edgewater Good Samaritan Posner had encountered on the scene. Santangelino. Numbers. Forlinos. Police speculate. All bodies accounted for. Except for the one standing in the paper store, thought Posner.

The phonebooth was in the back. Far from the window, but just as far from the door. Posner walked to it slowly, listening behind his back for any sudden sounds. As he dialed, he kept his eyes on the front.

'Lopes Investigations. Al B.Lopes speaking.'

'Lopes. It's your old buddy, Joe Posner.'

'Hi, Posnuh. Everything work out O.K. last night?'

'Well, I'd like to discuss that particular matter with you at your earliest convenience.'

'What's the gag, Posnuh?'

'That's what I want to know. And who the fuck thinks it's funny.'

'I don't know watchuh talkin' about.'

'Just tell me when we can get together today, and if you can convince me of that, I might not break your fucking legs.'

'What's a matter? Didn't nobody show up last night?'

'Will you be in your office another fifteen?'

'Uh-uh. I'm on my way to court. Be there till at least noon.'

'Fuck. Meet me at two. Same place as yesterday. O.K.?'

'No good. Gotta keep your habits unregular, y'know? You got a lot to learn in this racket, Posnuh. Meet me at the candy store at Loon Avenue just south of Tenafly. Know it?'

'Whatever you say, hot shot. Just be there.'

'I'll be there. Just take it easy.'

'Pick up the Metro edition of the *Post* and see if you'd be takin it easy if it were you. See you at two.' Posner banged down the phone and zipped up his leather jacket. Take it easy, he shuddered. What a swell idea. Keep moving and stay low seemed better.

Traffic going away from the bridge was light, and it was only about nine-thirty when Joe Posner rolled into the parking lot of the Human Learning Space. None of the three cars he'd seen the day before were there. Next to the psychedelic garage, though, there was a huge, filthy, white '66 Oldsmobile. Posner parked the Dart over by the entrance to the school and got out into the rain. A window was open on the second story of the garage, and saxophone music poured out. It was 'Lush Life,' one of Posner's favorite tunes, and it was no recording. The music felt like hot soup after a blizzard. If someone could be playing 'Lush Life' on a sax at ten am on a cold rainy spring morning, the world couldn't be all bad.

On one side of the garage, Posner found an open door and a stairway behind it. It smelled like sawdust. He took the steps two at a time, hoping to get to the top before the music stopped. At the top of the stairs Posner found himself in a rough, but surprisingly well-equipped recording studio. Posters of Charlie Parker, Elvin Jones, and Jimi Hendrix were mounted on the walls. Paper cups and bags from McDonald's and Chicken Too Good were heaped in all the corners and around all the chairs. At the far end of the room a tall, emaciated man stood, facing a corner and playing a tenor saxophone. His blond hair was very

51

long and straight and tied in a pony tail beneath a brown and white South American knit cap; Peruvian, Posner guessed. His playing was good (especially, Posner thought, for a white guy) – sort of Ben Webster breathy with a little Archie Shepp sinew. He was just starting the release when Posner got there, and the detective, encouraged by all the adrenalin his anxiety had left on hand, and more than a little desperate for some kind – any kind – of bond, sang along in his half-tongue-in-cheek Johnny Hartman style. *'Life is lonely,/Again, and only last year/Every thing seemed so . . .'* He could never remember that word. The sax player turned, eyes wide and smiling, and kept playing. Posner kept singing.

'Now life is awful
da-dum, a troughful
Of hearts could only be a bore.
A week in Paris would ease the bite of it.
All I care is to smile in spite of it.
I'll forget you,
I will, while yet you
Are still burning inside my brain.
Romance is mush, stifling those who strive
I'll live a lush life in some small dive.
And there I'll be, while I rot with the rest
Of those whose lives are lonely toooo.'

The saxophonist laughed and clapped his hands together. 'All *right*. All *right*.'

'All right yourself,' Posner answered. 'You can really play.'

'Well, thanks, man. I do my best, you know?'

'What's your name?'

'Hawk, man, glad to meet you.' He held out his hand and grasped Posner's in a 'soul' handshake. 'What's yours?'

'Joe.'

'Glad to blow with you, Joe.'

'You teach music at the school here?'

'Yeah, man. That's my story. What's yours?'

'I'm looking for Alice Cabot. You seen her?'

'Uh-uh, man. Not lately. Heard she was splitting the scene here, though. What you want her for?'

'I'm her brother.' Joe Posner didn't feel like lying, but he hadn't been doing too well with the truth. It felt like a luxury, and Joe Posner felt poor that morning. Real poor. 'I was by her place, but she wasn't home.'

'Her brother, huh?' Hawk seemed more amused than suspicious at the lack of family resemblance. 'Nice to meet you, man. Sorry I can't help you out. She ain't been here today, I can tell you that. Only me. Blues in the mo'nin'. I come to practise.' The lids sank in modesty over his gray eyes.

'Say, Alice was a little funny on the phone about why she's leaving. She can be like that, sort of evasive, you know?' Hawk didn't answer. 'I think she's upset about it, and I'd like to help her out, but I could help her better if I knew what was going on. You know anything about it, Hawk?'

'Well, you know, man, I don't really. I know it was kinda sudden. She just dropped it at a faculty meeting about three or four weeks ago. She's splittin' at Easter Vacation, she says. That's all I know. There's a lot of gossip around this place, but I try to stay away from it. You know what I mean?' He slid long fingers down his thin, pale, boney nose. His teeth were a little crooked.

'What kind of gossip?'

'Like I say, I try to keep away from it.'

'I heard about that student dying of an overdose. What was her name? Melody?'

'Yeah, man. That was really too bad.' Hawk bent over and started fiddling in his saxophone case. It was new – even though the sax itself was old and dented – and the buckles and hinges looked like real brass.

'What was she like?'

Hawk answered quickly, automatically. 'She was ambitious, man.'

'Ambitious how?'

'Just ambitious, man.' He didn't look up from the case.

'Well, what kind of thing did she do to make you feel that way?'

'I don't know, man. I can't explain it any more than that.' An edge of nervousness had crept into his voice.

'Alice told me there was a big party at the girl's place the other night.' Hawk made no comment. 'Were you there?'

'Everyone was there, man.'

'Did anything happen there that night?'

'Happen? I don't get you, man. What d'you mean, "happen?" ' Hawk was getting peeved, and Posner knew he was asking too many questions about Melody Gold for Alice Cabot's brother. He wanted to ask about the box, but couldn't figure out how to bring it up. He'd have to wait. 'I don't know. Alice seemed upset when I talked to her Saturday morning . . . I thought maybe something happened at the party.' Hawk still had no comment. 'Well, thanks for the music. I gotta find Alice. See you around, Hawk.'

'Later, Joe.'

'Say, do you ever play gigs?'

'Sure.'

'What's your last name? I wanna look out for you.'

'Brennan. Hawk Brennan.' He was smiling again.

'Great. Nice to meet you.'

'You, too, man.'

'Say, you think Les will be in soon?'

'Wouldn't know, bro.'

'You have his number, by any chance?'

'Not on me. Norma'll be here soon. She'll give it to you.'

'Great. Thanks, man. I'll see you.'

'Later.'

Being with Hawk felt safe – relatively safe, anyway – and as Posner left him, he felt the chill from outside sweep up the dark staircase and through his bones. He wished he could see the parking lot before he went down the steps and out the door, but he couldn't. He stood at the top of the steps for the few seconds it took to realize that he really had to go sooner or later. Then he took a breath, launched into a scat version of 'A Foggy Day in London Town,' and bounced himself back outside.

He didn't see a hitman. He didn't see a black sedan. He did see that the orange Datsun he guessed to be Norma's had arrived. It was about the least sinister car he'd ever seen. The light in the office was on, and Posner headed for the entrance. Just as he got to the steps he saw a tall, thin black kid, about seventeen, walk into the parking lot. He wore matching maroon slacks, jacket and 'Big Apple' cap and black sneakers. He walked quickly, with a jaunty gait in a straight line aimed at the garage. The day before, looking at the photographs, Posner had noticed only three black kids. Only one of them was a boy. And they were all dressed mountain style. This kid was definitely someone else.

Joe Posner was torn between his curiosity about the kid and his desire to get to Norma before Les arrived. He decided to take a chance on Les's being late, and once the kid was inside the garage, he jogged back across the parking lot. He eased the door open and slipped inside, standing in the landing at the foot of the stairs. He heard Hawk's voice from the floor above. The musician was trying to keep his voice low, but it was distinctly audible from Posner's listening post.

'Are you fucking crazy? I should cut your ass *off* for this, man.'

'Hey, man, I'm sorry. I told you. But my man's sick. He couldn't wait till tonight.'

'I haven't got anything now.'

'Can't you get something? Just a little. He needs it.'

'All right. Forty-five minutes. Davis Park. Be waiting.'

'Oh, man. You're beautiful, man.'

'Now get the fuck out of here. And if you *ever* come back to this place, you're through. You got that?'

'I swear man.'

'And if you don't have that Haydn down solid on Thursday, I'll kick your butt.'

Posner ducked out the door and ran back to his Dart. Lying flat on the seat, he left the door ajar to avoid the sound of slamming it. After a minute or two he heard the roar of an old V–8 starting and knew it was Hawk's Olds. He sat up as it pulled out of the lot and headed south. For once, the Dart didn't stall, and he got onto the road while the Olds was still in sight. His hands trembled on the wheel.

The rain had stopped, but the wet roads still reflected the red lights of the cars of mid-morning shoppers and errand runners. Posner followed the Olds through the single shopping street in Leonia. Then, two blocks on the other side of the main intersection at Broad and Fort Lee Road, it went left into one of the handsomer residential side streets in the area. The houses, all pre-war, but none older than fifty years, sat atop a hill that rose steeply from the street. Long ribbons of steps connected them to the sidewalk. They were large, comfortable-looking wood and stucco houses, but not opulent, like that clumsy Gold fortress or the more confident nineteenth-century wood frame mansions that dotted the area.

Two blocks down, the Oldsmobile turned another corner and stopped in front of the third house in. It was a bit larger than the rest and built with dark green beams in a mock Tudor style. Ivy reached three-quarters of the way up its three stories. Posner pulled his Dart over before turning the corner, and watched Hawk Brennan get out of his Olds and walk up the long stairway to the house. The door opened, and a man with gray hair and a thick gray moustache opened the door. He was dressed in khaki trousers and a rust crewneck sweater. It was too far away for Posner to make out much else. When the door closed behind Brennan, Posner pulled around the corner and read the number on the door as he passed the house. 347. 347 Woodmont Lane. At the next corner he turned around and parked, facing the direction he had come, and waited for Hawk to emerge.

It took only five minutes. Hawk came bouncing down the steps, slid behind the wheel of the Olds, and took off. Joe Posner followed him back to the school. He parked the Dart across the street from the school parking lot and watched as the lanky blond man loped up the steps to his studio. A few minutes later, he ran back to the Olds and restarted the engine. Posner ducked below his dashboard. He wondered how long he'd be able to keep this up without being spotted. If Hawk was doing what Joe Posner thought he was, he was being awfully careless. Drug pushing seemed to be the kind of thing teachers would try to stay away from. And if they couldn't stay away, he thought, they ought to be more careful than this. Posner gave the music teacher a big head start, since he had an idea of where he was going and didn't want to be too obvious. The difficulty would be to get close enough without being spotted once they got to the park.

Several residential streets ran perpendicular to the road Davis Park was on. Joe Posner turned up the one closest to the park and found an empty driveway next to a split level, four houses from the corner. He left the Dart there and sprinted toward the park. He was as tight as he had been limber the night before. Before the Lan-more. He was tight alright. After about thirty yards he had to slow down to a fast walk. He was too late. The Olds was already pulling back on the road. An equally beat-up Pontiac Bonneville went off in the opposite direction. Before he ducked behind a mailbox to get out of Brennan's view, Posner caught a glimpse of maroon in the driver's seat of the Bonneville. Hawk Brennan's Oldsmobile sped past the mailbox and around the bend. Joe Posner stood up. He hadn't seen the transaction, but he had little doubt about what was going on. Hawk Brennan was at least one germ in the 'heroin epidemic ravaging area youth'. Of course, he had no proof. Just a fragment of a conversation that *might* have meant something completely different. And a meeting in a park too short for anything but an exchange of some sort. If he could only get a little bit more on Brennan, he could force him to talk about Melody Gold. And he'd bet that Brennan would have something to talk about. With an imaginative bluff, he could probably make him talk right away, but that would mean tipping his hand. He'd sit on it for a while. Maybe it would be long enough to figure out what, if anything, the Forlinos had to do with it.

Then there was the question of the police. Posner had sold too many ounces of pot in his youth to want to get small fry like Brennan busted. Even for heroin. Selling junk. To kids. He didn't like it. Not at all. But he didn't like getting someone busted for small drug stuff, either. It had been one of the reasons he'd quit customs work. Whoever was in 347 Woodmont Lane, however, might be a different story.

11. Maneuvers

When Joe Posner got back to the Human Learning Space, the orange Datsun was still the only car in the parking lot. On his way to the office he stopped at the payphone in the corridor and jotted down the number. He found Norma in the same position as the day before.

'Hi, Joe! What're *you* doing here?'

'I just couldn't stay away. Whatcha typin', Norma?'

'Just about a million pages of evaluations.' She waved her long, red nails at a tall stack of handwritten pages.

'Evaluations?'

'We don't give grades. The teachers write out what they think about each student, instead.'

'Really. Sounds like a good idea. Kind of tough on you, though. Huh?'

'I don't mind. Some of them are pretty interesting, you know?'

'I can imagine. What kind of evaluations did Melody Gold get?'

Norma's face got sulky. 'Uh-uh. You've got to talk to Les about that.'

So much for working on Norma. 'He's not in, is he?'

'Uh-uh. I don't think he's coming in today'.

'I was really looking for Alice Cabot. Know where I might find her?' Posner scanned the bulletin board behind her and spotted the 'Faculty Contact List.'

'Joe, you seem like a really nice guy to me. But this Melody Gold thing could be bad for the school.' Her wet, brown eyes could have melted a dog catcher.

'I don't want to do anything to hurt the school. I just want to talk to Alice Cabot.'

'You never know, Joe. Anything you say, no matter how unrelated, could be very important.' She spoke her words as she might a catechism. She'd been well coached. 'It's just too sensitive. I don't think I ought to talk to you at all. The best thing would be to talk to Les.'

'Fine. How can I find him?'

'I really can't give that information out.' Posner could see the pain it gave her to have to say no again.

'Can I use your phone for a second?' He tilted his head at an extension on a table in the far corner of the office.

'Sure, go right ahead.'

'Thanks.' He sat down by the table, opened the Bergen County telephone book, pretended to find the number he was looking for, and dialed the number of the payphone down the hall. Its ring echoed through the corridor.

'Oh, *darn* it.' Norma stopped typing. 'Excuse me, Joe. I have to get that.'

When she left the office, Posner dropped the receiver on the table, slipped behind Norma's desk, and grabbed the mimeographed address list. He folded it in quarters without looking at it and stuck it in his back pocket. Then he ran his fingers down the folders in the file cabinet till he came to the one marked 'Melody Gold.' He shoved the whole folder inside his jacket and pulled the zipper up.

On his way out he passed Norma in the hall. 'Can you believe it? There wasn't anybody there.'

'No kidding.'

'That stuff really burns me up.'

'I know what you mean. I gotta go, Norma.'

'Take care, Joe.'

Joe Posner hesitated for a few seconds at the school door. It had started to rain again. He pulled his jacket up and his head in and skipped down the steps to his car. Falling behind the wheel, he shivered and cursed the cold wet. Still, he felt good about his little flim-flam. He pulled out the folder, put it beside him on the seat, and pulled the Dart out of the parking lot. When he'd put a few blocks between him and Norma he stopped under a mammoth, newly-leafed elm to survey his booty.

Melody's file contained transcripts from the local public elementary school and two private ones, three private junior highs, and Bergen Valley High, the local public high school, which she had attended, or, as the record indicated, hadn't attended, for the first term of the previous year. Her grades had started as mostly As and Bs in elementary school, then, from the fourth grade on, had fallen steadily. After eighth grade she hadn't lasted anywhere long enough to receive grades.

Teachers' comments in every grade at every school were different combinations of 'unmanageable,' 'high strung,' 'selfish,' 'destructive,' 'dishonest,' and 'unhappy,' with a sprinkling of 'underlying potential,' 'better than average aptitudes,' and 'might do better in a different environment.'

Her Human Learning Space record covered a year and a half. Her first 'evaluations' had been strikingly more encouraging than anything since third grade. One, from Alice Cabot, in a class entitled 'Death,' noted that while 'you should of come to class more than six times, you were really involved. Your memories about when your grandmother died were really great, and we all enjoyed them a lot. I'm definitely looking forward,' she went on, 'to getting to know you better and have you in more classes.' Another evaluation from that term, for a class listed as being in the History Department and called 'Early Beatles,' was written by one Geoffrey 'Elvis' Smucker. It lauded Melody for being 'fun to have in class' and made special mention of her 'too-much hair and eyes,' though it took her to task for 'talking a little too much to Dessie when we were discussing lyrics.' Elvis also looked forward to having her in more classes.

One of the evaluations from that first term struck Posner because, unlike the others, which were typed (by Norma, he assumed), it was written in a large, floridly artistic hand that seemed strangely familiar to him. The language, too, had a familiar ring. It was for a class called 'Studio,' and it was the least laudatory of those he'd looked at: 'Your Herculean efforts to escape, evade, and generally elude anything in the slightest sense resembling work, responsibility, or consideration for others, though placing you unquestionably within the mainstream ethos of the class, represented for me a sad squandering of human capabilities. Would that some of this formidable energy could have been turned to more productive ends.' The signature at the bottom told Joe Posner why it seemed familiar: Alan Apfelbaum.

Apfelbaum was an artist who had lived in the same apartment building in Washington Heights as Ellen, Posner's last serious girlfriend. They had been friendly neighbors, and Posner had spent several evenings in Alan's spacious, river-view apartment drinking German brandy and listening to his improbable and hilarious stories and harangues. Posner had some vague recollection that Alan had been teaching part-time at some school in Jersey. He hadn't seen him in the two years since Ellen had moved to Boston and he'd moved to Jersey, but he was fairly sure that Alan would remember him. He checked the faculty contact list for a phone number, but Apfelbaum wasn't on it. Posner hoped that Information could help.

Posner leafed through the file a little more avidly, now, having found so promising a lead. Melody's fall term that year got mixed reviews. Alice praised her in Mexican Cooking: 'Even though you could of been a little more cooperative and helpful at clean-up, and you missed too many classes, I felt *super* good getting to really know you. It was a growing experience for me. And your great sense of humor and energy made the class great for all of us. Love, Alice.'

The math teacher, though, a Mary Ann Scapelli, refused her credit for Algebra I. 'The class agreed that three cuts would mean no credit. You cut 7 times, or 19.4% of all classes. This makes your lack of concentration, attention and cooperation besides the point.'

But she received three credits, one in English, one in psychology, and one in human studies, for her participation in Advanced Intimacy Workshop, taught by none other than Les Coniff himself. 'You're beautiful, and you know you're beautiful. I'd have been more comfortable with your participation in this workshop if we could have got you sharing more with the others. The work we did in private was major and beautiful, but next time I want you to struggle for more disclosure. The material on your mother is so important, and the work you're doing with Marjorie-Lynn is so great, but we know that the other issues are still there. Next time will be great. Love, Les.' Like our President, Posner thought: A great communicator.

He wished he had everybody's files. It was great reading. But he wanted to get to a phone. He leafed through an assortment of letters that didn't seem like much. One, from a Marjorie-Lynn Feldman-Goldberg, C.S.W., in Teaneck, was addressed to Les Coniff. It was short and to the point.

Dear Les,

Couldn't get you on the phone. Melody's mother is giving me a hard time about paying for the sessions. Can you put some pressure on from your end? Thanks.

Love
Marjorie-Lynn

Now that was a promising lead, Posner thought. Nothing like a disgruntled shrink for spilling family secrets.

Posner started the Dart and rode down to a luncheonette on the fringe of the business section to make some calls. Halfway there, he realized he'd stopped checking his rearview mirror for possible hit men, but he wasn't sure if that was good or bad. The Human Learning Space seemed as far from the Lan-more as Disneyland from the Bowery, and what the connection could be, he sure as hell didn't know. Except that if there really was one, it had to be Melody Gold.

Once inside the luncheonette, he stood by the door for a moment, trying to shake off the damp chill. He turned around to see an enormously fat woman, about fifty, staring at him from behind the counter, with a wide but unfeeling grin smeared across her face. Tiny black eyes, inert as frozen blackberries, peeped from under the bangs of a frosted hairdo. 'What can I get you?'

'I just wanted to use the payphone, thanks.' Posner nodded at the phone by the door.

'Sorry.' Posner could tell it was her favorite word. 'No phone calls without an order.'

'What?' Posner was stunned.

'No phone calls without an order.' She underlined each word with sensuous delight.

'I'll have a cup of coffee.'

'You want it at the counter or at a table?'

'The counter.' Posner hadn't expected that making the call would involve such elaborate negotiations.

'Dollar minimum at the counter.'

Posner looked around the luncheonette. There was only one other customer, who seemed to be meditating on a bowl of soup. 'Minimum at the *counter*? How 'bout if I have it at a table?'

'That's a two-seventy-five minimum.'

He looked hard into her eyes to see if she was joking. 'You mean it's gonna cost me a dollar-ten just to make a phone call from this place?'

'Don't get smart, mister. The phone call's only a dime. The *minimum*'s a dollar.'

'How 'bout if I give you fifty cents and don't order anything? Just use your phone?'

The offer perplexed her. 'I'll ask my husband.' She maneuvered her wide load through the kitchen door. Posner was beginning to wonder if he was dreaming. On the wall behind the counter a large tag board sign was hung. 'The Hippo Club' was lettered across the top. A list of about twenty names went down the left side. Vertical lines divided the chart into weeks, forming a box for each week next to each name. A number was written in each box with a plus or a minus. Another smaller sign was hung next to it which read 'Congratulations Hippo Club! The Hippos lost *113* pounds in March! Let's keep it up!'

A fat man wearing an apron came out from the kitchen. He wasn't as wide as his wife, but his stomach made up for it. 'You givin' the missus a hard time, buddy?'

'Look, mister, I just want to make a call, and I don't want to eat anything. That's not usually a crime.'

'O.K., wiseguy, make your call and get the hell outta here. And don't come back. We don't like your type around here.'

Posner stifled his impulse to attempt a retort. Making the call and getting out of there was, after all, his primary objective. And as for not coming back, they were in complete harmony. He was curious to know what type he was, but fought off the feeling.

He dialed Information in New York and got Apfelbaum's number. It was the same exchange as Ellen's had been, so Posner guessed he was still in the same apartment. When the operator told him that the call over the Hudson was going to cost a dollar-ten, Posner grimaced at the irony, then panicked at the thought of having to ask at the counter for change. He felt an almost religious gratitude when he found a dollar-fifty in change in his pocket.

'Hello?' Alan Apfelbaum's voice had a familiar European lilt.

'Alan? This is Joe Posner; Ellen's friend?'

'Joe! Good to hear from you. How have you been?'

'I'm O.K., thanks. Listen, Alan, I wondered if you'd have some time for a chat.'

'Sure. Come over now if you want. What's it about?'

'I don't want to go into it on the phone, really. Do you teach at a school out here in Jersey?'

'Did, my good friend, did. You mean the Yooman Learning Space?' He pronounced it in a snide imitation of a Brooklyn accent. 'I got out last June. Three years was more than enough. Why do you want to know about that? And what do you mean "out here in Jersey?" Are you calling from Jersey?'

'Yeah, I am. I'll tell you about it when I get there.'

'Are you coming now?'

'Well, I was going to try to get a hold of this Coniff guy . . . '

Apfelbaum groaned at the other end.

'Look, Alan, If I don't call you right back, I'll be there in twenty minutes. O.K.?'

'Good. I'll make some lunch.'

'No. Don't bother.' Posner's mouth was starting to water at the thought of lunch at Apfelbaum's. Alan was a superb cook, and Posner knew his polite refusal would be brushed aside.

'No bother. I have some soup from yesterday.'

'Sounds great. See ya, Alan.' Posner pulled the hook down and dialed Coniff's number from the staff list, but got no answer. He took the student list out of his back pocket, and found Tony Bagliano's number. Then, underneath it, he saw

64

something on the list that raised his eyebrows a good way up his balding forehead: Blittstein, Larry. 347 Woodmont Lane, Leonia. Parents: Marty and Susan.' Marty Blittstein of Leonia. Posner had heard of him. He was a small time entrepreneur on the off-beat culture scene and pretty well known within the miniscule bohemia of Bergen County. The gray hair and the bushy moustache fit. But had Hawk gone to see Blittstein senior or Blittstein junior?

Posner dialed Tony Bagliano's number. A woman answered.

'May I please speak with Tony?' Posner asked.

'You want Big Tony or Little Tony?'

'Little Tony, I guess.'

'He's not here. Who's calling please?'

'I'm a friend of a friend. Do you expect him later?'

'Not particularly,' she sounded uneasy and a little angry. 'May I have your name?'

'He wouldn't know it, actually. Is there somewhere I can reach him?'

'Not that I know of. Who is this? Is he in trouble?'

'No. No. Thanks, anyway.' Posner hung up. Then he dialed Marjorie-Lynn Feldman-Goldberg from the number on her letter in the file.

'Hello?' The voice was flat, but tenderly breathy.

'Hello? Is this Marjorie-Lynn Feldman-Goldberg?' Posner asked in his most depressed and anomic voice.

'Marjorie-Lynn Feldman. We got divorced.'

'Oh. I'm sorry.'

'Don't be. We're both much more actualized because of it.'

'Oh. Good, then.'

'Thank you. To whom am I speaking?'

'My name is Billy Strayhorn, and I was hoping I could see you for a . . . a . . . talk sometime very soon.'

'I think that would be possible. How did you get my name, Billy?'

'Ethel Levine referred me.'

'Ethel Levine?'

'Her daughter goes to the Human Learning Space. I think she knows you from them.'

65

'Oh, I see. O.K. How about tonight at nine? It's my late night.'

'That would be good. Thank you so much.'

'Do you have the address?'

'38 Kappachung Road?'

'That's it. See you then, Billy.'

'Thanks. Good bye.' Posner practically tossed the phone back onto the hook. Things were looking up.

12. Culture

The rush hour traffic into the city was long gone, and in fifteen minutes Joe Posner was going down the exit ramp from the George Washington Bridge into Washington Heights. Despite the overcast sky, the air was clear. Manhattan was majestic in slate gray profile against the light horizon. The bottom of the ramp brought him directly facing the gargantuan Columbia-Presbyterian Hospital complex and the brute basalt cliffs that serve as its foundation. Its massive solidity left no doubt that he was entering a land of a different order from the one he had left. This is New York, it said. This is weight.

Apfelbaum's building was only a few blocks south of the bridge exit. Posner fitted the Dart into a line of double-parked cars on 160th Street. The concrete and brick block ached like a bruise under the cold wind off the river. Broken glass and dog-shit trimmed the edges of the cracked sidewalks.

As Posner looked out across the Hudson at Edgewater, images of the Lan-more Luncheonette flashed across his mind, and he remembered again why he'd been feeling so anxious all morning. Like when a woman leaves you, he thought, and you feel bad all the time, and just about once every half hour you remember why you feel so bad, and that feels worse. Good to get it straight, though, thought Joe Posner, as he walked into Ellen's old building.

Nelson Velez, the Puerto Rican super of the building, was

standing by the door that separated the inner and outer lobbies. He was looking at a lock cylinder in his hand and an empty hole in the door as if they had fallen from another planet. Joe Posner took a nostalgic look around the lobby. Marble sheets from a more prosperous past remained on the walls. On the ceiling, intricate frieze work was barely visible under layers of cheap paint.

'Hey, Nelson. Remember me?' Posner's question was heartfelt. The super screwed up his eyes and tilted his head to one side.

'You fron' the Unibicajun Church?'

'No. I'm Joe. Remember, I used to visit Ellen Silber in Fifty-three?'

Nelson rolled his eyes up while he searched his memory.

'Fi'ty-t'ree?'

'Yeah.'

'Oh, *yeah*. I remember now. She no libbing here now.'

'I know. How's Mrs. Velez?'

'She *good*. Yeah. *Sure.*' Velez enjoyed the enthusiasm of his own answers. 'Who you come to see now?'

'Alan Apfelbaum.'

The super's face went blank for a second, then relit with an idea. 'In fi'ty-fi'?' Apfelbaum had lived there for over six years.

'That's it.'

'Ohhhh. O.K.'

Nelson stepped aside, and Posner squeezed through the open door to the inner lobby. 'Thanks, Nelson. See ya.'

'O.K.'

When the door to fifty-five opened, Posner was hit with the dark, sweet aroma of cumin and fond memories. Alan Apfelbaum's round ruddy face, red bristly beard, and wry brown-toothed smile were unchanged.

'*Mr.* Posner. A long-awaited pleasure. Please come in,' he crooned in a soft baritone, and waved his hand in a facetious European bow. Apfelbaum was overly mannered, but in a sly, self-mocking way that Posner enjoyed.

'Thanks, Alan. You're a sight for sore eyes.'

'Come. Come.' Apfelbaum ushered him into the spacious

light-filled living room. It faced the Hudson, overlooking a broad expanse of gray water, gray sky and brown, leafless palisade which somehow both belied and reflected the mean squalor of the neighborhood. Joe Posner remembered summer sunsets from Ellen's apartment with a flashing pang of regret. The bittersweet harmonies of Thelonious Monk coming from Apfelbaum's record player didn't help.

The walls were covered by huge canvasses on which flowers, women, fruit and heavy machinery mingled voluptuously in vital colors and angles. Posner had always liked Alan's paintings, but one glance at this more recent work told him that the angry and slightly acid quality of his earlier paintings had given way to a cheerier, more optimistic outlook. Joe Posner took this as an encouraging oracle for the eighties. But then, he told himself, he was always looking for encouraging oracles for the eighties.

Apfelbaum plucked a bottle of German brandy from the coffee table. 'As I recall, you had a particular fondness for this concoction. Am I right?' He laughed at himself and his parodied pomp.

Posner couldn't help smiling. How in the hell had he remembered that? 'Aren't you always?'

'On the contrary. Please sit.'

'How's Nadia? And the little one?' Posner sank into an old couch. It was a bit threadbare, but in a beautiful floral print, and not at all seedy. The perfect piece for the carefully nurtured atmosphere of impoverished nobility that pervaded the apartment.

'As always, Nadia is great. She's killing me with her greatness. The little one is not nearly so little, and so beautiful it hurts to look at her. Yes, the spectre of incest haunts me daily. And how are you? You still living downtown?' He poured brandy and then soda into each glass, finishing each portion with an expert twist of the bottle. He hitched up his French workman's overalls and sat down in an easy chair facing Posner.

'No. I'm living in Jersey now.'

'Quelle horreur!' he intoned in an intentionally broad American accent. 'Still with Customs?'

Posner studied his shoelaces. 'No. I'm a detective.'

Apfelbaum did a double take. Real interest and a hint of admiration twinkled in his eyes. 'Really?'

'Really.'

'That's fantastic.'

'It's not. It stinks. I think I'm going to have to find something else soon. It's all fucking divorces.'

Apfelbaum put his hand over his eyes. 'Ach. I'm getting the picture. Into the bowels of suburban depravity.'

'Something like that.' He took a long sip of the brandy and soda and shivered at its dusty rich flavour.

'And how, may I ask, in the creator's master plan, did you come to such a pass, Pilgrim?'

Posner massaged his eyeballs with the thumb and index finger of one hand. 'I moved to Jersey two years ago . . . ' He looked through half-closed lids at Apfelbaum to see if the date got a response. If it did Apfelbaum didn't show it. Posner had hoped it wouldn't and was disappointed that it hadn't. 'Six months after that, in a state of serious depression . . . '

'That's what it is, friend,' Apfelbaum interrupted.

'What?'

'New Jersey: a state of serious depression. I'm sorry. Go on. I'm incorrigible, I know.'

Posner smiled. 'So . . . I figured I needed a change. I'd been at Customs for five and a half years. I couldn't take it anymore.'

'You know,' Apfelbaum interjected again, 'I never knew how you got into Customs, if that's not too much of a digression.'

'That's easy,' Posner explained dryly. 'I didn't have a job coming out of college, so I took the civil service test; they offered me a job at Customs; it seemed easier than cab driving and less boring then graduate school. And for five years it was. Just. After that I quit. Grad school seemed more interesting by then, but harder, so I went back to cab driving for a while – three weeks to be exact – during which time I went from seriously depressed to suicidal. Then I saw this story in the *Record* about how Jersey had changed its requirements for a private investigator's license. It had been five years police experience, and they changed it to five years of any kind of investigative experience. I figured that might include investigating suitcases, so I called up my supervisor at Customs – did I ever tell you about him? Ben Duberman? Anyway, the guy liked me a lot: never had a son, etc. etc. So, he wrote me a recommendation they couldn't refuse. I still had a couple of thousand saved that I used for the office deposit and a few months' rent, and here I am.'

During the story, Apfelbaum had been slowly stroking his beard and watching Posner's eyes. 'Fascinating' was his only comment. 'And how did you happen upon the Yooman Learning Space?'

'I was hired by Melody Gold to locate some stolen property.'

'Melody! Oh, Melody! That sweet post-pubescent peach! The mere mention of her name ignites my loins and turns my stomach.'

'She's dead, Alan.' Posner was surprised at how offended he was by Apfelbaum's joking. He wanted to freeze Apfelbaum, and Apfelbaum froze.

'What?'

'She's dead.'

'That's terrible. How did it happen?' He was concerned, genuinely, it seemed, but not bereaved.

'Well, it looked like an o.d.'

'Of what?'

'Heroin.'

'Heroin?' Apfelbaum was incredulous.

'My reaction exactly. Do you think she could have been using heroin?'

'Could? Sure, *could*. But I didn't think any of those kids were using heroin. Everything but. Maybe an experimental snort or two on the lunatic fringe, but never needles. And not Melody at all.'

Joe Posner felt like he'd finally found a friend. A badly-needed one. 'Tell me about her. Did she use anything to your knowledge?'

Apfelbaum laughed. 'Are you kidding? Melody Gold, the Queen of Coca?'

'She used cocaine?'

'Used, sold, and gave away. To students *and* teachers.'

'Jesus Christ,' Posner said in befuddlement. 'What kind of place is that school?'

Apfelbaum laughed again, pleased to be getting a strong reaction.

'Look, Alan, I went up to Harriman yesterday. They had this Advanced Survival Experience thing on . . . '

Apfelbaum looked up at the ceiling impishly. 'Pierre Cardin faces the elements.'

'Yeah,' Posner went on, 'but more. I mean, all these girls were nude, stumbling around stoned out of their skulls, and this guy Jake, who I took to be some sort of teacher or something, bribing them with pot . . . I mean I've read Summerhill and all, and I never thought of myself as a prude, but . . . Jesus, man, I don't know. What's it all about?'

'*That* is a long story.' Apfelbaum sighed, but a twinkle in his eye reminded Posner that long stories were the painter's forte and suggested that this long story was a good one.

'I've got time.'

Apfelbaum rubbed his face with the palms of his hands. 'Have you been to the school?'

'Just for a few minutes. I met Norma. And Alice Cabot.'

Apfelbaum looked into his eyes for signs of laughter. 'But not Les?'

'I can't catch up to him.'

'Not surprising, the snake. Well, what shall I say? In some ways it's a good place, really. Or was. It's gotten a lot worse over the years.' Apfelbaum stopped. He was having difficulty getting started. 'O.K.' He pulled himself together. 'Most schools are based on crushing the curiosity and creativity of students, right?'

He didn't wait for an answer; he was getting into his stride. 'They're factories for socializing young people. Young people – some young people, a lot of young people – are unhappy; alien-ated. They don't like their schools, their teachers, their parents, their lives. Their behavior becomes a pattern of resistance; of pure negativism and self-destruction. This is just as true today as it was in the fifties and sixties.' Apfelbaum swelled on his words; but through the posing and histrionics, Posner could see that politics mattered to Apfelbaum. It was something he respected him for. Ellen was the same way. He hadn't met too many people like that since she'd left. 'The good core of the Space is that it tries to help kids find something they want to do in themselves, for themselves. Not against someone or something else. The method, in theory, is to eliminate all rules and requirements and to surround the kids with stimulating role models,' Apfelbaum paused for the first time to take a bow with a nod of his head, 'emotional support, and an interesting curriculum. Personally, I think it's a good theory. Or, at least it's a better way to run a school than a lot of others. It's on the right side of things, as it were. Unfortunately, the Space has some insurmountable problems.'

Posner knew he was expected to ask for elaboration. 'Like what?'

'Those kids are probably the most culturally deprived kids in the world today.'

'I thought they were from upper middle class suburban families.'

'I rest my case.' He gave Posner a moment to chuckle, and Posner did. If he wasn't an appreciative audience, he wasn't going to get the full show. Meanwhile, the cumin smell coming from the kitchen hadn't quit, and Posner was thinking how pleasant it would be to continue their discussion over lunch. Apfelbaum sailed on.

'That fucking wasteland out there is a vacuum; a black hole of catatonia. What the fuck do you think you find when you find the "true self" of most of those kids? Monsters, that's what. They're little fucking creeps, who, *if* they ever get their miserable "shit together," as they say in their imaginatively impoverished lingo, if they *do*, they will most certainly grow into *big* fucking creeps like their parents, who, I assure you, are some of the world's *biggest* fucking creeps. Avaricious, venal exploiters and parasites. Philistines!' Joe Posner started to laugh. Apfelbaum's practically sensual pleasure in his own jeremiad was irresistably infectious.

Next, stalking to the window, he threw his arms into the air, and searched the heavens. 'Is this what I was made for? To scrape the hippy tarnish from the future president of Goldfarb Belt Buckles Incorporated? To motivate him to learn enough math successfully to swindle his competitors and squeeze his workers? Oh, just Unmentionable One, no!' He wheeled and gaped, eyes bugging out of his head, lowering his hands to his chest, his fingers curved to claws. Then, as if to demonstrate his virtuosity, he modulated seamlessly back to normal.

'Of course, there are exceptions. That's what kept me there for three years. Every year there are a few kids who have a fighting chance to become human beings, and that place makes it relatively easy to help them. Institutionally, at least. You don't have any asshole curriculum planners or dress code enforcers, or any of that to worry about. But giving free rein to the degeneracy that has already been produced in these kids by the time they get there . . . well, it can get to be a pretty debilitating environment in its own right. It's the kind of place where you can sit around all day and do nothing but drink coffee and chat and come home exhausted.' Apfelbaum poured himself back into his chair, as if to demonstrate the point.

Posner inhaled deeply through his nose, as if concentrating and wondered what kind of soup Alan had made with the cumin. 'I don't see how this means that teachers would buy drugs from students. What kind of role model is that?'

'That, my friend, is attributable to the "Law of Pernicious Creeping Rot". Originally, teachers and kids would now and then smoke a little pot and drink together.' Posner frowned disapprovingly, and Apfelbaum interjected apologetically, 'After school only.' Then, realizing the insufficiency of the defense, moved up in his seat and flared his nostrils. 'Remember, I said *stimulating* role models, not upright. One fact is inescapable: drugs define the world of the alienated teenager. You won't get them to stop. Not as a group. Either they share it with you, or they hide it from you. Period. So, if the teachers are going to get close enough to open these kids up, they've got to be open about their own behavior in such matters. An occasional joint or some wine between students and staff was encouraged, in fact. Unofficially, but openly. We were supposed to be giving the kids examples of how drugs could be used in moderation; responsibly; without self-destruction. But . . . the teachers lost track of the function of the "anything goes" philosophy and became participants. That I blame principally, no pun intended, on good ol' "Love Man" Les. Now there's a degenerate for you. If there's anything rotten out there, you can bet he's got a finger in it somewhere.

'How do you mean?' Posner pinched his upper lip.

'Let's just say he uses his position to advance his own interests at the expense of the school and the students.'

'C'mon, Alan. Details.' Joe Posner thought he might be getting a whiff of sour grapes.

'I don't know too many particulars, to be honest. It was an attitude. First, I don't believe administrators should fuck teachers. It's messy.'

'Who was he fucking?'

'Are you sure you're a detective?'

'I'd rather not answer that.'

'Take a guess.'

Joe Posner only knew one female teacher, and he remembered her crotch against his leg again. 'Alice Cabot?'

'You *are* a detective!'

'How serious is it? Or should I say "was it"?'

'Could anything involving Les and Alice be considered serious?'

C'mon, Alan. You know what I mean.'

'I don't know. I doubt it was very serious. I don't even know how long it was going on, or if it still is.'

'What else? That sounds like the simplest, not the most serious accusation to make.'

'We all suspected he was siphoning off money, but nobody ever got to see the books.' Apfelbaum tossed this allegation off rather carelessly, but then came the venom. 'Worst of all, he uses his position as a confidant of the kids for his voyeurism. That's what used to disgust me the most. He'd egg them on to ever greater depravity because it gave him vicarious pleasure to hear them confess. I tell you, the guy is a confidence man, and his racket is education. That's all there is to it. He's picked up some jargon the same way a phoney diamond seller has picked up talk about carats. He's defiling something good. Something hopeful. I don't believe this type of stuff is inherent in alternative education. I don't, Joe.'

Joe Posner had believed in this stuff himself, once. As far as he'd thought about it. He'd opted for pass/fail whenever possible at college, but that had been as much laziness as principle. *Time* magazine said progressive education was out; and so, Posner figured, it couldn't be all that bad. Still, all this sounded crazy to him. And he wondered how Alan had fit in as well as this final outburst of uncharacteristic sincerity had suggested he had. 'Is that why you left?'

'More or less. I was there three years . . . it was enough. It was . . . corrosive. As I said . . . debilitating.'

'Tell me about Hawk Brennan.'

Apfelbaum smiled sardonically. 'That nincompoop. He can play sax. That's it. Somehow, he secured himself a part time job at the public high school, too. Teaching a chamber music group after school. I could never figure that one. Talk about drugs. That guy was always high.'

'On what?'

'On anything. Mostly pot and coke, I suppose. Even during school. And that *was* forbidden. But nobody ever said anything. I guess it made him seem like a real jazz musician.'

'What about heroin?'

'I don't know. I wouldn't be surprised.'

'Did you ever know him to deal?'

'No. Well . . . now that you mention it, I think he and Melody were in on a cocaine deal that I heard about.'

'Where did Melody get the capital for these deals?'

'I haven't the foggiest. But she was always flush. And I know she got very little from her parents.'

'What about her family?'

'Let's have some soup.' Posner had almost given up hope. They moved to Apfelbaum's bright blue kitchen and sat at a weathered oak table.

'The father does public relations for the government of South Africa.' Apfelbaum raised his eyebrows in what Posner took as an acknowledgement of evil, and ladled steaming, pungent-smelling cabbage soup into dishes that had been laid on the table earlier. 'It's the mother's father's business, though.'

'Come again?'

'Another irony of patriarchal nomenclature, my friend. The father, né Burton Gold, is an officer of Finkel, Finkel, and LeBarron, the public relations and lobbying firm; the president of which is Bernie Finkel, father of Phyllis Gold, née Phyllis Finkel; who is president of Gold Antiques.'

'How do you know all this?'

'I had the dubious distinction of being Melody's advisor for a term. She went through the entire male faculty. Looking for her father, I suppose. She finally settled for Les. Anyway, in my tour of duty I suffered one family conference with the three of them.'

'Go on.' As Posner gobbled the soup, he reminded himself to pay some attention to its full cumin and cabbage succulence. He didn't often eat this well.

'Well, Melody hates – I mean hated –' Apfelbaum paused as he tried either to feel or not to feel some pain at the thought of the girl's death. Posner couldn't tell which. 'She hated her mother. And vice versa. Melody told me they had tried to kill each other at least once. I never knew whether to believe her or not. She had a crush on her father, but he was never around. Not a coincidence, I'd venture. He'd meet her places: Hawaii, the Canaries, Paris. For a weekend or a week. Usually on a day or two's notice and never with any regard for her school schedule. But of course she was always delighted to go. What the mother got from him was never clear to me. And beyond his position at Finkel, Finkel, and Le Barron, I don't know what he got from her.'

'Alan,' Posner asked somberly,' 'I saw a photo of Melody looking badly beaten, and the night she died, somebody hit her hard enough on the chin to leave an ugly bruise. Do you have any ideas on that?'

'None. She'd only been at the school for a year when I left, and I don't remember anything like that then.'

'Was she going with a kid named Tony Bagliano when you

were there?'

'That little slug. No. I don't think so. But teaching the tykes was bad enough. I didn't pay much attention to their couplings.'

'What about him?'

'I never had much to do with him. He was one of Les's most devoted acolytes. With more courage he might have made a second-rate juvenile delinquent.'

'How about Melody's friends?'

'What about them?'

'Well, I've talked to Dessie Levine . . . '

Apfelbaum clapped his hand over his eyes. 'Don't believe it.'

'Don't believe what?'

'Anything she told you. She's a compulsive liar.'

'Really?'

'Really.'

'Can you suggest another friend of hers I could talk to?'

'Well, anyone with that much cocaine at a high school is going to be very popular. Who her closest friends were, I'm not sure. You know who you might try? Judy Williams. She works after school at the deli down the block from the Space. She's a good kid. Tell her Old Sacroiliac says hello and she'll tell you everything she knows. And she generally knows everything.'

'Great.' Posner spooned up the last of his soup with regret and grudgingly let it slide down his throat. 'That was fantastic, Alan.'

'Would you like some more?'

'No, no, no.' It was a purely reflexive refusal, one born of some distorted sense of propriety developed in childhood. There was a pause. Joe Posner could see that Apfelbaum couldn't bear the silence for more than a few seconds.

The painter piped, 'There. Now I've done your job for you, hah?' Posner didn't answer. Apfelbaum pressed on. 'What exactly is your job?'

'I'm just trying to find out what happened. I'm not sure why myself. Nobody's paying me. *That* I'm sure of. I just don't think she took that shot herself, and I want to see if I'm right, I guess.'

'No man ever had a nobler ambition, my friend. I hope I've

been of some service, but it's time I got back to work. I've got a model coming. We must get together sometime and have a good talk.'

'I'd love to, Alan. One last thing. Alice Cabot disappeared on me a few hours ago. Any idea where she might have disappeared to?'

'Disappeared?'

'Moved out. Everything. Gone.'

'Hmm. Her parents . . . '

'Oh yeah. And someone with an old Saab with New Hampshire plates was maybe with her.'

'Oh. That's Elvira. Last I heard she was living in Nyack.'

'Elvira.'

'A friend of Alice's. Elvira Fishelman. An old, close friend. She used to hang around the school when Alice first started. I used to think they had a thing, but I don't know.'

'Alice is bi-sexual?'

'I really wouldn't know, but I'd guess "polymorphously perverse" would be the operative phrase.'

'Nyack, huh?'

'The jewel of the Hudson. Where, I have no idea.'

'It's a start.' Posner pushed his chair away from the table and stood up. 'Alan, this has been fantastic. The food and the info. The soup was delicious.'

'It was delightful to see you. You must come for dinner sometime. Nadia would like to see you. Have you heard from Ellen?'

The question had been a long time in coming. 'No.' Posner would leave it at that. Apfelbaum would let him. 'I'd love to come to dinner sometime. Give me a call.' Posner knew he wouldn't, but wished he would.

Apfelbaum showed him to the door and tossed out a 'stay in touch' as he closed it.

13. Les's Lair

Joe Posner had never heard of the street where Les Coniff lived. There was nothing strange in that. Bergen County is riddled with discreet cul-de-sacs and loops unknown to all but their inhabitants. Although the address on the staff list said it was in Cresskill, Posner found it on his Fire Department map about midway between the center of Cresskill and the center of Demerest. It didn't matter to him. He was equally unfamiliar with both towns. They were in that part of the county which had always seemed to him less New York City sprawl than colonial heritage, smalltown America. Not his turf.

Before folding the map and putting it away, he looked around 160th Street from the driver's seat of his still-parked Dart. He used to leave this corner early in the morning. When the high rises across the river reflected the orange rising sun. After a night with Ellen. He let himself remember now, but only for a few seconds. The soup was still warm in his belly, but the feeling of having an ally was fading fast. He kept his eyes away from Edgewater.

A stray dog, only a year or so old, with an injured, or maybe deformed rear leg and a serious case of the mange hopped up the broken street, nonchalantly bouncing its bald rear end between the bits of garbage and broken glass. Joe Posner reflected that he was only twenty minutes from the manicured green of Cresskill, where nobody ever sees stray dogs with mange, or even much garbage. He hated reflecting on paradoxes like that. It made him feel like one of those over-the-hill T.V. reporters who become philosophical 'news analysts' on their way to pension land.

The Dart stalled several times before Posner could get out of 160th Street. He patted the dashboard and spoke to it. 'I know, old pal, I miss it here too. Jersey's a drag. We'll come back soon. I promise.'

By the time he was on the Palisades Parkway, Posner noticed with relief that he had stopped feeling like a TV commentator and talking to his car. One thing that could be said for Jersey was that it seldom made him sentimental.

The Parkway was still very wet from the morning rain and he could hear the periodic splashes under the chassis, as the tires cut through puddle after puddle. With the wetness, Posner was a little nervous about the 55mile per hour shimmy and tried to keep the Dart down to around 50. He didn't need any more anxiety.

At the first exit he switched over to Route 9W. Every time he drove this road it reminded him of a joke from his Junior High Algebra class: 'Question: what question has the answer "9W?" Answer: Do you spell your name with a "v," Mrs. Wagner?' It was a particularly stupid joke, but with its contorted, cloying absurdity, it was wonderfully evocative of his Junior High experience; and it stuck in his memory like an advertising jingle that he couldn't stop humming.

Route Nein W took him by several country club-like corporate headquarters. Long, low, and modern. Lipton, Scholastic Magazines, Volkswagen America. Once he had heard that there were no land taxes along this stretch, and that that was why so many companies had their offices there. And why there were no public schools in the township of Englewood Cliffs. He had never found out if it was true, but it sounded right.

He took the road off Nein W down the hill, through Tenafly, and into Cresskill. Thanks to the map, he found the address, 7 Culloden Crescent, with little difficulty. It was a dark, heavily wooded cove, and the house, which was small and had a log cabin exterior was set far back into the tress. A long gravel driveway, covered with last fall's leaves, well into decay, went down the left side of the house as far as the back door. There were no cars in it. Posner parked the Dart at the far end of the Crescent, where it would not be visible to someone entering from the south, and walked back to number 7.

He knocked on the door and rang the bell. Neither got an answer. Posner hopped down from the doorstep and peered through the widow. Inside, the walls were of bright blond pine, edged by heavy black timbers. Antique looking furniture cluttered the small room with no apparent stylistic unity. It was like a hunting lodge version of the Golds' house.

Both front and back doors were locked, but the large window in back was ajar. It was easy to slide it up and slip in. The kitchen was like a set for a little ol' cookie maker commercial. Only six by eight, it had enough frills to dress a Tennessee homecoming parade. Under the counter an old fashioned country store grain bin with glass doors was filled with granola, pecans, pistachios, and – Posner gasped – chocolate chips. Expensive high carbon pots and pans hung from the walls. A large color photo of a snow capped mountain was framed next to the refrigerator. Posner figured that he was supposed to know what mountain it was, but he didn't. He didn't know from mountains.

A closer look at the living room furniture confirmed his impression that it was antique, expensive, and almost comically heterogeneous. The only modern piece was a high-tech slimline stereo system. A metal ladder led to a small loft platform built next to a second-story window. A little alcove built under the loft was lined with several hundred paperback books. 'Human Learning Space' was stamped on all their spines. Under a window, in a space carved out of the bookshelves, reposed a huge rolltop, natural oak desk. It was a beauty. Posner had always liked rolltop desks and had once priced them at antique stores in Brooklyn. This one, he knew, was far more expensive than the ones that were far too expensive for him. It was unlocked, and he rolled back the top, more to admire the workmanship than anything else. Then he checked the papers piled in the middle. He got a glimpse of an airline ticket folder and pulled it out. TWA had issued tickets and made reservations for Les Coniff and Melody Gold on flight 63 for Cartagena, Colombia at 10.45 the following morning. Joe Posner would not have liked to admit it, but he felt more envy than outrage at his discovery. He wrote down the ticket numbers and looked through the other papers. Pinned to the inside wall of the desk were four business cards of antique dealers. Two were in Nyack; one was in New Hope, and the last was on Atlantic Avenue in Brooklyn.

Nothing else looked interesting.

He nosed around the place a bit. Not only did Coniff have a lot of kitchen utensils, antiques, paperback books, and stereo equipment, he also had a lot of crockery and postcards. He seemed to have a lot of everything he could think of having a lot of. The fetishism of it all didn't really surprise Posner, but he wondered how Coniff financed it all on a high school principal's salary.

The bedroom was at the end of a short hallway. It was small, and dominated by a king-sized waterbed covered with fake fur. It smelled of the cheap rose incense Posner hadn't smelled since his college dormitory days, when it was believed to be equally effective at stimulating sex and covering the smell of pot. Three expensive leather suitcases were lined up on the far side of the bed. They were empty. An antique oak bed-table had a drawer, which Posner tried, and found locked. It seemed strange to leave the windows unlocked, but lock a bed-table drawer. A small bookcase faced the foot of the bed, filled with hardback books. Posner browsed over the titles, and noticed a thick one, entitled *Hampton's Encyclopedia of Antiques*. He checked the index and found the entry 'Boxes, Jeweled, 487–92'. He flipped the pages to 487, then turned them one by one, looking for some mention of amethyst and amber. It was all he had to go on. He didn't find it. Pages 489 and 490 had been ripped out. He closed the book slowly, wondering what that might mean, when the sound of two cars pulling into the driveway, made him jump.

He moved quickly into the living room, up the ladder to the loft, opened the window, and drew the curtains. Then he lay flat by the window at the back of the platform, and prayed he couldn't be seen from below. Too late, he realized he'd forgotten to close the desk again.

A cluster of voices burst through the kitchen door. Above them all was a high pitched, though thick, man's voice in laughter, rolling between a whoop and a cackle. The other voices were younger and male. One whined, 'Leehhhs, ya *gotta.*'

The man sneered with glee, 'I don't gotta do anything!'

Another voice joined the first in complaint. 'No, *really*, Les, You *prom*ised. You're being a total fuck.'

'I never promised anything,' Coniff laughed, 'you just don't want to deal with consequences.' Posner identified his accent as being from an outlying borough of New York—Brooklyn or the Bronx—and probably the source of Apfelbaum's satiric 'Yoo-man Learning Space.'

A new voice was bitter and trying to sound much harder than the others. 'Smirnoff is totally piss. You can fucking drink it if you want, but I'm not drinking anything but Stolich.'

'Fine,' Coniff taunted.

'Come on, Les. Stolich would be so totally excellent now.'

'Please, Les. It's only a coupla miles. At least give us your license.'

Coniff answered with finality. 'I'm wasted. If you wanted Stolich, you shoulda said so when we were at the liquor store. There's perfectly good vodka in the kitchen. Especially for mixing with cranberry juice. I'm not going anywhere. And I'm not giving you my license. Nobody's gonna believe you're 47.'

'Fuck it. Light up a bone,' the hard guy said.

'Hey!' Coniff sounded irritated. 'Who's been fucking with my desk?'

Nobody answered.

'This was closed when I left here. I know it. I always close it. It's bad for the wood to keep it open all the time.'

Still nobody answered.

'Weird,' Coniff exclaimed. 'Totally weird.'

'Let's have that bone,' the hard guy repeated.

'Gimme a back rub,' the first voice had become a touch langorous.

'Me too, Tony,' chimed in the second.

'How the fuck am I gonna give you both fucking back rubs?'

Coniff had the answer. 'Alternate. One, then the other. I'll roll the joint.'

'O.K., but use the Sens. That Bo sucks.' Hard guy again.

'The Colombian is excellent, you asshole,' Coniff answered, 'But if you want the Sens, I'll give you the Sens. I'm not smoking anyway. I've got to do some work at the Space in an hour.'

Posner heard a loud, wet smack that sounded a lot like a kiss.
'Fuck off, Fatty,' the hard guy complained.
'I love it when you talk dirty,' Coniff joked.

The first voice piped up in excitement. 'Y'know what would be totally excellent? Let's do it nude in the loft!'

Posner's heart stopped. He knew he had to move immediately. Without a sound he raised himself to a squat. As he made the move, he got a glimpse of the three boys. Two had shoulder-length straight hair, one blond, one dark. The other's was brusquely cropped, punk style. They all wore jeans and flannel shirts, already unbuttoned. They were all skinny. Coniff had gone into the back, presumably to get the pot, and Posner couldn't see him. He parted the curtains and lowered himself through the open window. Spaces between the logs allowed him to plant his toes securely. He only had to make six or seven feet, because one of the cars parked in the driveway was a van, with its roof directly below the window. The last voice he heard was Coniff's. 'Go on up. I'll put on a record. I got the new Ramones yesterday.'

Joe Posner's knees were shaking as he lowered himself onto the top of the van. Then, holding onto the luggage rack, he lowered himself to the bumper, and he was down. Behind the van, an old cream-colored Mercedes convertible was parked. The back door to the van was open. Posner climbed in.

He had seen plusher vans, but he thought this was pretty nice. If you liked that sort of thing. Four Jensen speakers and an upmarket Hitachi tape machine were the main attractions. The back was carpeted, but unfurnished. Some tools lay in a pile on the left side. Posner took a look at them. There was a crowbar, along with a few heavy mallets, a hacksaw, and some chain clippers. They weren't car tools.

Joe Posner still wanted to talk to Les Coniff, but decided to wait till the principal was back at the Human Learning Space. It would give him a chance to calm down a little and think over some of this new information. Besides, Coniff was unlikely to be in a talking mood with three naked boys smoking pot in his loft.

14. Bad Influence

The girl behind the counter at the delicatessen was cute and bright-eyed. Her light brown hair was pulled straight back from her open, lightly freckled face into a pony tail. Scampering around behind the delicatessen counter in her long apron, she looked to Joe Posner like a throwback to an era before even his own youth, now already an era away.

'Hi. Can I help you?' She said it with the kind of friendliness that Posner usually took as necessarily insincere from strangers; but something about this girl carried it off. He wanted to like her. He guessed everybody did.

'Are you Judy Williams?'

'Uh-huh.' It didn't seem to bother her that he knew her name. 'Who are you?'

'My name's Joe Posner. I wanted to talk to somebody about the Human Learning Space, and Alan Apfelbaum suggested I talk to you. We're old friends. He said to say that Old Sacroiliac said hello.'

Posner wouldn't have thought it possible, but at the mention of Apfelbaum the girl's face got even brighter than it was already.

'Alan? You know Alan?'

'Uh-huh.'

'Oh, God! How is he? I miss him.'

'He's good. Do you think you'd be able to talk soon?'

'Well, my break's not for another hour, but maybe I can get it early. Wait here.'

She ran to the rear of the store where, Posner was surprised to see a fat bald man in his sixties had been sitting motionlessly the whole time. The man turned slowly to look at Judy, who bent from the waist, bringing her face close to his.

'Mr. Englehard, I know it's early, but do you suppose I could take my break now, just this one time?' The words spilled out of her fast, sweet, and bubbly.

Deep wrinkles started to gather slowly in Mr. Englehard's forehead, like a time-lapse photograph of an earthquake. Posner was sure he was building to a refusal, but Judy knew what she was doing. Before he could get his speaking apparatus in gear, the girl cut him off. 'Thanks, Mr. Englehard, you're a sweetheart. Still my boyfriend?'

She turned and ran back up the aisle behind the counter to where Posner stood. Mr. Englehard's face sagged back to its original position of resignation and repose. Judy fiddled behind her back and crossed her eyes in comic frustration; then spun around, showing Posner her back. 'Would you please undo my apron strings? They're all in a knot.'

The apron strings went three times around her narrow waist and were tied in a knot that rested on the surprisingly full curve of her rear end. Her blue jeans were faded and the denim was soft and thin. Her body was compact and athletic; shapely, but not voluptuous. He got the knot undone, and Judy unwrapped herself and smiled at him. Her eyes were very large and dark chocolate brown. She hung the apron on a hook, then splashed coffee from a pot on a warmer into two styrofoam cups. 'Do you take milk and sugar?'

'Just milk.'

She poured milk in both cups, then added four packets of sugar to one, and tilted her head at the door. 'Let's go.' She pulled a purple and gold athletic jacket emblazoned with a 'V' over a 'B' around her shoulders, and took the coffees. 'Is it OK to talk outside? I know it's cold, but I get so cramped up in there.' They were already on the street.

'Sure. Anywhere.' Judy handed him his coffee, and they began to stroll.

'Ol' Sacroiliac. What a pissah,' she said in an exaggerated, but precise New York accent that wasn't her own. It made Posner smile. 'How come you wanna know about the Space? Do you want to send your kids there? You really should. It's the best school.'

Posner shrugged off his shock at being placed so easily in a parental generation. 'Well, like I said, I'm a friend of

Alan's . . . ' he was sure it was his best lead. ' . . . and I wanted to know something about Melody Gold . . . '

'Oh, God. Melody. Isn't it awful? But you shouldn't think bad of the Space. I never once heard of anybody doing heroin there.'

'You go there now?'

'Uh-huh. It's my last year. I'm so glad to be graduating from high school – my poor parents never thought I would – but I almost hate to leave the Space.'

'What's so good about it?'

'First off, the teachers are really nice. I mean some of them can be pretty flakey, but, you know, not like public school, where they're mostly like . . . ' She twisted up her face into a startlingly effective imitation of a rigid old crone.

'I get the picture.' Posner smiled again.

'And they don't tell you what to do or try to force you to learn. You know? They tell you it's up to you, and it is.'

'You learn a lot that way?'

'Oh, *tot*ally,' Then she stopped. 'Well, pretty much. I should really work harder. I still don't read much. And I just can't do math. It's really embarassing at the deli. I'm always making mistakes giving people their change wrong. But at least I'm trying. At public school I really never did anything but get high and get into trouble.' She looked up sheepishly from her coffee. 'I was always in trouble there. My teachers hated me. One year they suspended me forty-two days. They said I was sick and a bad influence.'

Posner didn't much like the way she said 'public school'. It sounded snobbish to him, himself a product of public education. But, remembering his own high school experience, he had little doubt that most regular high schools, public or private, would have tried to clip this girl's wings – with chainsaws if necessary, and he liked that a lot less.

'Did you know Melody?'

'Sure. I know it's horrible to say, but I didn't like her too much.' She had that sheepish look again. 'I guess I was sort of jealous. She was so rich and all. That's the worst thing about the Space. So many spoiled rich kids. It's practically got my parents in the poorhouse to pay my bills there, and I'm on half scholarship. And Melody, you know, had so much money and all. You know, her Firebird and . . . ' she stopped short.

'And what, Judy? Alan told me she used a lot of coke.'

'Oh. You know. Well, she did. She'd always share it a lot, I have to admit it. But, you know, she always acted so totally superior about it and all. I guess she had her own problems, right? Everybody does. I really am sorry about what happened to her.'

'She was dealing, too. Wasn't she?'

'Hey, you're not a cop, are you? Oh, I'm sorry.' She put her free hand over her face. 'Alan wouldn't be friends with a cop.'

'Right. I'm no cop. I just want to know about it.'

'Were you a friend of hers, or something? I'm sorry if I said anything rude.'

'No. Not really. I'm a private detective.'

'Intense.'

'She hired me to try to find a box of hers the day she died. Did you ever see an antique box of hers?'

'A box? Uh-uh.'

'When was the last time you saw her?'

'Last Friday. At school.'

'You weren't at her party the night?'

'Uh-uh. It was my dad's birthday.'

'*Was* she dealing coke?'

'Sure. A lot. This year it got really bad. Before it was just to friends, you know? Then it got really intense. She was like practically a wholesaler, or something. I was scared to be with her sometimes. She'd have like a half pound of coke, you know, or something, in her car, and like I'd always think we were gonna get busted, you know? Can we turn around? I better get back.' They started to retrace their steps along the street.

'Who were her closest friends, Judy? Dessie Levine?'

'Dessie? You know, they were *pretty* good friends. I wouldn't say like *really* good friends. 'Course Dessie thinks everybody's *her* best friend. I wouldn't necessarily talk to her. She's like such a total liar. Tony Bagliano was Melody's boyfriend. Did you talk to him?'

'Not yet. Does he have a van?'

'That's him. Him and Billy Margolies and Johnny Parducci are always bombing around in it. They're total d's. They think they're so cool.'

'How did Melody fit in?'

'It was weird. I wouldn't of taken it. It's so disgusting, you know? Tony would like pretend that she wasn't even like there if Billy and Johnny were around, you know. I hate it when boys do that. It's so stupid. But I guess Melody sort of used him, too.'

'How do you mean?'

'Well, I don't think she respected him too much. He's such a d, you know, a jerk. And she knew it.'

'What did she use him for?'

'I don't know. You know, like to have a boyfriend, sorta. But still . . . I wouldn't of . . . '

'What, Judy?'

'I think he used to hit her. I mean I saw him once in the hall. He didn't exactly punch her, but he like pushed her, you know, really hard, into the wall. I freaked, you know?'

'When I was at school, I saw a picture . . . '

'*I* know,' she cut him off. 'The one from the camping trip. That's what I mean. I mean she told everybody she fell down the stairs, but I always thought Tony did it to her. But anyway, you should really talk to him if you want to know about Melody.'

'I've tried calling him at home.'

'He's never there. You should try over at Salt's.

'Salt's?' It sounded familiar.

'Dawn Salt's house. People always hang out there. He'll be there, probly, tonight. I guess you'd call it a party. I know! Why don't you go there with me? I told my friend Ann I'd see her over there, and I could use the ride.'

Posner felt just the slightest squirt of adrenalin. A brief quickening of the pulse. He told himself it wasn't a come-on. If he hadn't wanted it to be one, he told himself, it never would have occurred to him. On the other hand, he told himself, if he wasn't so ashamed that he wanted it to be one, maybe he'd know that it was. Maybe she didn't know either. 'I don't know if I can . . .'

Judy wasn't bothered. 'I get done at 9.45. If you want to, pick me up then. If you can't make it, I'll get over there on my own.'

'Great. Sounds good. Thanks. Umm . . . ' He remembered what he was doing. 'Was Melody especially close to any of the teachers?'

'Alice. And Les. The three of them did a lot of stuff together. They went camping together over Thanksgiving.'

'With Tony?'

'Uh-*uh*,' Judy wagged her head. 'Alice and Tony hate each other. Like intensely.'

'How come?'

'I don't know. I mean like, you know, Tony's so crude and all, and Alice is, you know, sorta sensitive.'

'Yeah. So how close were Melody and Les, d'you think?'

'I don't know. Pretty close. I don't know what you mean.'

'What do you think about Les? As a person.'

Judy thought for a minute, then shrugged her shoulders. 'I think he's a d. I shouldn't say this, cause he started the school and all, but . . . I think he's disgusting. All that intimacy stuff . . . I mean, I don't exactly want to *know*, you know? And I think he lies.'

'What about?'

'I don't know. You know. Anything. Like he tells you you can graduate in June and then he tells you you have to wait like till next December and all. He did that to a friend of mine. It's just . . . I don't know. I just don't trust him. He's always got sex on the brain . . . and his laugh. Iccchh!'

'Do you think he even might have had sex with Melody?'

Judy twisted her face in a grotesque knot. 'Gross.' Then she let her face relax again and considered the question. 'I doubt it, but I suppose it's possible. I don't know.'

'Was Melody close to Hawk?'

'No, I don't think so.'

'Did she *ever*, as far as you know, have anything to do with heroin or people who used it?'

'No. I don't . . . well, wait. You know, I forgot about this.

Last month, when I was at the Bergen Steak House with my mom and dad, she was there with Luther Davis.'

'Who's that?'

'Luther? When I was at Bergen Valley High, he was *the* one to talk to about heroin.'

'Did the teachers know?' Posner no longer had any concept of what constituted propriety in these precincts.

'At Bergen Valley? You must be crazy.'

'How many kids would you say are on drugs at Bergen Valley?'

'Everybody. I mean, you know, a lot. An awful lot of kids are totally high and fucked up all day. You almost have to, the classes are so boring. But not heroin. Mostly pills and reefer and booze. Only twenty or thirty, I'd say, are into heroin.'

'How about coke?'

'Nobody's got money to do coke at school. Some kids can afford it for partying, you know, now and then.'

'Luther doesn't wear a maroon cap, by any chance, does he?'

'No, that's Donnie Taylor. You know Donnie?' It sounded like she liked him.

'Not really.'

'If you want to talk to Luther, go over to the high school at three or three-fifteen, when they're just getting out. They had vacation last week. He'll be standing next to a green '73 Baracuda. D'you have a piece of paper?' Posner fished the pad and pen out of his jacket. Judy dropped her half-empty cup into a trash can and wrote a note slowly in an infantile script. 'Give him this and he'll talk to you. Otherwise forget it. He's totally paranoid.'

'How do you know him so well?'

'I used to go with his best friend.'

Posner was shaken by this admission, and Judy picked up on his dismay. 'I used to do a lot of really fucked up things, but Willie was sweet. Really. And Luther was always totally nice to me.'

They had reached the deli. Judy gave Posner back his pad and grabbed one of his hands in both of hers. 'Maybe I'll see you tonight. If I don't, say hi to Alan for me, O.K.? And good luck with whatever you're doing. Bye, now. See ya later. Maybe,' she called back as she ran back into the deli. Through the window Posner could see her give Mr. Englehard a bear claw tickle to the midsection as she threw her jacket on a chair.

Some kid, Posner thought. Some kid.

15. Education

Loon Avenue was no place for a candy store. The supermarket, the drugstore, the pizza place were all, if not new, at least modern. Suburban. The candy store belonged in the Bronx. Or so it looked to Joe Posner from across the street, where he sat in the Dart watching it, and thinking it had a lot in common with the Lan-more Luncheonette. Too much in common.

He got out of the Dart slowly, keeping his eyes moving up and down the block: an old lady on her way into the laundromat, a pin-up boy for the Acne Fund coming out of the pizza place, a couple of young mothers with loaded shopping carts heading for their cars. From the candy store, no movement. Joe Posner crossed the street.

The entrance was even darker than the gray street. He moved carefully through the aisles cluttered with dingy toys, games, greeting cards, and wrapping paper, all looking like they'd been stocked a decade or more ago. There were no customers.

Posner sat on a stool at the lunch counter and looked at the proprietress, who was staring into space. She looked just the part: her bloated face and square mouth, with its stubborn meanness, was a living explanation of how 'petty bourgeois' got to be one of history's great insults. Her robin's egg blue apron, frilled at the edges, was probably one of two she'd bought in 1948 and maintained in mint condition ever since. Her rotund body, he guessed, could only have obtained its excess fifty pounds by diligently cleaning every scrap of toast, velveeta, tuna fish, and English muffin left on every plate for thirty years. Places like this made Joe Posner sour. So did waiting for Al

B.Lopes.

He grunted his coffee order, and she poured it for him into a plastic cup in a holder, wrote up the check, and slammed it on the counter without looking at him. Posner kept his eyes on the door.

A few minutes later Lopes came through it and sat on the stool next to Posner, but didn't acknowledge him. Instead he spoke to the woman. 'Heya, Gladys. How's tricks?'

She turned to face him slowly, and her rectangular mouth opened slightly into a sickly grin that showed terrible teeth. 'Hi, Al,' she said without enthusiasm. 'Need some lunch?'

'No thanks, sugar. Bit a cow out in Hackensack. Just some of that special java juice, beautiful.'

Posner thought he might puke. When Gladys had poured Lopes's coffee, Posner turned to him and said flatly, 'Take your coffee,' and tilted his head at the two small booths with tables next to the counter.

Lopes sat in the booth and sneered at Posner, to whom he still hadn't spoken. Posner sat across from him and stared back.

'Well?' Lopes asked carelessly.

'Who set me up, Lopes?' Posner kept his voice soft and even.

'Set you up? Look, I'm sorry nothin' panned out for you last night, but set up? I don't get it.'

'You read the paper?'

'Yeah. So, old Santangelino got it at the Lan-more. Scary coincidence, huh?'

Posner sat for a minute staring at Lopes. After a few seconds of looking into Lopes's eyes, Posner decided that he was probably stupid enough not to be lying. 'How in the hell do you make a living, Lopes? That's what I don't get.'

'Posnuh, I wish you'd . . . '

Posner leaned across the table and grabbed one lapel of Lopes's trench coat. All the miserable anxiety of the past twelve hours poured out of him. 'Listen, you greasy asshole. Whoever hired you knew about that hit last night. They wanted me to be in there waiting so I could get hit, too. Get it now? They wanted me *dead*, shithead.' He held onto Lopes's lapel, his hand balled into a quivering fist, and stared into his face, watching him come to terms with what Posner had just said.

Lopes got it. Slowly, but he got it, and became genuinely shocked. 'Holy Christ, Posnuh. It can't be. Wait a minute . . . First, you gotta know that I woulda nevah of sent you there if I'd known anything like it was dangerous. Second . . . I can't believe it. Maybe you're paranoid, huh? I mean my client wouldn't do nothin' like that. I mean he's . . . ' Lopes stopped.

Posner let go of the lapel. 'He's who, Lopes? Tell me.'

'I can't. He's a good client. Listen, I know he's gotta have an explanation. Let me call him. OK? I'll get it straightened out.'

Posner looked into the back of the store where two old fashioned wooden phonebooths stood together. 'OK. I've got to make a call, too.' They both went to the phones. Posner put his ear next to the shared wall, and as he'd guessed, he could hear everything.

'Hello? Yeah. This is Al B.Lopes. Lemme talk to Senator Bagliano. No. Look, it's very important and highly sensitive, get it? OK, OK. But you be sure to tell him I called, and I got to hear from him *soon*. *Today*. Got that? Al B. Lopes. He's got the numbah. Yeah.' Lopes put down the phone and got out of the booth.

Posner picked his up and pretended to be talking to someone. Then he looked at Lopes through the door and said, 'Gotta go. Call you later,' put down the phone and got out to face Lopes.

'Well?'

'I couldn't get him.'

Posner frowned.

'Look, Posnuh. I swear to you. There's some mix-up. I'm sure this guy didn't know nothin' about that hit. Probly the guy who was s'posed to meet you got scared off by the cops or somethin'. I mean, this guy . . . '

Posner stopped him. 'You're an idiot, Lopes,' he said, trying to sound forgiving. 'I've got to remember that.' Then he let his voice get angry, but it almost went all the way to hysterical. 'Because idiots can be dangerous.' He started for the door and didn't turn around to hear Lopes's 'Aw, you're just sore.' He wanted to get out of there. He wanted to get out of everywhere.

When Posner got to the Human Learning Space, he saw the Mercedes he'd seen at Les's house in the parking lot and pulled in.

He paused in the corridor to look at the photo of Melody again, but somebody had taken it down.

Inside the office, Norma was holding down her position at the typewriter, clacking away. He stood in front of her desk for a short while before she noticed him and looked up nervously. She'd let her hair down since morning and it made her look slimmer and a good deal prettier. Posner admired her cobalt blue chain knit sweater, which he hadn't noticed that morning.

'He's here, right Norma?' Posner asked sharply.

'Well, Joe,' she stammered. 'He's awfully busy. I don't . . .'

The door to the inner office opened part way and out came a large head with thick black rimmed glasses and thick middle-aged features. A shoulder-length mane of white hair cut in the exaggerated shag of a rock star framed it incongruously. 'Nawma,' it said, then noticing Posner, turned to him. 'Can I help you?'

'I hope so. My name's Joe Posner. I've been trying to get a hold of you for a few days.'

'Joe!' cried the head. 'C'mon in!' The door opened more widely, revealing an enormous pear-shaped body covered in many yards of courduroy and plaid flannel. Stretched out, Posner estimated, he'd be at least six-four. When Posner had passed through the door, the principal closed it behind him. Then, in a motion that seemed to originate more in the involuntary than voluntary nervous system, he fell backwards into a reclining desk chair, and crossed his tree trunk legs. On the end of each leg was a rubber hunting boot, identical to those Alice Cabot had worn. Sixty-five bucks from L.L. Bean. Plus tax and handling. Seldom wet and never been hunting. Behind him, mounted on the wall was an assortment of handicraft products (weavings, crochetings, macrames, 'cat's eyes'), drawings and paintings. Several bore inscriptions Posner could read. 'To Les, I love you more than you could know', 'To Les, I'll always love you,' 'Les, you saved my life.' There were no diplomas.

Joe Posner tried to take a look at the man the way one considers an optical illusion. Somehow, a visual nexus kept eluding him. The massive monument to adipose tissue that was his body; the dramatic, long nose, the thick glasses, and heavy brow of his face; the frostywhip topping of the silly hair-do, suggested a mixture of Woody Allen, Mick Jagger, and Haystacks Calhoun.

Coniff leaned back into his chair and smiled. 'What can I do for you, Joe?'

'Well, Mr. Coniff . . . '

'Les,' the principal corrected him. 'Last names are kinda cold. And they're really about our parents, not us, right?'

Joe Posner didn't answer. He liked his last name. 'Well . . . ' Posner started again, but Coniff cut him off.

'I understand you'd like the Golds' address.' He held his heavy nose high and looked over it with an expression that might have been meant to be mirthful, or maybe just confident.

'Yeah,' Posner said dryly and looked over the blubberous principal slowly. 'I did, but I got it.'

Coniff didn't seem to like having his body looked at, but managed an uncomfortable smile. 'Good for you. Then what can I do for you?' He stretched his large, beefy hands over his huge thighs and rubbed the corduroy covering them.

'Well, there are a number of things about Melody's death that don't make sense to me, and I've heard that you were quite close to her – closer, perhaps, than even her parents, and I was hoping you might be able to explain a few things to me.'

Coniff removed his glasses and rubbed his eyeballs ferociously. By the time he looked at Posner, they were red and wet. 'The pain is still fresh,' he explained sadly. 'Yes, we were very close. Excuse me for asking, Joe, but I'd be more *comfor*table with this if I knew your connection.' From his pronunciation of 'comfortable,' which was like '*Kampf*' (as in *Mein Kampf*) plus 'tble,' Posner pinpointed his accent as Brooklyn. The slightly unctuous sincerity of the voice resonated from vocal chords aged to rich mellowness in pastrami fat that no amount of crunchy granola could ever scrape away. 'I don't really know who you are.'

'I'm a private investigator.'

'And you're working for the Golds?'

'I'd rather not go into that. What I was hoping . . . '

'Joe, Joe,' Coniff shook his head and held his hands palm upwards. 'I can't tell you anything at all unless I know your tie-in. Let's be serious.'

'OK. Melody hired me. The day she died.'

Coniff raised his brows and pulled his head back, compressing his chins against his neck. 'Why would Melody hire a private investigator?'

'I'm afraid that's where the "private" part comes in.' Posner said softly, almost apologetically.

Coniff scratched his head. 'I respect you for that. But I still don't understand your involvement. Whatever Melody hired you for . . . it's over now. True?'

Posner clenched his jaws and thought things over. Coniff was keeping a straight face, betraying very little satisfaction over having got the upper hand. 'I understand you're going on a trip tomorrow,' Posner said pointedly.

Coniff didn't flinch. 'Yes. And . . . ?'

'Well, it's just that Melody was planning a trip then, too.'

'Uh-huh. It's vacation time. A lot of the kids go away.'

'Sure, but do a lot of the kids go away to South America with the principal?'

Coniff let loose with a silly, high-pitched giggle, 'Ah, Joe, I like you. You've got a lot of vibrato, you know? And a lot of creativeness. Like buying the student list from little David. And stealing Melody's files.' He stopped and stared at Posner, but got no reaction. 'I could call the police, you know.'

'Maybe you should,' Posner shrugged, 'There are a number of things about this place that might interest the police.'

Coniff lowered his eyelids nonchalantly. 'Like what, for instance?'

'What would they be interested in, or what do I know about?'

Coniff cackled his falsetto laugh again. 'You *do* have vibrato.' The grin melted from Coniff's face and his eyes went all puppy dog. His voice took on an almost reverent tone. 'Look. Joe. I can't see what you're trying to do, really, but I can sense that it's coming from a basically good place. Still, honestly, it would be beyond my legitimacy to tell you anything. Anything I might know about Melody would be totally confidential. And confidentiality is a basic of a yoomanistic environment. If you had some *official* connection, I'd have to struggle with the issues.' Not without pity he added, 'But you don't.' He smiled like a lawyer enjoying both the knowledge that his argument is a winner and the coincidental luxury of believing it himself. 'It would be totally derelictive for me to discuss it with you. I really shouldn't have talked to you at all. Not about Melody or any other student.' Coniff sat back into his desk chair, barely able to keep the grin from his lips, and folded his hands on the summit of his belly.

Joe Posner felt pretty badly beaten, and he didn't like it. He wished he'd planned his strategy better. This guy was no Al B.Lopes. 'O.K. Let's forget the students. Do you know where Alice Cabot is?'

Coniff was surprised by the question. 'She's not home?'

'She flew the coop. Moved everything out. Just this morning.'

Coniff shrugged as if he didn't care. 'I knew she was moving, but I didn't know it was so soon.'

'How come she left in the middle of the year?'

'She had some personal problems.'

'Really? What kind?'

Coniff shook his head. 'That's really none of your business.'

Joe Posner winced deeply, and hoped it didn't show. My business, he said to himself, what the fuck is my business, anyway? 'I guess you're right,' he sighed out loud.

Without getting out of his chair, Coniff leaned over, stretching his huge torso across the small room, and opened the door. 'I really have some work to do, Joe.'

Posner didn't get up. He tried one more jab, hoping to hit a nerve. 'You know, I've been thinking about buying some antiques, and I hear you know a lot about them.'

Coniff didn't exactly fall to pieces, but Posner was certain that he'd seen something like worry flash across the principal's eyes. 'That's right. I'm into a little collecting. Maybe we can talk when I get back from vacation . . .'

'Mrs. Gold is into antiques, too. Isn't she? You know, she

said something funny yesterday. She thought I was a teacher at first, and said that it would take a lot of nerve for someone from the school, here, to show up there. What d'ya suppose she meant by that?'

Coniff's face went rigid, taking on the petulance of a cab driver in an accident. 'I don't have the vaguest idea.' Then catching himself in a defensive posture, he eased back into his fraternal intimacy mode. 'But I can see why she thought you'd be a good teacher.' He held out his hand for Posner to shake. 'It's been good. Listen, why don't you come back sometime we could just talk? You could give a one-day mini-class. The kids would love to hear about being a detective. I *know* you'd be a good teacher. It's that vibrato. Kids love that. Now, I've really got to get to work.'

Posner stood slowly, and smiled. The small travel clock on Coniff's desk said five to three. 'So do I,' he said, as he shook the principal's hand. 'It was nice meeting you, Mr. Coniff.' He sneered the last name, just slightly. It was a childish act of spitefulness which he regretted immediately, but Coniff smiled at him with equal parts of pity and forgiveness, and hung on to his hand.

'Oh, one thing, Joe. We do have to have that file back.'

Posner pulled his hand free and started through the door.

'I don't know what you're talking about. Honest.'

Norma gave him a hurt and angry look, and Coniff called after him, 'I'm serious, Joe. I'm serious.'

Posner kept walking, remembering Apfelbaum's rhetorical question: 'Could anything involving Les and Alice be called serious?' It almost made him feel better.

16. The Way the Man Sell It

Bergen Valley High School was on the other side of the tracks. Before he had moved out to Jersey, Joe Posner had never actually experienced this phenomenon of tracks and their sides. Here, there was nothing metaphorical about it. East of the railroad tracks was upper middle income, lower upper income, middle upper income, and upper upper income. East of the railroad tracks was virtually all white. West of the tracks was middle income, lower middle income, upper lower income, and low income. The more prosperous sections of the west side were integrated. The poorest sections were virtually all black.

To get to the school, Posner passed through the Sixth Ward, one of the poorest sections of the town. Mostly, it was composed of dilapidated wood and shingle houses that reminded him of Roxbury, New Haven, or any number of northern slums – more closely packed, though, than the almost rural poverty of Edgewater. Breath steam rose from men of assorted ages, gathered on corners; in front of bars and empty, boarded up storefronts; at gas stations. Talking, story telling, passing time. The *Bergen Record* said that local unemployment was up to thirteen percent. Posner knew that meant thirty to forty percent for blacks. Sixty to eighty for black kids.

One area, a few blocks square, was all institutional concrete. The projects: small boxes with the occasional capricious angle that testified to the good commission some architect got for designing them, built after this section of the Sixth Ward had been burned in response to the assassination of Martin Luther King. The concrete was already starting to crumble, and Joe Posner wondered whose brother's contracting company had made it with too much sand and not enough cement.

Once out of the Sixth Ward, the houses got sturdier and tidier, though still close together and small by east side standards. Temperate brick churches reposed on every other corner. Black people and white people walked the sidewalks and waited for buses. The mood was easy.

Bergen Valley High School sat in the middle of a broad, rolling lawn. Its neo-gothic architecture and two ivy-covered towers made it look more like an Ivy League college than a public high school. In the middle of the lawn, classing up an already classy act, two elms posed for each other. Clusters of kids dotted the area, casually carrying out the rituals of teenage society.

Posner nosed the Dart into the parking lot, which he found to be the center of activity. Kids threw frisbees and baseballs, splayed themselves on car hoods, revved engines, ran, shouted, rehearsed dance steps, smoked cigarettes. Mostly, they just hung out. A few clusters were racially mixed, but most of them were predominantly white or black. The few Asian kids seemed to hang out mostly with the blacks.

Posner edged the car forward a couple of feet at a time through the crowd, which seemed completely nonchalant in its reaction. Finally, he found an empty berth, pulled into it, and got out of the car.

As Judy had said he would, Posner found Luther Davis sitting on the hood of a green '73 Baracuda. He was by himself and acted like he wanted it that way. He stared into space, as if in intense concentration, and sucked deeply on a Kool cigarette. The pack in his hand was upside down, and a hole was torn in the bottom for access. He wore a short, tan suede jacket too light for the cold weather, green polyester slacks and black Puma sneakers. Posner walked up to him, but Luther didn't show any signs of noticing him.

'Luther Davis?'

'Who wants to know?' Luther answered, still staring straight ahead.

'I'm Joe Posner. Judy Williams sent me.' He handed the kid the note that Judy had given him.

Luther's eyes darted quickly toward Posner, then back. He held out his hand, took the note, unfolded it, and took a quick look. 'That's cool. Rap.'

'I'm trying to get some information about Melody Gold.'

'Melody.' He blew out a lungful of smoke. 'That was some cold shit, man.'

'Did you know her?'

'If I didn't know her, man, you wouldn't be aksin' me questions.'

'Judy said she saw you with Melody at the Bergen Steak House.'

'So?'

'Do you know if she was using heroin?'

'I guess she be usin' it the other night, sucker.'

'Do you know if she was using it before that night?'

'What make you think I know that?'

'Look, Luther, Judy told me about you dealing, but that doesn't . . . '

Luther turned to look at him for the first time. '*You* look, Joe Poster, Judy don't know shit, dig? I'm finished fucking with all that shit. *Been* finished for a while. So don't be tellin' *me* what *you* know about *me*.'

'I'm sorry.' It seemed to be all the deference Luther had been waiting for, and he started talking without emotion. 'Melody never used no junk. She always be comin' to me aksin' where I get it from, but she never wanted none to do for her own self. Not even for free.'

'Why did she want to know your source?'

'Well, she be dealin' coke to the white kids already. Maybe she just wanted to diversify, if you get my meaning.'

'Did you tell her?'

'After a while. That's what we doin' at the steak restaurant. She took me there for thanks.'

'Will you tell me?'

'Why should I?'

'Was it Hawk Brennan?'

'Melody never wanted to do no business with Hawk. She be wanting to do business *instead* of Hawk. Dig?'

'She wanted *Hawk's* supplier?'

Luther dropped his cigarette on the asphalt and looked at Posner out of the corner of his eye, but didn't say anything.

'Hawk's supplier is Marty Blittstein, isn't it?'

'You not so dumb as you act, sucker. You know so much why you aksin' me?'

'I didn't know Melody knew it, or wanted to.'

'She knew it. For 'bout a month.'

'Tell me something, Luther.'

'What I *been* doin', man?'

'Why do the white kids do coke and the black kids do heroin?'

Luther laughed, then suddenly stopped and said seriously, 'First off, "black kids" don't "do heroin". *Some* black kids do.

Dumb ass niggers like I used to be. And they do coke when they can make the price, which is not too often. The white kids do coke on account of they got the bread and they not bad enough to fuck with smack. They just like to look bad. That's the way I see it, anyway. Main thing is, the man sell it that way, you understand. He be sellin' junk down in the projects and blow on the hill. So that's what the peoples buy.'

'When was the last time you saw Melody?'

'That night at the steak place.'

'How did you know her in the first place?'

'She went to school here for 'bout a month before she went off to the Sick School.'

'The Sick School?'

'You know, man, the free school. Man, you couldn't *drag* my ass in there.'

'How come?'

'No discipline. Can't learn nothin' if you ain't got no discipline.'

'You learn a lot here?'

'I'm gonna. The teachers ain't got no respect for the students, and they prejudice, too. But it's all up to your own self, man. Dig? It's up to the individual. That's what Jesse Jackson says.'

'I don't get it. Is it discipline or self-discipline you're talking about?' Posner felt like being contentious.

'Don't be fucking with my head, now. Anyway, they don't want no blacks up there. "If you white, all right," as they say. They just want a place to hang out till daddy hands over the business. Place ain't set *up* for people who really got to get over. And I got to get over.'

'Well, I hope you do, Luther.'

'What you hope ain't got nothin' to do with it.'

'Guess you're right. Thanks for the help.'

'Later.' Luther Davis lit another Kool and resumed his pose of meditative concentration.

17. Patriarchy

The sign was the only thing missing from the Bagliano house. A neon sign and it would have been a dead ringer for a Holiday Inn: two three-story beige brick rectangular wings joining in an L shape; long, six foot high windows curtained in white gauze; pool in the front in the center of the semi-circular driveway; square balconies with plain black iron railings. It sat on at least half an acre of hill – not far from the Golds – that was, except for the putting green lawn, unlandscaped.

Joe Posner surveyed the situation from behind the wheel of the Dart. The Baglianos hadn't bought that place on a state senator's salary. More likely, the house and the state senator's office had both been bought with the proceeds of some more profitable occupation. Tony's van was nowhere in sight. A sapphire blue Porsche sat at the top of the driveway, in front of the two-story wood front door.

The place looked too stupid to be dangerous, but Posner still thought he ought to be scared. But scared or not scared, he wasn't about to let Bagliano know he was on to him. He dragged himself from the Dart and made the hike to the front door.

The huge oak door was opened by a young, plump, yellow-uniformed Latino woman Posner assumed to be in the country illegally. Piano music and singing came from inside somewhere. He asked for Mr. or Mrs. Bagliano and the woman said reverentially, 'Jew gotta wait here, O.K.?' Posner nodded and chuckled nervously to himself for the way he'd flinched at her pronunciation of 'you.' She showed him to the middle of the two-story foyer. The walls, all the way up, were bare. The second story corridor overlooked the entrance. The floor was marble tile. The maid left him and went into a spacious, powder blue carpeted living room, where a dirty-blond woman was playing a white grand piano and singing.

She sang slowly, her low alto quivering, and taking deep

dramatic breaths between words – not phrases – over a dirge-like repetition of one block chord:

I reach out to touch you – my heart's so alone.
I knock on your so-o-oul, but is anybody home?
Oh, philosophers may call you a fatso,
But I say it ain't so.
Somewhere in your blubber.
I know there's my lover.

Then, the chord stayed the same, but the tempo tripled.

Won'tchoo won'tchoo won'tchoo get to know-o-hoh me.
Don'tchoo don'tchoo don'tchoo even ca-he-he-haire.
My heart is raging
My face is aging,

Abruptly, the slow tempo returned.

'I search eternity for you, my precious love, but you're not
there.'

Four more repetitions of the one chord closed out the piece, and the woman leaned forward, resting her head on the piano. The maid, who had been waiting for the end, whispered in her ear. The woman sat upright and looked over at Posner, got up, and hurried towards him, pushing a crumpled kleenex into her eyes.

'Yes? I'm Mrs. Bagliano,' she smiled widely, her eyes thick with mascara, now running over cheeks painted with pale make-up. She was slender, almost boyishly built, her white jeans tight on her narrow thighs and belly, and her white cotton top falling loosely over her waist without showing the presence of her breasts. Her free hand was clenched into a tight ball. She wore no jewelry.

'Hello. My name's John Reed. I was looking for Senator Bagliano.'

Mrs. Bagliano stood motionlessly, the wide, unlipsticked grin frozen beneath her surgically buttonized nose.

'You see, it's a matter . . . ' Posner started, but she cut him off.

'I don't care what it's about,' she smiled, 'he's not living here right now. It's supposed to be a secret. You're not a reporter, are you?'

'No, ma'am.'

'Too bad.' The smile was still unchanged. Posner figured she'd be getting cheek cramps soon unless, as was likely, they were in shape from plenty of exercise. Dizzy Gillespie, Posner thought, should still have such chops. 'I don't know where to reach him, either. Except at his private office number, which I'd be only too happy to give you. It's 752–0471. Be sure to tell him I gave it to you. Unless it's good news you want to tell him. Wait. Are you investigating him, maybe?'

'Investigating him? Me?' Posner heard his voice hit the mezzo-soprano range, got his heart back down in its place and tried to play it cool. 'Why would anyone want to investigate him?'

'I wouldn't know. He never tells me anything about his work at all. It's just with all this Abscam stuff . . . it was just a thought. Big Tony behind bars. Think happy thoughts – that's what they say, right? Keeps you young forever?'

Young forever, Posner thought. Like a dead thirty year old detective. 'I've heard that. But I'm hardly involved in anything investigative. Now, that was 752–0471?'

'Uh-huh. What *is* your business, John?'

Posner's hand wouldn't stop shaking as he took out his pad and wrote down the number. 'I'm with the Explorers, Mrs. Bagliano, and we're looking for prominent fathers and their sons to take part in our program. How do Anthony Sr. And Anthony Jr. get along? Think they might be interested?'

Mrs. Bagliano laughed bitterly. 'Recently they haven't been getting along too well.'

'Recently?'

'I'd say for about five or six years.'

'Oh, I'm sorry. Irreconcilable?'

'They don't talk. As far as I know they haven't set eyes on each other for six months.'

'As far as you know?'

She laughed again, but this time she was starting to cry. 'As I said, Anthony Sr. doesn't live here now. Anthony Jr. is supposed to, but he's never around. *I* haven't seen him in over a week. There, now you can tell the boy scouts all our tragic little problems.' She was laughing and crying now, full tilt.

'I'm sorry, Mrs. Bagliano. I really didn't mean to intrude. Guess I'll be going now.'

'A pleasure to meet you.' She crossed to the door and opened it. 'Have a nice day, John,' she sobbed.

'You, too, Mrs. Bagliano.'

Joe Posner stood on the step as the door closed behind him. He looked out across the swimming pool and half acre of sod at his old Dodge Dart, with its lousy suspension, sticky butterfly valve, and broken radio. It looked just right.

Joe Posner expected to have to do some pretty fancy apologizing to get through Phyllis Gold's front door. But, when the door opened, she beat him to it.

'Oh, Mr. Posner, I'm so glad to see you. You must forgive me. Please come in.' She ushered him through the museum-like foyer into the living room. 'I was dreadful to you yesterday. I do apologize. But I was terribly upset, as you could imagine, and, well . . . that's the way I am when I'm upset, you know? It's sort of a transference process . . . or maybe I mean an avoidance mechanism. That's it. An avoidance mechanism. Please sit down. Here, take the Morris chair.'

'Thanks, Mrs. Gold.'

'It's English, of course. Morris chairs are. It's like Morris dances, I suppose.'

'I thought it referred to William Morris.'

Phyllis Gold burst into boisterous peals of laughter. '*William* Morris! The talent agent!' She gave him a sly look. 'You're a very witty man, aren't you?'

Joe Posner didn't know what to say.

Phyllis Gold sat down on a French looking sofa. Her snugly fitting gray wool skirt had a long slit down the side, and when she crossed her legs, Posner was reminded of Melody. The mother's legs were a lot older, but they were good.

'Anyway, Mr. Posner, my husband and I discussed your visit the other day – was it only yesterday? – anyway, he made me realize how utterly crummy I had been to you. He's out right now, but I know he'll want to talk to you when he gets back.'

'That's O.K. I think I understand.'

Phyllis Gold got deadly serious. 'You couldn't really. But . . . '

'Yes?'

'I . . . Burt and I thought it would be better if he talked to you about Melody. I get so upset.' She bit her upper lip hard enough to start the tears she was ostensibly holding back.

'Sure. Sure.' Posner agreed as sincerely as he could.

'Actually, Mrs. Gold, there was something else I wanted to talk to you about.'

She looked at him in pain and confusion.

'I know it's a bad time, but I'm afraid to let it wait,' he continued. 'It's about the robberies at your antique business.'

'The insurance detectives went through all that. They couldn't find anything.' She wiped her eyes with a crumpled, lipstick-smeared kleenex that she had extracted from a pocket in her skirt.

'Well, they can be pretty perfunctory about something like this. Believe me.'

'Are you looking for work? Is that it?' Her condescension bordered on pity. Posner was touched.

'It's just that, quite by coincidence, I came across something that might really lead to a solution of that case. Would it be all right if I asked you some questions about it?'

'Fire away.' The mention of a possible solution to the robberies dried her tears more thoroughly than a whole box of kleenex.

'When were they, exactly?'

'The last one was three weeks ago. Is that exact enough? That was the one that was here.'

'Here?'

'Yes. Didn't you know? They broke in downstairs. I had about five thousand dollars worth of Louis XV chairs waiting to be picked up. It was amazing. They were only here four or five days.'

'Is that all that was taken?'

'They ransacked the bedroom, but only found a box I had given my husband. And a matching brooch of mine. The rest of my jewelry was in the safe.'

'A box and a brooch?'

'Yes. Beautiful. All amethyst and amber. I'd given the box to my husband for our anniversary. It's identical to . . . ' Phyllis Gold's voice cracked and her nostrils flared, ' . . . to one . . . I gave Melody for her birthday. Burt was very upset that his was lost. He can be sentimental on occasion. Rare occasions.'

'I'm sure. What about the other robberies?'

'Two others. One in October, one at Christmas. Both were at the warehouse in West New York.'

'What was taken those times?'

'Never a lot, but always top-priced pieces. It was obviously someone who knew antiques and didn't have much hauling capacity. Let's see. In October it was early colonial stuff. A table and chairs and some small tables and some brass and pewter. About twenty thou' all together.' Posner whistled in amazement.

'Well, the newest piece was about 1790,' she explained. 'That kind of stuff don't grow on trees, you know.'

'And Christmas?'

'Japanese. Eighteen hundreds. That one was a fortune. Fifty thousand. Ever since *Shogun* Japanese has been hot. I've got a list. Would you like a copy?'

'Please.'

Phyllis Gold got up, smoothed her skirt and paced over to a colonial desk in the corner. 'It all belongs to the insurance company now, but I'd love to find who the bastards are. Otherwise they may try again.' She pulled a couple of xeroxed sheets from the top drawer, returned to the sofa, and handed them to Posner.

'Thanks. I might be able to use them. I've got a few ideas.'

'Like what?'

'I'd rather not say till I've had a chance to check a few things out.'

'You're a cagey one, aren't you, Mr. Posner? Do you have a first name?'

'Joe.'

'Phyllis.' She cracked a smile that was meant to be alluring, or at least to prove the capacity to allure.

'Do you have any books that might have pictures or descriptions of any of these things, Mrs. Gold?'

Guffawing lightly, she put her hand over her mouth. 'Not here. Nothing at all. It's all at the office.'

'Oh. Where's that?'

'In the city. Thirty-fifth Street.'

'Mmm.' Posner was disappointed.

Phyllis Gold cocked her ear. 'That sounds like Burt.'

Posner heard a car door slam, then a few seconds later the front door swung open. Burton Gold was home.

'Sorry it took so long, Phyl. The line at the deli was so goddamn slow,' he called out from the foyer before passing into the kitchen.

'Mr. Posner's here, dear,' she answered with a blast that almost shook the vases on their pedestals.

Burton Gold launched himself into the living room with a rustle of black check silk trousers. He was a large man, thick set, with big features. He wore a green and brown tweed jacket that clashed with his trousers, and a cashmere plaid shirt that clashed with both. His collar was open to show a muscular neck, which sported four or five gold chains of varying widths and styles. Gradiant tinted aviator glasses sat on his thick, pitted nose, and a curved Meerschaum pipe was clenched in his wide, square jaws. His hair was cut youthfully short and flecked with gray. He reached out at Posner with a huge, hairy hand. 'Hey, very good to meet you,' he bellowed, flashing a blinding capped-tooth smile. 'If I'd of known you were here I would of hurried even more.' Then turning to his wife, he grimaced, 'That damn deli gets so damn crowded.'

'It doesn't get crowded when I go there.'

'It was crowded as hell today.'

'Oscar's? He doesn't get crowded this time.'

'I didn't go to Oscar's. I went to the Leonia Deli.'

110

'Why in the hell did you go there?'

Posner sat silently fascinated by their dialogue, watching it as he would a tennis match.

'Oscar's strudel is soggy. The Leonia Deli gets strudel from the city. Liebner's. Real Hungarian.'

This, thought Posner, was something worth knowing. It seemed to satisfy Phyllis Gold, too, and Gold's disloyalty to Oscar, if not forgiven, was dropped.

Burton Gold extended his arm toward a door at the far end of the living room. The watch on his wrist had been allocated enough gold to balance the New Jersey state budget. 'Say, Mr. Posner, come with me to my study. O.K.? I'd like to talk to you about a few things.'

'Call him Joe, honey.'

'Why not?' answered her husband.

'Why not?' answered Joe Posner. He stood and maneuvered his way through the maze of antiques to the study. Gold opened the walnut door for him.

The study was all ultra-modern: chrome, leather, walnut and glass, with black shag underfoot. After the museum of antiques outside, it was like a pool of ice water after a sauna – refreshing in theory, but painfully excessive in practice. Gold motioned Posner to a huge black leather chair and dumped himself in a huger one behind an aircraft carrier of a desk that was covered with papers that had printed letterheads: the Dreyfus Fund, Friends of South Africa, Boys Clubs, United Jewish Appeal, New Jersey Citizens for Law Enforcement. On the wall behind him were a half dozen framed eight-by-ten photos of Burton and Melody Gold embracing each other in different faraway places. In all of them, Posner could see the father's huge hand wrapped around his daughter's slender upper arm. That perfect arm again. Clutching it. Engulfing it.

Burton shook his head slowly from side to side and rubbed his hands together. He had been periodically kneading his hands since arriving at the house. 'Joe, I know I don't have to tell you that this has been the worst week of my life. To lose my precious . . . what can I say? There are no words. Now, Phyllis told me that Melody hired you for something, and you wouldn't say what. Is that right?'

'I guess it is.'

'And voluntarily returned one *thousand* dollars in *cash* that she gave you?'

'That's right.'

'Well, I think that shows a lot of integrity. A hell of a lot.'

'It's no big deal.'

'The hell it isn't, Joe.' He started writing in his checkbook. 'Integrity is the biggest deal of all where I come from.'

Something about this guy made Posner feel like being a wiseguy. 'Where's that?'

'Where's what?' Gold didn't get the sarcasm. He couldn't think and write checks at the same time.

'Where you come from.'

'It's an expression.'

'Uh-huh.'

Gold tore the check out of his checkbook and pushed it across the desk to Posner. Posner picked it up and looked at it. In an extreme left-handed handwriting, the check made one thousand dollars payable to Joe Posner.

'We want you to have it.'

'That's very generous of you, but . . .'

'Now why did she hire you?'

Posner dropped the check on the desk. 'Maybe I can earn this. I might have a line on some of Mrs. Gold's robberies.'

'I don't think you understand, Joe. I *need* to know what my baby was up to that day. It's hard enough to accept that my doll was a dope addict. But if there are any unanswered questions about that day, I've *got* to get the answers. Can't you understand that? I've got to.'

'As a matter of fact, I've got plenty of unanswered questions about that day . . .'

'I want my questions answered, Joe. Not yours. You're not the father.'

'Still, maybe you shouldn't be so sure she was a dope addict.'

'Joe, Joe. I see she touched your heart, too. It's not surprising. No one who knew my Melody would think it was possible. But I'll tell you, Joe. Oh, I'll tell you, Joe.' His voice rose in quivering anger. 'It's no mystery to me what killed my little girl. That school killed her. That goddamn school. They turned my baby into a drug addict and a whore.' He shook with anger, and he wrenched the words from his gut. 'Shocked to hear me say it? About my own baby? Me, too. But it's true. It's goddamn true. Those hippy bastards ruined her, as sure as they held the needle, they killed her. And I'll never forgive myself for ever letting her go there. I knew from the start they were sick. That . . . Les.' He almost choked on the name. 'But she insisted. She refused to go anywhere else. Just wouldn't go. I even sent her to that public school full of *shvartzes* for a while, and if you think I liked that, you're crazy. A white girl with a pair of tits like hers around those animals? But she wouldn't go there anyway. She wouldn't go anywhere but that goddamn Human Learning Space. I guess it's my fault, really. I could never discipline her. I loved her too much. And Phyllis . . . ' he sighed, 'They never got along. She was daddy's girl.'

'You shouldn't blame yourself, Mr. Gold.' Joe Posner couldn't remember the last time he'd said something with less sincerity.

'I suppose you're right. So, Joe, please tell me. O.K.?'

'I'm sorry, Mr. Gold. I guess I just have too much integrity.'

'O.K., Joe, O.K.' Gold was just managing to keep his anger beneath the friendly veneer. 'Why don't I keep the check for you in case you change your mind?'

'That would be very generous of you, Mr. Gold. Mrs. Gold said I should talk to you about this . . . I know you weren't here, but Mrs. Gold doesn't feel up to talking about it. Do you know when the last time Mrs. Gold saw Melody was?'

Gold lit his pipe with an electric torch from his desk. 'Why do you want to know that?' he asked between puffs.

'Well, there was a bruise on Melody's chin when they found her. Mrs. Gold told the police that Melody had hit it on the swimming pool. But I saw her at four-thirty, and she was at a friend's by five and stayed there until seven, and . . . I can't figure when she had time to come home for a swim . . . unless it was almost immediately prior to her death.'

Gold's pipe was crackling briskly, and the room was filling

with aromatic smoke. 'The numbers don't sound too solid to me, Joe. But here's the point: Mrs. Gold is a very highly high-strung person. Very nervous, in fact. You might say,' he paused for a few more deep pulls on the pipe, 'she's not a well woman. Her relationship with Melody was not exactly the greatest. Now, when the police asked her about the bruise, she had two electives. One was to tell the truth, or, in other words, that she didn't know how Melody got that bruise, and open the possibility of a messy, sordid police investigation. Still, make no mistake, I think she should of done just that. But Phyllis . . . Phyllis has a lot of guilty feelings about Melody, let's say, and she . . . well, she might of thought she had more to hide than she actually did, if you see what I mean. Why do you think I'm not suing that school back to the stone age? Phyllis. That's why. She couldn't take the strain. She holds herself responsibe for Melody's drug taking, sleeping around, all of it. Now, I think that's crap, but what can you do? It's psychological. So, all alone – I was unfortunately out of the country – she made a mistake. She made up the story about the swimming pool. Can you blame her, really?'

Joe Posner waited before answering. 'I'm not interested in blaming anybody, Mr. Gold. But I still wonder where she got that bruise from.'

Gold banged his pipe on an ashtray. It wasn't out yet, and the tobacco burned on. He looked at Posner flatly. 'Melody ran in bad circles. They don't fool around with heroin at the Temple Sisterhood. Who knows which one of those jerks she knew gave her a poke? Sure, I'd like to find out what little bastard watched her die and ran away. I'm sure she wasn't alone. But that won't bring her back, and the trouble it'll bring, the grief to Phyllis, the shame . . . this way, Melody's dead. That's it. Nobody knows anything is wrong with Phyllis's story, and, if you don't tell them, nobody will. Get it, Joe?'

'Sure, Mr. Gold. I got it.'

'So, tell me . . . what's your lead on the robberies?'

'I'd rather keep it under wraps till I can get a better line on it. You'd be surprised how upset people can get about being suspected of committing crimes. Mrs. Gold mentioned you had something stolen yourself.'

Burton Gold seemed confused, like he wasn't sure how to react to Posner's statement. He sat, blinking his eyes for a few seconds and then said slowly, 'Yes. That's right. A little box Phyllis gave me. It had a lot of sentimental value, but the other pieces were a lot more valuable. I kept cufflinks in it. They were expensive, but the insurance covered it. Why do you ask?'

'Just trying to get an idea of what was taken.' Joe Posner stood up. 'It's been nice meeting you, Mr. Gold.'

'Call me Burt, why don't you?' Gold stayed seated and didn't offer his hand. He was still distracted. Joe Posner left him there and crossed through the living room on his way out. Phyllis Gold wasn't around.

A midnight blue Continental was parked in front of the house. The sticker on the bumper read, 'Visit South Africa – For the Good Life.'

18. Hep Cat

Joe Posner decided to put some of the information he'd picked up at the Golds to immediate use. Liebner's strudel at the Leonia Deli was something that cried out for verification. It wouldn't be cheap, but, then, he'd saved on lunch.

The clouds had long since finished raining and were slowly sliding apart, making room for occasional shafts of sunlight. Apple blossoms and dogwoods caught the rays like ballerinas in spotlights. The suburbs did have their advantages.

The Leonia Deli was not crowded when Posner arrived. A short, wiry old woman with peppery gray hair tied back in a bun stood with her hands on her hips behind the counter. She looked at him as if she had been expecting him and he was late.

'Nu?' she said, with left eyebrow raised.

'I hear you got Liebner's strudel. May I have a slice, please?'

'No.' She said it simply and without rancor. 'Darling, if I had, I'd give to you. But, unfortunately, I don't. I sold the last piece

115

maybe an hour and a half ago. Yeah,' she agreed with herself. 'Something else, maybe?'

'You sold the last piece to Mr. Gold?'

'It's strudel, honey. Not codeine. I didn't make him sign for it.'

'A big man. Tan. Tweed jacket and plaid shirt. Glasses.'

'That's him. You gonna try to buy it from him?'

'No. It's O.K. I'll wait till you get more.'

'Sure.' She approved of his good sense. 'I got their humentashen. You want?'

'No thanks. What else you got good?'

'What else I got good? I should have maybe something bad? Everything I got is good.'

'How 'bout some cheesecake?'

She stood motionless for ten or fifteen seconds. Then she shrugged her shoulders and started walking toward the refrigerator case, slowly shaking her head.

'The cheesecake's not so good?'

'Did I say the cheesecake's no good?'

'Well, you . . . '

'The cheesecake's fine. My husband picked it.' Posner was satisfied. She pulled a large round of cheesecake from the refrigerator and raised a knife. She stopped an inch or two from the top of the cake. 'You're diabetic?' she asked. 'This cake is good cheesecake for diabetics. Not much sugar. Or cheese.'

'Maybe I'll have something else.'

The woman nodded her head severely, agreeing on moral principle. 'Myself, I like Liebner's cheesecake, but my husband says it's too expensive. So he gets from an Italian, yet, here in Jersey.' She shrugged her shoulders in resignation.

'I'll tell you what. Let me have just one humentash for now. You got mohn?'

'What then?'

'And wrap me up a salami sandwich for later.'

'What you want is what you get.' She threw herself into her task with vigor and determination. Posner watched her small boney hands wield salami and slicer with consummate professionalism. Slice after slice. 'This is your dinner?' She was worried.

'I'm gonna be too busy to cook tonight, I think.'

'You cook for yourself?'

'Who else?' He knew what she meant. She shrugged her shoulders and kept on slicing. When she had enough for four or five sandwiches, she stopped and piled the mountain of salami on to a large piece of rye bread, topped it, sliced it, slipped in a pickle, and wrapped it. Mustard went into a separate small cup, so the sandwich 'shouldn't be soggy.'

'Salami sandwich and one humentash. Three dollars and sixty-five.' Posner paid her and said goodbye.

'*Gae gesunt*,' she replied. 'Try on Thursday. We'll maybe have the strudel then. Around twelva clock.'

'Thanks. Thanks very much.' Posner backed out of the door. No strudel, but hardly unlucky, he thought. He felt like he might have turned a corner. He'd gotten the antique list, he hadn't let Burton Gold push him around, the sun was coming out, and he was the owner of the fattest salami sandwich in Bergen County. In fact, his mood had risen slowly but steadily for the past two hours or so. He was only a few blocks from 347 Woodmont Lane. He'd see just how good his luck really was. Marty Blittstein was bound to be a pretty slick operator. Posner would just feel him out. He dropped his bag in the Dart and walked over.

The temperature was still cool and the occasional gusts of wind were cold, but the colors of the wet young grass and the fluttering pink and white petals that seemed everywhere raised his already high spirits. He turned onto Woodmont Lane about ten yards behind a teenage boy carrying a notebook and a small stack of books. When the kid started up the steps to 347, Posner called out to him. 'Hey, you Larry Blittstein?'

The kid turned. His face was dark both in complexion and mood with thick black eyebrows furrowing over clouded brown eyes. Birthmarks floated like satellites around his wide, purple mouth. A short, clumsily cut shock of black hair topped it all. 'Yeah. Who're you?'

'I'm here to see your dad. Is he here?'

'He's supposed to be.'

'And your mom?'

'She's working. Somebody has to.'

'You coming from the library?'

'No. I just flew in on the space shuttle.' He turned and started up the steps.

Posner followed him up. 'I just mean that I thought you went to the Space, and I know they're closed . . .'

Larry didn't answer him, but stopped at the front door, found his key, and opened the door. 'C'mon in, if you want,' he said sullenly, without looking back. Once inside he shouted ferociously, 'Marty, there's someone to see you!' There was no answer. 'He's probably upstairs listening to his damn earphones. That's all he ever does. Go on up, if you want. I'm leaving. I just came to drop off the books.'

'O.K. Thanks. Uh, Larry . . .'

'Yeah?' This kid was really petulant.

Posner thought for a second. Anything he asked the kid was likely to get back to his father. He'd wait till he'd gone a round of the main event before tipping his intentions. 'Never mind. Sorry.'

'What the hell are you sorry for? You haven't done anything. See ya.' He went back out of the door and slammed it shut.

Posner looked around from where he stood at the foot of the stairs. The dining room was on his left and the living room was on his right. The furniture was old, but not antique. The woods were dark, almost black. The sofas and chairs were overstuffed and upholstered in burgundy velvet. Modigliani and Chagall reproductions hung on the walls. The living room was not quite dirty, but looked much used. Newspapers sat in several piles. Ashtrays were not full, but not empty. A coffee cup sat on the piano.

Posner climbed the carpeted stairs silently. It was an odd feeling – like he was creeping up on someone.

'Mr. Blittstein?' he called out, but got no more of an answer than the kid had.

The kid hadn't said which room his father would be in. Posner looked in the first to the right of the stairs. It was a bedroom. The bed was very high and unmade. A poster for a Paris production of *The Balcony* hung over it. Further down the dark hall a narrow band of dusty light slipped through the crack in a slightly open door.

'Mr. Blittstein?' Posner asked again outside it. The tinny buzz of music from earphones came from inside. Posner pushed the door open slowly. The earphones weren't on Marty Blittstein's head. They were wrapped around his neck, the cord pulled tight. His face was more gray than blue, except for the eyes that bugged so far out that Posner could see hundreds of broken blood vessels around their edges. Blittstein's small, slender body hung like drapery over the sides of a reclining desk chair that was tilted all the way back.

Posner wasn't sure how long it was before he could move. Or breathe. Maybe ten seconds. Maybe ten minutes. He knew it wasn't soon enough to stop anyone from doing the same thing to him that'd been done to Marty Blittstein. But no one did. Not yet. Not there.

Once he could move, Posner found he could think, too. But he didn't much like what there was to think about.

The kid had seen him. Could identify him. He hadn't given his name, though. He really didn't want to get tied up in this. Even if they believed him, it would mean spending the rest of the day at the police station. It would make the papers. It would tip off anybody and everybody that he was involved. It would be a mess.

He lightly raised one of the fingers on Blittstein's right hand. No *rigor mortis*. He picked up the phone with a kleenex from a box on the desk, and dialed with a pencil. He looked at the digital clock on the bookshelf.

When the police operator answered he spoke slowly, but without pauses. 'Send a car to 347 Woodmont Lane. A man has been strangled. It is 4.26. I just found him. He was already dead when I got here.' He hung up the phone, and put the pencil and kleenex in his pocket. Behind Blittstein's chair a framed photograph had been knocked crooked. It was Marty Blittstein, playing a C-melody saxophone thirty-five or so years ago. His bushy moustache had been jet black then. His eyes had been young and clever.

Joe Posner walked quickly out of the house. He looked around. There was nobody on the block. He walked back to the Dart, started the engine, and drove away. He didn't know where. He wasn't feeling so good anymore.

19. Treasure

Joe Posner figured it was a good time to go to his office. He could think there. He could sit for a minute, collect his thoughts, and try to steady his nerves. A few steps from his front door he had a different thought. And stopped cold. He could also get strangled there, shot there, blown up by a bomb, knifed in the belly or just beat to shit there. He considered never going to his office, or his apartment again, but only for a couple of seconds. He walked to the front door carefully. There was a note taped to it. It was printed in pencil and said only, 'Package next door.'

Next door was a vegetarian restaurant, Root and Brunch. Posner kept his eyes moving as he walked over. Through the window in the front door he could see – to his profound relief – Nathan Small, the proprietor and one of the world's least dangerous people, sitting in the lotus position on top of one of the tables. Alive, in a manner of speaking. His eyes were open, but seemed to be vibrating. He did not see Joe Posner.

'Nathan? Er . . . excuse me,' Posner ventured.

Nathan seemed to undergo a spiritual cellular division whereby his otherworldly spirit gathered in one part of his consciousness and his Bergen County spirit gathered in another. Posner didn't really believe in those things, but the feeling was uncanny. The Bergen County Nathan turned to Posner, leaving the astral Nathan in meditation.

'Hell, man. What's the buzz?' He said tranquilly, behind still fluttering eyeballs.

'I got a note that said there was a package for me here.'

Nathan's eyeballs fluttered on while five or ten seconds

passed. 'On the coat-rack, man.'

'Do you know who left it, Nathan?' Posner felt like mission control struggling with an intermittent radio link.

'I think it was a person, man. I'm not sure.'

'A person, Nathan? What are you talking about, Nathan?' Posner wasn't in the mood for this nonsense.

'Ask Andrea, man. In back.'

Posner went to the coat-rack and found a small rectangular package wrapped in brown paper. There were no markings on it. It wasn't ticking. Bombs don't have to tick, Posner knew. But there were lots of easier ways to kill Joe Posner than sending him a bomb, he told himself. He picked up the package and carried it into the kitchen behind the dining room.

Andrea, Nathan's wife and helpmate, stood behind two mountains of carrots, one whole, one sliced. 'Hiya, Joe.' She seemed more fatigued than tranquil. Her normally limp brown hair was wrapped in a bun, exaggerating the severity of her gaunt, sunken face. She was about thirty, but looked forty. She had been a sculptor, but had given it up to carve carrots in hopes of cleansing the colons of northern New Jersey. She was a proselytizer.

'Hi, Andrea. Were you here when this package was left?'

'Yeah. I was washing the pots back here. Nathan was doing his morning meditation.'

'What time was that?'

'Oh, about seven, I guess. Are you alright? You look kinda nervous. Have you been getting enough grains?'

'Probably not. Listen, did you see who it was?'

'Well, not too good. It was a lady. I think. She was short and had real short hair. That's about alls I can remember. Like I said, I was back here. Is it important?'

'I don't know yet. I wasn't expecting anything. I better go next door and open it. Thanks for keeping it.'

'Don't mention it.'

'O.K. I gotta get going.'

'Bye, Joe. You should come for dinner tonight. Special's alfalfa loaf.' The way she said it, it was like a fundamentalist preacher announcing a prayer meeting. 'It's real good for

121

nerves.'

'No thanks. I've already got something for dinner.' Posner remembered the salami sandwich in his car and its millions of little cholesterol molecules waiting to move into their new home in his arteries. 'Gotta go, Andrea. Take care.'

'Bye, Joe.' She sighed deeply and started slicing another carrot.

Posner hurried through the dining room, where Nathan's physical being was still on a table top. When he got to his front door, he stopped hurrying. He tried to open the door soundlessly, but, as he knew it would be, that was impossible. The wood stuck and the hinges creaked, but after that, not a sound. A single piece of mail lay on the floor under the mail slot. He crouched to it slowly, thinking that his knees creaked louder than the hinges. It was a flyer asking for contributions to the Policeman's Bulletproof Vest Fund. Neither the door nor the lock had been tampered with as far as he could make out, but he still took the steps one at a time. At the landing outside the curtains to his office he waited a few seconds. He couldn't hear anything. He stuck his nose through the curtains. The place looked the same. The light on the answering machine was not on. Webster hadn't called. Or anyone else, for that matter. Nor had anyone bombed, burned, or ransacked the place.

He dropped the flyer on his desk, put the package down gingerly, and unwrapped it carefully. Before he got the paper all the way off, a shaft of sunlight coming through the window ignited a strip of amethyst. This was it. Stripped of its paper, out on the table, the box glittered. Purple and yellow. Almost translucent. Posner raised the lid. The inside of the lid had a photo of Phyllis Gold. With the eyes gouged out and a ragged 'x' scratched into the face. Other than that, the box was empty. Posner checked the wrapping paper for a note, but found none. Then he sat down in his desk chair and looked out the window.

He picked up the phone and dialed the police. When the police operator answered, he changed his mind and hung up. Then he dialed Information in Rockland County. 'Nyack, please. A listing for an Elvira Fishelman.'

'I'm sorry, sir. I have no listing under that name. Oh, wait.'

Miracle of miracles, Posner thought, a resourceful information operator. 'I do have an E. Fishel*woman* in Nyack.'

'That's it.' He wrote down the number, but he really only wanted to know if it was listed. The address was what he was after. 'Is that at 14 Dwight Street?' he bluffed, hoping to be corrected.

'We're not allowed to give out addresses, sir.'

'Yeah. Thanks.' He took out his notepad and dialed Senator Bagliano's private number, but hung up on the first ring. What would he ask him? Confronting him would be too scary. He'd have to figure out another way.

He locked the box in his desk drawer, and sat back in his chair. He didn't reach for the T.V. He wished it was twilight. He did his best thinking at dusk, but that was still an hour away. He'd have to think in broad daylight.

Somebody had strangled Marty Blittstein. Somebody had given him, Joe Posner, the box that had been stolen from Melody Gold. Or Burton Gold. Or both. Les and Melody were supposed to go to South America together. Melody's boyfriend smoked dope in the nude with Les. Melody's boyfriend's father had tried to get Posner murdered. Dessie Levine said Melody's boyfriend had taken the box from Melody, but everyone said she was a liar. Alice Cabot had a brooch which was also probably stolen – from *Mrs.* Gold – and had run away or moved. Or been abducted. Maybe to Nyack with or by someone who called herself Elvira Fishelwoman. Hawk Brennan sold drugs. Probably heroin. Melody had sold drugs, not heroin, but had wanted to. Had he left anything out? Oh, yeah. Melody's boyfriend had burglar tools in his van.

Joe Posner figured he knew a lot. A lot more than he'd known twenty-four hours ago. But he was a long way from knowing enough or figuring anything out. And he was scared. How could Bagliano have known about him by yesterday afternoon, and why had he tried to get him killed? Maybe Lopes was right. Maybe it was coincidence. But that still left open why Bagliano had hired Lopes in the first place. And if he wasn't supposed to have been killed at the Lan-more luncheonette, what was supposed to have happened there?

123

He'd go to Nyack and find Elvira Fishelwoman. Or Alice Cabot. Or both. It was about five o'clock. He'd hit rush hour if he left right away. He decided to go anyway. He made sure the answering machine was on and went downstairs as steadily as a drunken giraffe.

The salami sandwich had given of its seductive fragrance to the air inside the Dart. Posner thought about eating it then, but it was too early. And the way he was feeling made the odds on keeping it down extremely long. He took out the humentash, but couldn't even deal with that. He stuck it back in the bag and started the car.

Route Nein W was crowded. All the way up to Alpine it was stop and go, jerk and lurch. Posner hated that, but the sky had really opened up, and the late afternoon sun was doing beautiful things to all the young greenery along the road. Posner swore at the Dart's broken radio. It would have made a difference.

Above Alpine the traffic lightened. Even stopping for five dollars worth of gas, he made Nyack by six. Coming around the last bend before the turn off, he got a view of the Tappan Zee in its sundown shade of blue. It was the best he'd felt since finding Marty Blittstein, but he was still pretty shaky.

Two blocks into Nyack, Posner spotted a bar. He pulled over for a drink and a look at the local phone book. He parked two doors down from the bar, in front of an antique shop. When he got out of the Dart, he realized that all the other stores on the block were antique shops too. He examined their windows. The third shop in the row had mostly one style, which looked to Posner like it could have been American Colonial. The sign said 'Anderson's,' and Posner, though not certain, thought that it had been the name of the Nyack shop on the card in Coniff's desk.

He peered through the window. A fiftyish gent with shoulder length gray hair and old fashioned gray trousers, hiked up almost to his chest by striped suspenders, was tidying up inside. Posner took the list Phyllis Gold had given him out of his back pocket, gave it a look, and returned it to his pocket.

As he opened the door, it rang a bell more loudly than Posner expected and made him jump. It made the shopkeeper jump, too. 'Howdee doo. Help you?'

'I hope so. I'm interested in some American Colonial items.'

The proprietor smiled broadly. 'Well, good buddy, you come to the right place. Just what in perticiler didja have in mind?'

'Just something colonial. A small table, maybe. Or a chair. You have any colonial chairs?'

'Does the Pope have a rosary?' He laughed heartily, from beneath his diaphragm. 'Folla me.' He lead Posner to a set of three chairs.

'What's the date on these?' Posner asked.

'1827,' the man answered proudly.

'Mmm,' Posner frowned. 'Let me tell you . . .

'Fred. Fred Anderson.'

'Nice to meet you, Fred.' Posner extended his hand. 'I'm Bobby Bradford.'

'Bobby.'

'You own this place?'

'Sure do.'

'Well, Fred, let me tell ya. I'm innerested in something a bit older. You know, when I say "colonial," I mean colonial. That is, before the revolution.' Anderson started to laugh, but Posner cut him off. 'And it doesn't have to be a table or a chair. Just anything before 1790. I know I'm speaking of expensive items. It's for my grandmom, and, well, let's say cost is not really gonna be an issue. You think you can help me?'

Fred Anderson wasn't laughing anymore. He stood quietly for a while. Thinking. If he had something like that, Posner figured, he'd know it. If he was thinking, he was thinking about some other angle.

'I might have something for you. Hang on.' He went into the back again. Posner browsed around the shop. Nothing seemed to match the items on Phyllis Gold's list. Some of the stuff was pretty nice, though, he thought. But basically, Posner didn't like antiques. They were too old. After a good five minutes, Fred Anderson returned with a brass basin, just over a foot in diameter. 'Lancaster 1763' was stamped on the bottom.

'Oh, yes,' said Posner. 'This is exactly what I had in mind,

Fred.' He held it up and studied it inch by inch.

Fred Anderson was beaming. 'I'm afraid that's a pricy little item you got there, Bob. But it's worth every penny.'

'How much do you want for it, Fred?'

'Well, I'd have to get at least twelve hundred for it, Bob.'

'That sounds fair, Fred.' Posner kept his eyes on the basin. 'How'd you come by it, Fred?'

Anderson laughed uneasily. 'Trade secret.'

'Naw, Fred. I think you oughtta tell me.'

'Can't, Bob.' He laughed again. 'Sorry.'

'Naw, Fred. You gotta tell me, or *I'll* tell the police that you been buyin' stolen goods.' He turned to look at Anderson, who was frozen and speechless. 'I'm not really an expert on these things, but I'm sure that Mrs. Gold's insurance people could determine if this is the exact same 1763 thirteen inch Lancaster Brass basin that was stolen from her warehouse last October.'

'I don't know what you're talking about. I paid perfectly good money for this from someone I had no reason to suspect. If it's stolen, this is the first I know about it.' He was apologizing. Posner knew he had him.

'You're stretching my imagination, Fred. Who'd you buy it from?'

'A kid. Just some kid.'

'Just some kid comes in here with a thousand dollar piece of brass, and you buy it from him, no questions asked? What'd you think, he'd picked it up at Sotheby's to use as an ashtray for his reefers?'

'Well . . .'

'You'd seen him before, hadn't you, Fred?'

'Yeah.' Fred Anderson knew he was licked.

'With a regular customer, right?'

'Right.'

'Who, Fred?'

'A fella named Coniff. Known him for years. This kid was with him, helping him move stuff. Kid had a van.'

'Was Coniff with him when he brought in the basin?'

'No. He was alone.'

'Well, Fred. I'm gonna give you a choice. You see, I don't

particularly believe that a topnotch colonial antique dealer like yourself couldn't have done a better job of makin' sure that none of the colonial antiques taken in a well publicized robbery of colonial antiques in this area got fenced in your own establishment. I just don't. Now, if you want to try to explain your point of view to the police, why that's fine with me, and we can call 'em up right now. If, on the other side of things, you wanna just let me take this offa yore hands and return it direct to Mrs Gold – well, I can't make any promises, but I'd do my best not to mention where I got it from. What d'ya say, Fred?'

'Take the damn thing. Take it.' His eyes were glazed and confused.

'Now, Fred. What else did you get from that kid?'

'Nothing. I swear to God. That was the only piece.'

'You ever have an antique box, Fred? A jeweled one? Amethyst and amber?'

Anderson looked down at his hands. 'I wouldn't carry nothin' like that. Only one I know who would is Leibowitz. Turn right at the corner – third shop on the left. He might still be open.'

'Why thanks, Fred. Say, do you have any books, say *Hampton's Encyclopedia of Antiques*, around?'

Anderson looked at him like he was crazy. 'Bob, leave me alone, O.K. You're takin' my bowl; go on now. I ain't got *Hampton's* anyhow. Not my line of stuff.'

'Sure, Fred. Just one last thing. I think I better have a receipt.'

'A receipt?'

Posner took out his pad and wrote 'Received from Fred Anderson: one 13″ 1763 Lancaster Brass basin,' dated it, signed it, and gave it to Anderson to sign.

'I can't sign this. It's practically a confession.'

'I need it to cover myself, Fred. They probably couldn't convict you on it, but it might get me off if anything went wrong. Sign it or we talk to the cops now, Fred. That's the choice.'

Anderson just stared at it for a minute, then signed it. He didn't appear to notice Posner's real name. 'How in the hell did you find it?'

'I didn't find it, Fred. You brought it to me. And I found you by luck. Just plain luck.'

'Yours, not mine, I'm sure.'

'Good night, Fred.' This time when Posner opened the door, the bell didn't scare him. Fred Anderson didn't seem to notice it either.

20. Antiques and Curios

Judging from the window, Leibowitz's Antique Jewelry was even smaller and more cluttered than Anderson's. And it was closed. Shining from the back, though, a light told Posner someone might still be there. He leaned on the door buzzer and kept leaning until he saw a small dark shape moving through the dark to the door.

'What in hell's name? The British are coming? Pearl Harbor's bombed?' Posner heard through the door, while locks clicked. In the crack of the opened door a round, bald head appeared. 'You got an antique emergency? What're you, crazy?'

Posner smiled as winningly boychik as he could. 'I'm very, very sorry. Are you Mr. Leibowitz?'

'And if I was?'

'I had to get you before you left. I'm from out of town, and I just drove for two hours to get here . . . '

'O.K., O.K., you got me. You got me. So?' He kept the door open only a crack.

'I'm looking for a jeweled box – amethyst and amber . . . '

'Another detective?'

'Someone else was here?'

'Sure. Two weeks ago.'

'From an insurance company?'

'He didn't say so. Not a nice man.'

'Do you remember his name?'

'That's all I gotta do? You think . . . wait. He gave me his card.' The door closed, and a couple of minutes later reopened a crack. 'Lopes Investigations. Al B.Lopes. Feh. A greaseball.'

128

'What'd you tell him?'

'I told him about the girl – that's all I know.'

'What girl?'

'A young girl. She looked Jewish. Long black hair. She had a box just like that. Wanted to sell it.'

'When?'

'Maybe a couple of months ago?'

'Did you buy it?'

'Listen, sonny. You look a nice fella to me. Let me tell you something: never do no business with a kid. It don't pay. *They're* not protected; *you're* not protected. It's a mess.'

'That's good advice, Mr. Leibowitz,' Posner said gravely.

'I'm telling *you* it's good advice. What're you telling me?'

'You have any idea where she might have taken it next?'

'How should *I* know?'

'Well . . . you might . . .'

'No idea, sonny. Look, I'm late. My wife will worry.'

'O.K. Sure. Thanks, Mr. Leibowitz. Thanks a lot. Good night.'

'Good night.' The crack in the door closed, and the locks clicked again.

Joe Posner was overdue for his drink.

He stopped at the Dart and locked the basin in the trunk and went into the bar down the block from Fred Anderson's shop. It was dark, and still decorated for Christmas. Silver tinsel streamers crisscrossed the room, converging behind the bar on a shrine where a trio of portraits – Pope John Paul II (or J2P2, as Posner had heard him called), Frank Sinatra, and a young man in a Marine uniform – were surrounded by a four-tiered display of liquor bottles. Joe Posner sat at the bar two stools away from the only other customer, a shriveled old man in a cowboy shirt and a Mets baseball cap, who was listening to the barmaid tell an angry story. Posner thought it best to wait quietly for her to finish.

' . . . and it wasn't *me* who was too goddamned sick to cook *last* Easter, either, for Christsake. Sick my *eye*, if you know what I mean.' She was bent over, her elbows resting on the bar, in a stance that suggested utmost confidentiality, although her voice sliced through the air from one end of the place to the other.

"At's a load a crap,' the old man croaked in one sour tone and sipped his beer.

'Whose mother *is* it, for Christsake? And I *told* you about Thanksgiving last year, didn't I?' Posner learned something watching her bare arms shake with anger. He'd always wondered what those TV commercials meant by 'cellulite.' Now he knew.

'When Vinnie came to me with that sad story, and all that you-know-what about Deena's braces . . . I wanna tell you.'

"*At*'s a load.' It was time for another sip.

She stopped suddenly and glowered at Posner. His politeness had been in vain. She felt interrupted. But she forgave him. 'What can I getcha, honey?'

'I'd like a shot of house scotch and a beer chaser, please.' Posner knew it was the perfect combination to smooth his rough edges. It had been some day. The barmaid poured the scotch all the way above the top of the shotglass without losing a drop. Posner was impressed. She drew a glass of Schaeffer from the tap. 'Have you got a phone book I could use?' Posner asked.

'Sure thing, sugar.' She reached under the bar and thumped the phone book down, spilling a quarter of an inch off the top of his scotch.

'Thank you.' Posner took a sip of the whiskey and followed it with a swallow of beer. It helped right away. He thumbed through the phone book to 'Fishelwoman.' There was only one. 88 Oakdene Avenue.

The barmaid had gone back to her story, so Posner decided to wait till he finished his drink, or longer, before asking her for directions.

'And don't *my* arthritis act up? Dontcha think *I* got a husband to feed. *Noooo*. Not in *her* book.'

"At's a *big* load,' ventured the oldster.

Posner downed the second half of his scotch and followed it with the last two inches of the beer. He noticed a definite improvement in his state of mind.

'Getcha 'nother?' The barmaid asked.

'No thanks, but I could use some directions, if you don't mind.'

For the first time the old man turned to face Posner. He seemed interested in any matter involving directions.

'I'm looking for Oakdene Avenue. Do you know it?'

The old man squinted his eyes and twisted his mouth into a frown while he tried to place the name. The waitress chewed her lower lip for a second, then answered. 'Sure. Oakdene is off Poplar, ain't it, Buzz?'

Buzz? Posner thought.

'Sounds right to me,' Buzz agreed.

'Yeah,' continued the barmaid, 'go on up here for, let me see, one, two, three lights. Turn left two blocks and that's Oakdene.'

'Thanks very much. What do I owe you?'

'Dollar seventy.'

Posner paid and made his way to the door. The last of the sunset was gone. He took the basin out of the trunk and placed it on the front seat. He didn't want it getting dented. He wondered how many shops in Nyack had bits and pieces of Phyllis Gold's property. He also wondered what in the hell the insurance detectives were doing when they were supposed to be investigating her robbery. And what the hell Al B.Lopes was doing two weeks ago looking for an amber and amethyst box.

Posner saw the Saab parked on Oakdene as soon as he turned off Poplar, but not the VW. The house was a classic – right out of an Andy Hardy movie: wide, unscreened porch circling the whole house, gables and garrets sticking up here and there, white shutters, gray shingles. A closer look showed that it had been reconverted for multiple occupancy. E. Fishelwoman had the top doorbell on a stack of three. He pressed it, and in a few seconds heard steps on the staircase.

The gray door was opened by a short squat woman dressed up in a Groucho Marx costume: droopy morning coat, string tie, collar, glasses, greasepaint moustache and eyebrows. Her short, boyish haircut was greased flat across her head. Her bulbous, mediterranean face belied no embarassment at her get-up. 'Yes?' she asked comfortably.

'Elvira Fishelwoman?'

'Yes? Who are you?' she asked wryly, as if, in his own way, Posner looked more comic than she did.

'My name's Joe Posner. I'm looking for Alice Cabot.'

She looked at the floor beneath her feet, mugging surreptitiously, counting beats, then looked up. 'You're looking for Alice, huh? What's the matter, you get tired of using your hand?' she wisecracked, and started closing the door in Posner's face. Then she swung it open again, again looking at the floor, but this time in contrition. She looked up, straight into Posner's eyes. 'You look like hell,' she said dryly. 'Would you like a cup of coffee?'

'I'd love one,' Posner sighed in relief.

'C'mon in.' She turned her back on him and led the way upstairs. 'Ignore the outfit,' she called over her shoulder, 'I'm rehearsing my routine. I do an act.'

The apartment was one large room with a bathroom and a kitchenette. The ceiling slanted up from walls that were only five feet high. There were no chairs. Intricate, elaborate, free-form weavings hung on the walls. They looked bizarre to Joe Posner, but Ellen would have called this a defensive reaction to feminist art, and he would have admitted she was probably right. After a long fight. Maybe two or three days.

Three old leather suitcases and four or five cardboard boxes sat on the floor next to the bed. Elvira Fishelwoman poured coffee from a handthrown ceramic pot that was on a warmer plate. She didn't speak until she'd handed Posner his cup – also handthrown – and sat with hers on a large tasseled pillow on the floor. Posner stayed standing.

'As you can see, Alice is not here.' She lifted the corner of the bedspread and pretended to look under the bed. 'Not here.' She flicked an imaginary cigar.

Posner looked at the suitcases and boxes. 'But she was here?'

She pursed her lips and rolled her tongue around her teeth. 'Ahh *oui*.'

Posner sighed and took an overly large gulp of coffee. He didn't really know what the game was, and he was too tired to pretend. 'Do you expect her back soon?'

Elvira Fishelwoman raised her greasepainted eyebrows, wrinkling her forehead, and tried to look blasé, but a little too purposefully to be convincing, especially made up like Groucho. 'Who knows what to expect from Alice?' Then dropping her cavalier mask, 'She's so damn scared.'

'Of what?'

'Who knows? The bogeyman, I suppose.'

'Don't you mean the bogeywoman?'

Elvira cocked her head. 'You know, Posner, some things in life are more important than being clever. At least to some of us.'

Posner didn't know why, but he didn't have an answer for that, clever or otherwise.

'Alice is afraid of me,' Elvira went on, 'Probably. Or herself. Of what she really wants. That's why she's promiscuous. And why everyone uses her.'

Posner didn't want to get into that. Not at all. 'Where is she, Elvira?'

Fishelwoman drank from her coffee cup, her hand trembling. She wiped her mouth on her sleeve. 'I honestly don't know; and if I did, I wouldn't tell you. She split while I was at the store. Why don't you leave her alone? She doesn't need this, you know.'

'I don't know,' Posner said without sympathy. 'All I know is she called me last night, told me to come right over, then wouldn't talk to me. She told me to come this morning. I come. She's gone. So I figure maybe she's in trouble. I'm worried about her.'

'Like hell,' Fishelwoman sneered out of the side of her mouth.

'Where'd you get the box, Elvira? From Alice? Whose idea . . .'

'Forget it, Posner. Just forget it,' she smiled confidently and sipped her coffee. 'I'm not interested in any of that, I don't know about any of that, I'm not talking about any of that. You wanna know about it? Find Alice.'

'Why'd she leave school in the middle of the year?'

She stared deadpan at Posner for a few beats, then looked to her right at an imaginary audience, then back at Posner, letting her shoulders sag. 'Hey, Joey boy, remember me? The nice woman who invited you in for coffee? I didn't have to let you in here, you know.'

Posner was too tired to answer.

'Isn't there a ball game or a war or something on T.V. you can go home and watch. Forget Alice. Don't worry about her. Crabs aren't fatal.'

Posner drained his cup, set it on the stove, and walked to the head of the stairs. 'Thanks for the coffee, Elvira. Good night.'

'You bet your life,' Elvira Fishelwoman said, smugly sympathetic.

It was time for Joe Posner to head back to Bergen County.

21. Call Me Pisher

Joe Posner rode down the Palisades Parkway with his window open. The night air was wet and cold, and with the Dart doing fifty, the wind was strong enough to whip his hair around his head and into his eyes. He needed the air, though. He needed something. Another drink would have been the wrong idea. He needed some clarity. Clarity about this whole crazy situation, and, more immediately clarity about what it was doing to him. He wanted to be a detective. Or so he had thought. To get away from all the petty, routine, banal crap his work had been. Now he was on a real case. No doubt about that. And what he was finding was that he didn't *like* discovering dead people. Or almost getting shot to pieces. Or cornering minor transgressors like Fred Anderson. Or being patronized by fatherly lesbians and jewelers. He felt like shit.

The headlights of the Dart caught the nose of a police car, and Posner's heart skipped a beat as he realized he was whizzing by a speed trap. He reminded himself that he wasn't speeding, but it took another four or five minutes for his pulse to return to normal. A sure sign, he thought, of his poor cardio-

vascular condition. He made another pass at the salami sandwich, and again he backed down. He checked the rearview mirror for the police car, but all he saw was black. There were no
lights on the Palisades Parkway, and he was the only one on it.
The alcohol and coffee sloshed in his stomach. Pure ulcer juice.

He had felt good not getting pinned by Burton Gold. He
wondered why he disliked Gold so much. Because he was rich?
Boorish? Racist? Insincere? Working for South Africa?
Dressed badly and expensively? Had tried to buy him off?
Pawed-up his own daughter? Maybe the shrink would give him
some ideas. Posner had felt good about finding the basin.
Except for what it meant to Fred Anderson. He liked Judy Williams, but he didn't like it that he liked her. He tried to give
himself permission. After all, she ws a cute kid. A sweet, cute
kid. He, on the other hand, was obviously a lecher. Then there
was Alice Cabot. If anyone seemed likely to get themselves
killed, it was Alice Cabot, Archetypal Victim. He wondered if
she already had, and his stomach gurgled faster. He wondered
how he'd feel cornering Les Coniff. He wondered if he could.

Warm, homey light shone through the windows of the houses
on Culloden Crescent. Les Coniff's bungalow, though, was
dark, except for a blue glow in the bedroom window that meant
the T.V. was on. Sitting in the Dart, looking at the house,
Posner remembered neighborhood football games in cold,
pouring rain. After a huddle. Late in the afternoon. Already
bruised, and readying himself to feel more pain and wet and
cold and dirt. He felt that way now.

He walked slowly, almost imagining himself limping, over to
the video-lit window. Les Coniff was alone, stretched across his
bed, dressed in shorts and T-shirt, bathed in blue light, head
propped up by pillows. On the summit of his belly sat two containers of what looked like ice cream, each with a spoon stuck in
it. Next to him on the bed was a brick of pot – close to a kilo,
Posner estimated – and a large carved pipe. The ice cream car-
tons bounced on Coniff's belly as he alternately giggled,
cackled, and bellowed at the T.V. It didn't look like a real T.V.
show; it looked like a video tape. A group of teenagers – less
than a dozen – were sitting on a floor in a circle. A huge, round

135

back was on the edge of the screen. A girl was talking.

'I don't *know*. Just *cause*. It *is* gross.'

Coniff chuckled on his bed.

The back on the screen asked, 'Maybe you think it's gross because you want to try it and you're ashamed.' It was Coniff.

Coniff howled on his bed, jammed a serving-spoonful of ice cream into his mouth, and continued his howl as best he could with his mouth full.

One of the boys in the group interjected, 'Wait, Les. That's not fair. Probly Nancy does think it's gross. Not everybody's into it, you know.'

'No contracts!' T.V. Les turned on the boy savagely. 'Why are you protecting her? Do *you* think it's gross?' Bed Les chuckled.

'No . . . I don't particularly think it's gross.'

'Do you *do* it? Has anyone ever done it to you?'

Bed Les laughed harder.

'Well, not really.'

'Bullshit!!'

Bed Les was going nuts, and one of the containers fell off his belly onto his bed. 'Holy Moses!' he yelped, jumped off the bed, switched off the T.V. and the V.T.R. and waddled out of the room – for a sponge, Posner figured.

Off-balance seemed like a good state to catch Les Coniff in, and Posner went for the doorbell. 'Wait a minute,' Coniff hollered. Then after two or three minutes, a light went on in the living room, and Les opened the door. Four or five inches of hairy belly showed between the top of his blue satin running shorts and the bottom of his 'Grateful Dead' T-shirt. His heavy, middle-aged face still had the remnants of a leer on it, mostly in the corners of his mouth. His eyes were red and glazed, and clouded with surprised confusion, behind the thick black glasses.

'Joe. What're you doing here?'

Posner smiled. 'I was just in the neighborhood, and I thought it might be a good time to talk about those antiques.'

Coniff wrinkled his forehead, trying to gain some equilibrium, and pulled up his shorts to cover his belly, revealing the bulge of an erection. 'It's not a good time now, Joe. Why don't you come by the Space tomorrow?'

'I'd rather talk to you now. May I come in? I won't keep you long.' Posner shifted his weight toward the space between Coniff's stomach and the door frame. Coniff filled the gap with a half a step to his left.

'I'm sorry, Joe. This is my time for being with myself. It would disturb my flow if you came in now. Come by the Space tomorrow.'

'I've been talking to Fred Anderson, Les.' Like a straight arm, the statement pushed Coniff a step back from the door. Just enough for Posner to get into the room.

'This is a cute place you have, Les.' Posner collapsed into a Victorian armchair.

'Hey! What is this? What's your problem?'

'Oh, Les, I have lots of problems. I might even have a few for you.'

Coniff lowered himself onto a dining room chair and scratched his beefy chest. 'Well?' he challenged innocently.

'Where's Alice, Les?'

'How should I know?'

'You were having a scene with her, weren't you?'

'I don't see how that's any of your business,' Coniff answered sharply, clearing his throat of reefer phlegm.

'Maybe not.' Posner picked up a copy of *Psychology Today* from the coffee table and thumbed through it. 'And I think you were having a scene with little underage Melody, too.'

'Bullshit,' Coniff snorted.

Posner shrugged. 'You were going to South America with her.'

'That again. Look, I don't have to explain that to you. Who in the hell . . . '

'And I think *maybe* you were involved in stealing Mrs. Gold's antiques, too.'

Coniff got calm. 'Have you told any of this to anyone?'

'Why?' Posner asked.

Coniff grinned. 'Because if you have, I'm going to sue your balls off.'

Posner smiled back. 'Fred Anderson says Tony Bagliano sold

him a brass basin. Mrs. Gold says whoever robbed her knew antiques. That leaves a pretty necessary middle man position for you, doesn't it?'

'You're nuts, Joe.'

'Am I? Am I also nuts that you've got enough reefer back there to keep Trenchtown high till Friday? And that you've had students here smoking it?'

'Bullshit.'

'Is it?'

'Who told you that?'

'A very reliable witness.'

'It's not *true*.' Coniff's voice and eyes were all injured bewilderment.

'Look,' Posner reasoned, 'I don't care about this stuff. Really, Les. I just want to know about Melody. I need the blanks filled in. I already know about what you're doing – the sex, the drugs, the burglaries. What in the hell have you got left to hide, for Christsake? Unless you killed her, of course.'

'Killed her? Nobody killed her, Joe. She died of an overdose. Remember? What kind of a paranoid trip are you on?'

'Just tell me what you know. I won't mess up your scene. I promise.'

'All I know is you could use some professional help, Joe. You're hallucinating.'

'O.K.' Posner heaved a sigh. 'Let's try it the other way. You start talking or I *will* bother you. The Golds hear about the burglaries and the sex. The school board or whoever you're responsible to hears about the drugs, too. How's that grab you?'

Coniff didn't twitch a muscle. 'Call me pisher, Posner,' he sneered. 'I haven't done anything to be ashamed of. And if I had, you don't have half enough to prove it.' He stood from his chair and started pacing the room, arms dangling loosely at his fat sides, like a wrestler stalking the ring. 'Who you gonna tell? The parents? They won't believe you. The kids? They wouldn't care if it was true. The school board? You think they want to know? We take the incorrigibles off their hands, and at no cost to the state. That's what they care about. If you think you and

Fred Anderson can bust Anthony Bagliano, Jr., be my guest. What he does after school is not my responsibility. It's his father's. So what's left? I have some grass in my bedroom? Big deal. I can move it before you get to a phone, anyway.' Coniff was finished, but the heat of battle glowed in his stoned eyes.

'I wouldn't be so sure that the Golds . . . ' Posner started more weakly than he wanted.

'The fucking Golds are nothing. None of the other parents on the board pay them any attention. Everyone knows they're against the school.'

Posner sat in his armchair with one finger on his upper lip, trying to look like his position hadn't been kicked to hell. 'Tell me about Anthony Bagliano, Sr.' he said weakly.

'What about him?'

'Everything you know. Is he hooked up with rackets, or drugs? What's he like?'

'Why should I tell you?'

'Because I need you to. Because I think he's trying to get me killed. Because I'm scared.'

Coniff did a double take with his eyes. 'You *are* on a paranoid trip,' he sighed, shaking his head.

'No. It's true, Les. Please.'

Coniff shrugged. 'What do I know? He's connected. Too connected for someone like you to make a lot of trouble for Tony. As far as I know he's very anti-drug. Heavy into law and order. Very conservative. Honestly, that's all I know about him. I've always dealt with Lucille – that's the mother. I never heard anything about him being involved with rackets. Look, Joe. This Melody thing has obviously got you very fucked up. Nobody killed her. Nobody's trying to kill you. Why don't you go home. Get some sleep. Wake up tomorrow, and forget all about it.'

Posner thought about knocking Coniff's legs from under him by saying that somebody had killed Marty Blittstein, but he realized there was little point to it, got up, and went to the door. He stopped, with his hand on the knob, and thought about making some threats about getting more proof, but that seemed pointless, too. Instead, he just walked out into the night, which seemed a lot darker and a lot later than it was.

22. Therapy

Joe Posner was almost too tired to drive. This working-on-a-real-case business was hard. He should have been two hours into T.V. and at least forty-five into his mid-evening nap by then. Instead, he was driving to Teaneck on Route 4 – no place, Posner whined to himself, to be when you're tired.

Joe Posner hated everything about Route 4: three lanes of traffic squeezed into the width of two, lined on both sides by concrete barriers, pocked by thousands of potholes, and populated by a race of jalopy jockeys who passed from every angle and at every speed except those permitted by law. His stomach gurgled and burned like a Yellowstone mud hole. But Joe Posner tried to look on the bright side. It wasn't raining. Route 4 was even worse in the rain.

Kappachung Road was just a block off the highway and only two blocks long. He was just on time for his nine o'clock appointment. The houses were mostly mock Tudor, and the vegetation was mostly evergreen. It had its share of dogwoods, but Joe Posner wasn't in the mood for them anymore.

Marjorie-Lynn Feldman-ex-Goldberg's house was also brick and stucco mock Tudor. Posner rang the bell on one of the two front doors at opposite ends of the walk. A small card by the bell read, 'In time, we all ring our own bells.' The other door opened.

Marjorie-Lynn leaned out with small, watery eyes and a face composed in suffering. 'Billy,' she said sadly, and looked at Posner with pity. 'Please come in this way, O.K.?'

The door led to a small single room, maybe twelve-by-twelve. It was dimly lit, and the carpet, furniture, drapes, and walls were all browns and rusts. A framed plaque reading 'Life is Energy is Love,' a bachelor's degree and a master's of Social Work, both from Alwyn-Hayes University of Paramus, New

Jersey, hung on the wall.

Marjorie-Lynn, dressed in a violet tie-dyed pants suit, was on the large side, but not fat. Her orange hair hung in a somewhat greasy shag cut over her pasty oval face. Once Posner was in the center of the room, she came up behind him, putting one hand on his forehead and the other on his spine, underneath his jacket and loose shirt tail.

'Billy, Billy. You're really tied up, aren't you? I bet you've got indigestion right now, don't you?'

'Why, yes. How'd you . . .'

She grabbed some flesh on Posner's back in between her thumb and forefinger, squeezed it hard, and twisted it. 'Jesus!' Posner yelped.

'That hurt, didn't it, Billy?'

'It sure did . . .'

She did the same thing further down his spine and, at the same time, ground a knuckle against one of Posner's lower vertebrae. Posner howled again, and turned to face her, holding one arm up as a shield. 'Energy blockage,' she said seriously. 'I could see it from the way you walked in.'

'Look, Ms. Feldman,'

'Marjorie-Lynn. Last names are really about . . .

'I know, I know . . . our parents, aren't they? Listen to me. I have a confession to make. My name isn't Billy Strayhorn, it's Joe Posner, and I'm not here for therapy, I'm here to ask you questions. I'm a private investigator.' He almost added 'Please don't hurt me anymore,' but opted to hang on to a modicum of toughness.

She smiled at him understandingly. 'Resistance is part of the therapeutic process. I think Freud even wrote a book about it once. But if you're more confortable, let's talk first, before I diagnose you.'

'No, really. I'm not resisting you. Honest. I gave you the false name because I didn't want you to tell anyone I had contacted you . . . in case you might have mentioned it.'

Marjorie-Lynn moved to a chrome and brown leather chair and sat back into it with the poised, but esoteric posture of a yoga freak. She sat still, upright but relaxed, her hands spread firmly over the arms of the chair, and looked at Posner with groping, suspicious eyes. 'Sit down.' she mentioned to a tweed armchair, which Posner took. 'You *are* in a lot of pain. I can feel it all the way over here.'

A good deal more relaxed, now that Marjorie-Lynn was out of pinching range, Posner held his hands parallel in front of him, as if to demonstrate his steadiness. 'Be that as it may, my name is Joe Posner, and I made this appointment to talk to you about one of your clients. Melody Gold.'

Marjorie-Lynn didn't even blink. 'Yes. Go on.' Only her lips moved, and not very much, when she said it.

'I don't know if you know this, but Melody died last week.'

Marjorie-Lynn neither spoke nor moved.

'Did you?' Posner asked.

Still she didn't speak.

'Did you know that Melody was dead?'

'How would you feel if I did know?' she asked in an innocent, sing-song voice.

Posner shook his head and rubbed his eyes. 'No, no. Marjorie-Lynn, um, I uh . . . No. Listen. I was hoping you could tell me something about Melody and her parents. I know that professionally . . . '

'Tell me, Joe. Why are you so resistant to talk about your feelings about all of this? Imagine that you *did* tell me how *you* felt. What do you imagine would happen?'

'You know, I think it would be a really terrific idea to really get *in*to my feelings about *all* of this,' Posner did his best to imitate Marjorie-Lynn's nursery rhyme intonation. 'And I'd really like to get into *yours*, too. But just for *today*, I think it might be more *help*ful if we could just *fo*cus on something *else*.'

At last communication had been achieved. Marjorie-Lynn's mouth curved weakly into something like a smile. 'What do *you* want to talk about, Joe?'

'Somebody was beating up on Melody. Do you know who? Did she ever tell you?'

'Well, of course I can't really tell you anything about Melody at all. It would be terribly unprofessional of me. But I suppose in this case I can make an exception.' Posner nodded as if he

142

had some idea of what it was about this case that warranted an exception. She nodded back and went on. 'Melody had a terrible energy flow problem with her mother. There was near total blockage. Now in cases like that, where there's so much energy that's not getting discharged, you get a terrible situation we call the "I hate you–you hate me" mode.'

Posner rubbed his chin. 'You mean Melody and her mother didn't get along?'

Marjorie-Lynn smiled. 'In layperson's terms.'

'What about her father?'

Marjorie-Lynn nodded her head severely. 'You're perceptive, Joe. Very sharp. There was a small energy flow problem relating to her father, too. But in an opposite direction. I call that the "I love you–I need you–which?" mode.'

'That might be a little too sophisticated for me. Could you try to explain it in layperson's terms?'

'Well, I never actually met the father, but I know that . . . well, let's say Melody liked him more than she liked her mother. Now, that sets up what we call an energy im*bal*-ance . . . uh, I don't want to get into that. But it's not very good.'

'Could you elaborate on that?'

'How do you mean?'

'Well, like . . . how do you know Melody liked her father . . . what'd she say about him?'

Marjorie-Lynn nodded seriously. 'She told me. I remember, she said, "I hate my mother, but my dad's great." Is that what you mean?'

'Well, what about their *history*? Do you have any ideas how this situation developed?'

Marjorie-Lynn's lips curved and opened, and she exhaled weakly a few times. It seemed to be her version of a laugh. 'I get where you're coming from . . . we don't get into any of that. I've never found it helpful. We dropped most of that rigid Freudian kind of thinking in '73. We only deal with material that develops while the client is in therapy.'

Posner looked around for bookshelves, but there weren't any. 'This is fascinating, Marjorie-Lynn. Is there some school of philosophy that this is all based on?'

Marjorie-Lynn beamed. 'It's incredible, isn't it? We call it "Goldberging". It's named after my ex-husband, Dr. Ernest Goldberg, who ran the psych program at Alwyn-Hayes in the early seventies. It's highly eclectic.'

'It *is* incredible,' Posner cooed. 'Well, then, while Melody was seeing you, did Mrs. Gold ever try to kill her?'

'What does "try" mean, Joe?' She smiled sagely and sat forward in her chair, leaving her hands on the arms. 'I "tried" to write a book, but I didn't write it. Did I try, or didn't I?' She sank back in the chair again, eyes twinkling like a Hindu master's. Posner could not respond. 'Now this really *is* confidential,' Marjorie-Lynn went on, 'But Mrs. Gold did push Melody down the basement steps this past fall. And then she threw a knife at her a few months ago. And last summer, she came at her with an axe. But, to be fair, Melody did try to poison her mother two or three times this past year, too. I hope I can trust you not to tell anybody about this. It was a very, very bad situation. Probably the worst energy blockage in a mother daughter mode that I've ever seen. It was hard working with them, too. Her mother's analyst was this very traditional Freudian, and she undercut a lot of what I was trying to do.'

'When she pushed her down the steps – this past fall, you said – was she hurt?'

'Oh my, yes. Terribly. Her eyes were closed, she had some stitches.'

'Why did she do it?'

'Nothing special that I recall. Usually these things start out as a fight over something small – curfew, or cleaning up her room – then the blocked energy breaks loose, and kaplow! An explosion.'

'Did Melody ever talk to you about drugs. Heroin in particular?'

'No, no she didn't.'

'How about sex? Did she ever mention any boys or men she was sleeping with, or seeing?'

'No. Come to think of it, she never mentioned boys. Mostly we worked on the blockage with her mother.'

'Why did she come to you in the first place?'

'The school sent her. Les did. I've worked with other students, too.'

'And why did Les send her?'

'Well, Melody had told him some things about her and her mother, and he realized I could help.'

Posner smiled grimly. 'How lucky for everybody he knew you.'

Marjorie-Lynn closed and opened her eyes once, in lieu of a bow.

'Did Melody ever mention a box, a jeweled box, that her mother, or her father, maybe, gave her?'

'No. Nothing like that.'

Posner stroked his nose. 'O.K. I guess that's all.' He stood. 'Thanks very much. This has been very helpful.'

Marjorie-Lynn didn't get up. Her hands still hadn't moved from the arms of her chair. 'You should make an appointment, Joe. I could help you. If you want to stay for another fifteen minutes, and let me work on your back, you'll be convinced.'

Posner moved quickly to the door. 'I'll call you. I'm in sort of a hurry now. I'm supposed to pick somebody up at work.'

Marjorie-Lynn smiled sadly. Posner could see she knew he wouldn't call.

23. Helpless, Helpless, Helpless, Helpless

At a red light Joe Posner looked at himself in the rearview mirror. He did not look like a teenager. He didn't look like a college kid either. He looked even worse than usual. Elvira Fishelwoman had been right: he looked like hell. His thinning hair was long overdue for a haircut and extra ragged from the wind. It had been on a rainy Thursday morning, a month before, that he had accepted the bags under his eyes as a permanent part of his face. He didn't feel that way about the tire around his waist, but it had been there for a couple of years and didn't seem to be going anywhere. When he looked back at the road, the light was already green, and he drove on.

He was looking forward to seeing Judy Williams. A lot. Not only enough to be dangerous, but enough not to care. Enough to make him believe that seeing her might ease all the fear, the frustration, the physical and mental fatigue that was Joe Posner that night.

The salami sandwich in the paper bag was still sitting on the seat next to the brass basin. He was starting to think of it as an old friend. They'd certainly been through a lot together. Then it occurred to him that the smell might prove offensive to the eminently goyishe nose of young Judy Williams. He held the wheel with his left hand, leaned over, stuck the bag in the glove compartment, and rolled down the passenger window. Romance before friendship. He felt like a real idiot. 'Fuck you, you fuckers.' It was something he often said out loud when alone to break out of a humiliating reflection. And hiding a salami sandwich to make time with a schoolgirl was pretty damn humiliating.

The deli was the only shop still open on Ramapo Street. Posner pulled up in front. The clock outside the drive-in bank flashed 9.41. Through the window, he could see Judy wiping the glass display case with a paper towel. She held a bottle of window cleaner away from her body in her other hand. Her rear end stuck out. Just a little. Just enough. She was maddeningly, insistently pert. Posner put the basin under the seat and got out of the Dart.

Hoping to get Judy's attention without going in, he tapped on the glass door with his fingers. He would have stayed in the car, but he didn't want her to make other arrangements for a ride. Why he didn't want to go in, he didn't want to think about. Just chicken, probably. Judy looked over her shoulder and past her ass at Posner. Her whole face smiled at him. Ignoring his attempt to wave her off, she made for the door, opened it, and grabbed his hand before he could withdraw it. Her warm fingers made something somewhere pop.

'Hi, Joe. I'm really glad you came.' She tugged at his hand. 'C'mon in. I'm like almost finished.'

146

Posner held his ground. 'No, thanks, Judy. I'll wait in the car. I just wanted you to know I'm here.'

Judy looked a little puzzled. 'O.K. I'll be out in like about five minutes. Want me to bring you a cup of coffee? I mean you look really tired.'

'That would be great.' A stroke of genius, Posner thought, after flinching at the confirmation of his decrepitude. Coffee would be perfect. Just what he needed. What a thoughtful, perceptive kid she was. Unquestionably mature beyond her years. As he turned to go back to the car, Posner searched the pockets of his leather jacket for an old pack of Camels he remembered coming across earlier. He almost never smoked, but he wanted a cigarette now. He found the pack. There were three cigarettes in it. They were bent but not broken. He took one out and twisted up the end where the tobacco had fallen out. Then he realized that he had no matches. The cigarette lighter on the Dart hadn't worked for almost a year, but he tried it anyway. It still didn't work. He stuck the cigarette in his mouth. For the feel of it. It felt tired.

In the glove compartment, somewhere, he had a film can that held his emergency amphetamine supply. He rummaged around till he found it. There were two 25mg Preludins and a Dexamil left. After letting the saliva collect for a few seconds, he popped one of the Predulins. After all, he was going to a party.

He slumped behind the wheel and tried to get his mind back on business. How to handle Tony Bagliano? Push him hard. Use Anderson. His appointment with Melody. Accuse him of getting his father to try to get Posner killed. Try to force him to implicate Les. Panic him into running to Les and confront them together. Maybe it would work. If Les had already got to him, it probably wouldn't. He should have worked on the kid first. He needed to talk to Hawk again, too. What with Blittstein dead, maybe Hawk would be scared enough to open up. Unless Hawk had killed Blittstein.

'O.K. we can go.'

Posner almost swallowed his tongue in surprise. Judy Williams had hung her elbows over the edge of the open passenger window and rested her chin in her hands.

'Great. Get in.' That much took all the self-composure at his disposal. She got in. There was nothing intentionally provocative about what she was wearing – old jeans, the purple and gold Bergen Valley letter jacket, and sneakers – but Posner's skin was crawling. As he started the Dart, he thought he was picking up a whiff of freshly applied perfume. The sweet kind that young girls use. The same kind they used when he was in school. Could it be for his benefit? he wondered.

'Sorry about the coffee,' Judy apologized. Posner had forgotten anyway. 'All that was left was the drags, and I, like, you know, couldn't start a new pot.'

'Forget it. It was a sweet thought.' And 'drags' was cute as hell. 'Where are we going?'

'Up the hill. Make a left at the lights.'

'How was work?'

'It's always the same: You know, like I love it, but it's boring. Is that a joint?' she asked, looking at the twisted Camel hanging from Posner's lips. 'Let's light it!'

Posner took the cigarette from his mouth and looked at it. 'Uh-uh. It's just an old cigarette.'

'Bummer. I think I've got one, though.' She started looking through her cloth bag. Posner tensed a little. He'd never smoked with someone so young. Except when he was that young himself. So what's the problem? he asked himself. He had been smoking at her age. She had been four years old then. The bigger problem was what it would do to his concentration to get high. He could just see himself grilling Tony Bagliano and forgetting in mid-sentence what he was trying to find out. The speed would keep him together, though.

'Here it is.' Judy fished a thin, bent reefer from her bag, as Posner made the left and started up the hill. She lit it with a lighter from her bag, took a deep drag, and offered it to Posner. As always, he found the sweet and pungent smell of the reefer powerfully seductive, but that was just icing on the cake. He wasn't about to look any squarer or any older than he was. The smoke was smooth and spicy – good stuff – and he pulled it deep into his lungs. It was the best tasting pot he'd smoked in months. Maybe years. He handed it back to Judy.

'It's nothing special,' chirped the girl, 'but it's pretty good. How's your thing doing?'

'My thing?' Posner thought he felt a blush starting to tickle at his collar, and let go of the smoke. The pot got to him. Not a lot. But unmistakably. And on one hit. All the way down to his thing.

'*You* know, your . . . case, or whatever you call it. Melody. Did you talk to Luther?'

'Oh, yeah. That. Ah, well, pretty well, I guess. I did talk to Luther, and he told me some very interesting stuff.'

'Really? What? Make the next right.'

Posner debated whether he should tell her what he knew. She was an insider and might be able to make some new connections. But kids like to talk. Especially girl kids, or so they say. He didn't think he wanted just anybody to know what he knew. He made the right onto a dark, narrow road. It was the land of bigger trees and houses. The biggest. The headlights on the Dart were the only lights in sight. There was no sign of any houses on the road. Posner knew about the concealed driveways spaced at quarter-mile intervals, though. He'd been on roads like it before.

'Well, I don't know if I should say . . . '

Judy passed him the joint again and let her hand drop on his leg. 'C'mon. You can tell me. I won't say a word to anyone. Cross my heart and hope to die.'

'O.K.' A great prisoner of war he'd never make. He took another drag, but didn't hold it in. 'But this is some very heavy stuff. You've got to promise not to say a word to anyone.'

'I promise. Really. Can I tell my friend Ann, though? She's cool.'

'*No*! I'm serious, Judy. No one. I could get in a lot of trouble.'

'O.K., O.K., I promise. Not one person. Not even my mom.'

'*Especially* not your mom.'

'O.K.'

'Well, it seems that Melody was trying to expand from just dealing coke to dealing heroin, too.'

'Really? Who was she going to sell it to? There's never any junk on the hill.'

'I think she was interested in wholesaling and using the same distributors into the town that are there now.'

'Oh my god.' Judy was impressed. Posner told her more.

'But somebody – and this is the part I'm not sure about – somebody apparently didn't want her to; because she wasn't getting in. At first I thought whoever already had the local franchise might have wanted to kill her, but I think it goes higher than that.'

'Why?'

'Because somebody killed him.'

'Oh my *god*! Who was it?' She finished the joint and threw the roach out the window.

Posner felt very stoned. 'I can't tell you that. And if you figure it out later, remember you promised not to tell anybody anything.'

'O.K., O.K.'

'Do you think Hawk will be at this party?'

'Is Hawk part of this?'

Posner didn't answer.

'Oh, come on.' Again her hand was on his leg.

'Where is this place?'

'Coming up next. The driveway on that side.' She pointed to the left. Posner saw nothing. 'Go slow. There.' He could just make out the stone marker and the asphalt apron. He stopped just short of it.

'Hawk's been selling heroin to kids at Bergen Valley. I don't know exactly how, but I think he must be tied up in this somehow. I told him I was Alice Cabot's brother. I may need you to back me up on that. O.K.?'

Judy's eyes sparkled. 'Sure thing.' Then she sagged. 'Are you going to get him busted? I mean, is he really dealing? Or like just selling some?'

'I don't know. I don't really want him busted for selling nickle bags. But I'd like to see it stopped, and the people at the top busted. Wouldn't you?'

'Sure, I guess. I mean, like, you know, it's no joke what happens to kids on junk. I know.' The sadness in her voice convinced Posner that she did know. And that she'd been hurt herself, somehow.

'Willie?'

'Uh-huh.'

'What?'

'He's in jail. He tried to rob a liquor store.' She tried to head off her tears. 'Like, you know, it really wasn't fair. He broke his leg, and that like ruined his track scholarship – he was gonna go to Maryland – and then after that, like he just didn't care. God knows what'll happen to him now.'

Posner's jealousy over Judy's sorrow was, he knew, utterly disgusting. But he did feel sorry, too. Sorry for Judy. Sorry for Willie. 'Rich white people in the big houses up here get richer while poisoning black kids. And *their* kids get the coke and the four years at Columbia or Penn.' The pot was letting Posner get himself worked up. He hoped he hadn't put Judy off with his sudden political outburst.

'I'll back you up, Joe.'

Posner thought he might faint. Luckily, the dark concealed his blush.

'You know, my Uncle Larry went on all those old civil rights marches.'

'Really,' Posner pulled up the driveway. 'That's nice.'

Almost a quarter of a mile from the road, the driveway passed under a carport supported by fluted white columns and ended in a small parking lot. Next to the lot was a carriage house slightly larger than the house Posner lived in. The main house was huge and rambling. Artistically placed floodlights lit selected contours of brown wood and gray trim. Half a dozen gables stuck up from the roof, looking like a Cubist mountain range silhouetted against the sky. About a dozen late model cars, mostly foreign or sporty or both, filled the parking lot. Two or three spilled out onto the driveway. Posner parked there, too. He didn't see Hawk Brennan's Olds.

'Nice house,' Posner said, disguising his bitterness enough to avoid its being obtrusive, but hoping Judy would pick it up and agree.

'Wait till you see the inside.' She jumped out of the car and ran up to the front door. Posner wondered whether she did it because she was embarassed to arrive with him or was just energetic. After that joint, one thing he wasn't was energetic – the speed hadn't hit yet. Judy was inside the house before he could achieve sufficient mobilization to get his door open.

Judy had gone straight in through the unlocked front door. So, after a few seconds of fumbling, Posner did too. Neil Young's frail, quavering voice greeted him with its effete, self-indulgent pubescence from the stereo. The house was mainly spacious. What he could see of it. The foyer was wide and very high. To the right of it was a thirty foot dining room with a small kitchen table stuck in the middle. To the left was a living room with two long neutral tone sofas and a matching armchair. There were no carpets or wall hangings anywhere. About a dozen or so kids lounged around in a veritable seizure of enervation. The place reeked of pot. Beer bottles were scattered across the hard wood prairie of the floor. Posner wondered where the parents were. Probably on vacation, he figured.

He looked around for Judy, but couldn't see her. He didn't see Tony Bagliano, or the other two from Les's place, either, and he walked into the living room. Nobody paid him any attention. Splayed across the armchair, a boy and a girl, both with straight brown hair past their shoulders, licked each other's face. Posner had seen golden retrievers do it with more sex appeal. Three boys in denim jackets and jeans slumped, staring straight ahead, on one of the sofas. One wore a Grateful Dead T-shirt under his open jacket. The other had a button on his jacket which read 'Vegetable Power'. Posner was relieved that however pathetically depraved, modern adolescence could retain this smattering of irony.

The living room opened on a conservatory. A tall, very thin girl with long, dirty blond hair stood alone at the plants. She appeared to be the closest thing to a sentient being Posner had come across, so he attempted a communication. 'Hello.'

'Hi.' Her response was less than perfunctory. It was hostile.

'I'm Joe.'

'Does that make you happy?'

'Sometimes.'

'Good.'

'Who are you?'

'I'm trying to forget.'

'I see.' Posner hung on steadfastly to his pleasant tone.

'I'm looking for Judy Williams. Have you seen her?'

'No, thank god. Try upstairs in the pool room. There's usually an assortment of her type up there.'

'Thanks. Nice talking to you.'

She didn't answer. Posner went back into the living room, where Neil Young was still whimpering. 'Helpless, helpless, helpless, helpless/ Helpless, helpless, helpless, helpless.' Must be their anthem, Posner thought, as he passed back through the half dozen limp forms on the living room furniture.

From the foyer Posner saw a chubby boy, about fourteen, shirtless, stretched out on his stomach on the dining room table. Posner paused to watch him as he repeatedly dropped a small pen knife into the oak floor. Boy, Posner thought, wait till Mrs. Salt sees what's happened to her floor.

24. Notes from the Underground: Junk at the Space

The suggestion of a spring in Joe Posner's step as he went up the stairs told him the speed was starting to work. From the top of the stairs he could see smoke and light spilling from an open door down the hall. A torpid chatter fitfully echoed along the dark hallway. Posner couldn't make any of it out, but it didn't sound like anything in particular. Just talk.

He walked into the room and stood near the door. Three boys and two girls stood around a full-sized pool table while a wiry kid in a corduroy vest and no shirt lined up a shot. Beyond the light that shone on the table, half a dozen more kids sat talking on beanbag furniture along the walls. The air was thick with more than one kind of smoke. Nobody looked at Posner. Then, behind him, he heard a woman's deep voice. 'I don't know you, do I?'

Posner turned and looked at her. She was sitting in a chair that was really a large wicker basket hanging by a chain from the ceiling. Her hair was black and straight, with lots of gray streaks. Her lipstick was as dark as red could be without being black. Her glasses were tinted brown over eyes that bugged out slightly: a result, perhaps of the pre-faded blue jeans that were at least a few inches narrower than her hips. A very small boy, who could have been fifteen, but short for his age, sat on her knee holding a cue stick and a bottle of Pilsner-Urquell beer. She was holding him. 'I'm Joan Salt.' The kid at the table made his shot.

Posner's ears started to buzz. Or maybe, he thought, his eyes started to buzz. That is, if eyes could buzz. 'Mrs. Salt?'

'Joan.'

'Hi. I'm Joe Posner. I came with Judy Williams.'

The kid on her lap jumped off. 'It's my shot.' Joan Salt held onto his hand as long as possible before he pulled away into the smokey light around the table.

'Has she been up here?' Posner asked.

'Not yet. Try the basement. But why don't you stay for a while?' She slid over to one side of the basket. 'Want to sit down? There's plenty of room.' There wasn't.

'No. Thanks. I'm fine standing. Has Hawk Brennan or Tony Bagliano been here tonight?'

'I haven't seen them. You don't teach at the Space, do you? I thought I knew all the teachers.' She showed him a mouthful of very white teeth, which, in the dark room and in her dark face, seemed to float in the air.

'No. No, I don't. I'm, uh, interested in the Space, though. It's quite a place, isn't it?' Posner looked around the room as if what was in front of them was ample proof.

'You're telling me. You should of seen *me* before the girls went there. I was *closed*, and I mean *really* closed.' She said it like she was mad at somebody about it. 'Then, I went to Les's first parents' Sensory Awareness Workshop, and, *blam*,' she slapped her hands together, scaring the hell out of Posner, 'I was *open*. Look at me now.' Posner chose not to. He would have been unable to resist asking if she meant *really* open. 'My relationship with the girls is a million percent better. I can say anything to them, and they can say anything to me. And I mean anything. And my relationship with my husband is at least a thousand percent better. But most important, I *feel* now. And I mean really feel. From every part of my body. How much do you feel from the top of your head, Joe?'

'Not much,' Posner had to admit. He didn't see any reason to mention the tingling in his toes, fingers, and nose that was increasing by the moment.

Joan Salt nodded her head with equal parts of sympathy and contempt. 'I knew it. I do. *I* feel from the top of my head all the time.'

'What do you feel up there, Mrs. Salt?' Bigmouth, Posner said to himself.

'Tons of thing. Sensations. I feel from the top of my head to the bottoms of my feet. And I have Les to thank for all of it.'

'Gee, that's great, Mrs. Salt.' Posner was unsure of proper etiquette when being informed of major personality break-throughs. 'And you've got a really nice place here, too.'

'*Joan.* Oh, god, this barn? My husband and I bought it two months before he deserted us. That's why there's no furniture. Except for this pool table, of course. That we had to have right away. He wouldn't give me a penny for decorating after he shacked up with his girlfriend.'

Joe Posner was not happy to be hearing this story. But Joan Salt was obviously hellbent on opening up a bit further. The Preludin was like a small turbine, fueling his reefer high, making the whole room like a corny satanic apparition from a corny B movie. Joan Salt was the star and was not to be denied.

'Can you believe it? With a medical student yet. He's supporting her while she goes to *medical* school. What do you think the chances are she's going to stay with an old fart like him once she's a lady doctor?' She coughed out a desperate laugh. 'Sam's forty-seven, Joe. Anyway, it doesn't matter to me now. Thanks to the Space. Thanks to myself. Les just gave me the feedback I needed. He facilitated the emerging of what was always my me-ness. Now Sam can do any goddamn thing he pleases. He can make himself into the biggest fucking asshole in New Jersey. I don't care. It's his trip. I've got mine.' She smiled a wide, unhappy smile.

'That's great, Joan. Listen, I've got to find Judy. I'll try the basement. Nice talking to you.'

'Nice meeting *you*, Joe. You make good eye contact.'

'Thanks.' His feet walked out of the pool room, but his heart ran.

Once back on the first floor, it wasn't hard to find the stairs down to the basement. Somebody had started playing a trap set down below, and the thumping and crashing, though audible throughout the ground level, was loudest coming up the steps. Posner followed the beat. It was as elementary and imprecise as a drumbeat could be without sounding like the first time the drummer had ever seen a drum. Boom chi boom boom. Boom chi boom boom. Boom chi chi boom boom. Whoever was playing had party manners to match his virtuosity, but Posner felt like dancing.

Halfway down the steps, he could see the large pine panelled recreation room. It didn't surprise him much to see that the kid behind the drums was only nine or ten years old. What did surprise him a lot was seeing Larry Blittstein, chin on chest, barely conscious, on a green plastic sofa. On the table in front of him were a dozen or so empty beer bottles. Next to him, setting out lines of white powder on the back of a magazine, sat an extremely thin, jackalish kid with disheveled, greasy blond hair, dime store clothes, and thick horn-rimmed glasses. Across from them sat a girl, as darkly complexioned as Larry. She wore a white cotton top that stopped just below large breasts. She was heavy, and Posner could see unhappiness all over her.

Posner stood frozen on the steps. Larry could identify him, tie him to Marty's death. What in the hell was he doing at a party the night his father had been murdered? Maybe he didn't know yet. But Apfelbaum had said the kid never smoked or drank. He had to be upset about something. Just as Posner turned to escape back upstairs, Larry came to and hollered, 'Hey you!' waving his hand vaguely in Posner's direction. 'C'mon over! C'mere!' Posner went.

By the time Posner got down the steps and over to the couch, Larry's eyes were closed again. The skinny kid turned to Posner. His hands shook, and he seemed to have a slight tic around his mouth and eyes. 'He's wasted,' he said, as his face melted into a sick grin, which he held for a few seconds. Then it disappeared, and he returned to arranging his lines.

Larry's head rolled onto its side and his eyes fell on Posner. 'Hey. How ya doin'?' He was drunk, but not as drunk as he was acting. Like a lot of non-drinkers, he had imagined drunkenness to be something it wasn't, and was trying to make up for the difference. He rolled his head to the other side to address the kid next to him. 'Hey ya Franz, this is the guy who killed Marty.' Franz smiled his sociopathic smile again, and Larry turned back to Posner. 'I guess I should thank you, huh?'

'Listen, Larry, I'm very sorry about your dad, but I didn't kill him. Really. He was dead when I got there.'

'So who do I thank?' He lurched forward and picked up a half-empty bottle of Molson's and spilled most of it down the front of his chin. 'Here's to you, whoever you are.' Then he looked up at Posner. 'I gave you the credit to the cops.'

'You *did*?' Posner's heart started to drown out the drummer.

'Yeah. But I didn't give 'em a description. I wanted to give you a chance.'

Posner started vigorously rubbing the bones behind his eyebrows. Larry started grinding his teeth together and making a sort of low, growling sound. Posner saw nothing to do but what he was doing.

'Larry, I'm trying to find out who did kill your dad.' Larry didn't respond. 'Do you know if he ever knew Melody Gold?'

Larry's eyes rolled and his mouth fell open. 'Ahh. Melody. I'd like to *fuck* her. Wouldn't you like to *fuck* her? Can't now, though. Huh? Unless you're some kind of *fuck*ing necro*phil*iac. Marty *fucked* her, though. Hee-hee. Marty, the *fuck*er, *fuck*ed her. Old *fuck*er *fuck*ed 'er. Fucker fuckter. Fucker fuckter. Fucker fuckter . . . ' He chanted it in time with the not-so-steady boom-chi boom that came from the kid on the traps.

'Why do you say that, Larry? How do you know?'

'She came to the house. Twice. Three times. Mom at work.

Somebody has to. Stayed half an hour. With Marty. Door locked. Had to be fucking, right? She wouldn't even touch me, you know. Acted like I had leprosy. D'ja ever walk down a hall and a girl like almost pushes up against th' other wall? Like to get away, far, from you?'

'Can you remember the times she came to the house?'

'Nah. What's time? Last week. Every week for a month. Not before then.'

Franz had finished preparing the lines and offered them to Larry, who managed to get about a third of one up his nostril, blew the rest around the magazine cover, and sank back into his stupor.

'Is that coke?' Posner asked, startled by the quantity and waste.

Franz grinned again. His smile actually scared Posner a little. 'It's a little something I whipped up myself.' His hands were shaking like they were holding a motorcycle.

The sad girl facing them spoke for the first time. 'Franz's a genius. He makes speed in Chemistry Lab.'

'Is that why your hands shake?' Posner asked the Edison of the eighties. Franz twitched and smiled again, only a bit more sourly. He didn't seem to have a wide range of expressions.

'Uh-uh,' the girl answered for him, 'he never takes the stuff himself. He's just nervous.'

'Do you take it?' Posner asked her.

'Nah. It just burns your nose.'

'There's something in the molecule I haven't got right yet,' Franz explained without looking at Posner.

'It doesn't work at all?'

'Nah,' whined the girl.

'So how do you figure he rates the genius category?' It was a pointless question, but Posner couldn't resist asking.

'Could *you* do it?' the girl insisted.

Larry pushed through into consciousness once again to solve the riddle. 'We call it "Process over product" in the alternative ed biz. Doesn't matter if it doesn't work so long as you spend a lot of energy on it. Alternative ed biz.' He repeated it, liking the sound. 'Les sells junk you know,' he tossed off, one eye closed, one open, with the brow raised.

'What?' Posner was jolted. As if on cue, the kid on the drums started up a series of splashes around his ten and twelve-inch cymbals.

'That's right. To all the kids. He calls it "love" or "intimacy" or "trust", but it works just like junk. He gives 'em just enough of what they need, what they never got from mommy and daddy, to get them hooked. Then they want it all. Need it. They follow him around. They sit in his office. They go to his house. And all they want is just a little more. Contact. Attention. Special status. Boychiks and girlchiks. But no one ever gets it all – except for the chosen few. Like Melody. Or Tony Bagliano. And of course the very ugly ones don't get any at all. Isn't that right, Franz?' Franz smiled his dyspeptic smile. 'You ever go to Les's house, Franz?' The grin stayed on Franz's face as he shook his head. 'Did you, Felicia?'

The heavy girl pouted, 'Once. I was with Mary Melman. I never got to go back.'

'I rest my case,' Larry smiled wanly, waved his hand, and closed his eyes again.

Posner blanched at all the raw nerve endings being exposed, then tried to retrieve his line of questioning. 'Larry, did Melody or your dad ever say why she was coming to see him?'

Larry's eyes opened to slits. 'Marty said she had friends who wanted to get some poems published. But he was lying. I can always tell when he's lying. And Melody didn't have any god-damn poet friends. She never talked to me.' His eyes closed again, this time with finality.

Posner turned to the other two. 'Did you two know Melody Gold?'

'Stuck up bitch,' pronounced the girl. 'She never talked to me, either.' Franz smiled and twitched his head in a way that suggested a negative. It was a safe bet she hadn't talked to him, either.

'Well, nice talking to you kids. Have you seen Tony Bagliano tonight?' He addressed the question mainly to the girl, who was by then the only one of the three Posner thought capable of answering a direct question.

'Uh-uh.'

'Hawk Brennan?'

'Uh-uh.'

'How 'bout Judy Williams?'

'That stuck up bitch? I think she's out by the pool.'

'Thanks. See ya.'

Posner had gotten accustomed to the pounding of the drums, and when he got outside his ears rang with the relative stillness. The reefer was fading, but the speed was going strong. It made him feel younger, lither, taller. He didn't exactly know why he was looking for Judy. Or, he didn't exactly want to know. The party didn't seem to be a by-invitation-only sort of affair, and he knew what Tony Bagliano looked like already.

Maybe she liked him, too.

Some girls go for older men. Some girls can handle it. She was probably very experienced. Of course not as experienced as he. He started to do a quick calculation of how many times a seventeen year old could have had sex, figuring a start at thirteen, but he caught himself and didn't finish it. There had to be some limit to this craziness.

Why shouldn't she like him? He wasn't a bad looking guy. Especially on speed. And he was a detective. That could be somebody's turn-on. Somebody naive. His heart was pounding with embarrassing insistence as he rounded the corner of the house and saw the pool.

Judy was there, alright. Standing with her hand on the waist of a guy who was much younger than Joe Posner. And much taller. And much thinner and lither. And with much more hair, all of which was much blonder than Joe Posner's.

Posner suddenly had a desire to disappear. He found himself hurrying in the opposite direction. He was sure the fantasy he had just been constructing was even more visible than his decrepit, virtually middle-aged condition.

He got around the corner of the house out of the floodlights just in time to see Tony Bagliano doing a miserable version of a swagger up the front walk. Alone.

Posner's step suddenly had spring again, and he crossed the broad front lawn with athletic strides. 'Hey, Tony. Hold up, man,' he called out cheerily. He knew that nothing could soothe the sting of rejection like picking on someone else. Especially someone deserving; and not too big.

Tony turned and slouched in Posner's direction. One hand loose at his side, the other patting the small, but flabby, belly under his T-shirt, he could have been trying to pass for a young Marlon Brandon type. Except for his sunken chest, weak chin, and pimples, he might have had a chance. 'Who the fuck are you?' The voice was nasal. A bit of resonance would have made it a little threatening, but there wasn't even a bit.

Posner was up to him. 'I'm Joe. I'm a friend of Les's. He told me to talk to you.' Posner grabbed the kid's hand in a 'soul' handshake. Tony went with it, but still seemed leery.

'Talk to me about what?'

'Come on around to the pool. It's nice back there.' Posner guided him back toward the dark side of the house. 'I'm interested in antiques.'

Tony followed him with a puzzled look on his face. 'Yeah? I don't know bullshit about antiques.'

'That's not what Les says.'

'What the fuck are you talking about? Les is totally full of shit.'

Posner chuckled. 'You won't get an argument from me about that, but I'm talking about a special kind of antiques.' They were around the corner and out of the light. 'I'm talking about *stolen* antiques, Tony.'

Tony stopped walking. 'Hey. What is this?'

'In particular, antiques *you* stole from Phyllis Gold's business.'

'Fuck you.' Tony pushed Posner hard in the chest and started to move towards the front of the house. It was what Posner had been waiting for since laying eyes on him. He grabbed the kid's wrist, wrenched it behind his back, and gave it a strong extra push up to his shoulder blades. Tony fell to his knees, and Posner pushed his face into the damp grass. He kept the pressure on the arm and put a knee in Tony's lower back.

'Tell me about it, Tony.'

'Fuck you.'

161

He gave the arm another shove and Tony winced. 'Fred Anderson and Les have already told me a lot. Don't you want to tell me your version?'

'O.K., O.K. But, Jesus, you're breaking my fucking arm.' Tony Bagliano was crying. Posner loosened the hold on his arm, but didn't let go.

'What do you want to know?'

'Everything. From the beginning.'

'Are you a cop?'

'No.'

'How do I know you're not a cop?'

Posner gave the arm a long, insistant shove. 'I think you should be prepared to make a leap of faith, Tony. Start talking.'

'Melody wanted money. She knew when her mother had good stuff to steal. I had the van. Les knew where to get rid of it. That's all. Lemme go.'

'Was Les in on it all the way?'

'More or less. It was Melody's idea, but like Les went over the lists of stuff, you know, that Melody made before we got the stuff. He told us like what was, you know, like really worth something. And he picked the fences.'

'How much of a cut did Les take?'

'A quarter. I got a quarter, too. Melody took half.'

'What did she need the money for?'

'Coke.'

'That's all?'

'Sure. Her parents gave her money for clothes and gas. What else?'

Posner put a little more pressure on the arm. 'Did she have any future business plans other than coke deals?'

Tony yelped. 'Stop it, you fuck. *Please*. I don't know what the fuck you're talking about. I swear.'

'Did she ever do business with Hawk?'

'Only once that I know of. Last year. On an ounce of coke.'

Posner loosened his grip again. 'Did you see her the day she died?'

'Just for a minute. Around seven-thirty. She said she was going out.'

162

'Going out where?'

'She wouldn't tell me. She was doing like this whole number on me about, you know, this dude.'

'What dude?' Posner was growing exasperated by Tony's underdeveloped communication skills.

'I don't *know*. Don't you fucking get it, asshole? She was doing a trip on my head. Some totally far out dude. From South America. She gave me some bullshit about him bringing her presents from South America. I didn't know what the fuck she was talking about, but that was normal. I figured she was lying anyway. She was probly fucking some greaser from Pal Park.'

'So you hit her.'

'Yeah. So big deal.'

Posner gave his arm another wrench, and Tony groaned. 'Yeah. So big deal,' Posner repeated. 'And that was the last time you saw her? When she was going to meet this guy?'

'Yeah.'

'Where was she going to meet him?'

'Somewhere in Fort Lee. Fort Lee was all she said.'

'There was a box stolen from Melody last Friday night – at the party. What do you know about it?'

'Nothin'. I don't know what the fuck you're talking about.'

Posner adjusted his grip on Tony's wrist threateningly. 'Dessie says she saw you take it.'

'Dessie's a fuckin' liar.'

'It was covered with jewels, Tony. Purple and yellow jewels. Sound familiar?'

'Sure. The ones her mother got. She gave one to Melody and one to her father. We took his on the last haul.'

'Why?'

'*I* don't know. Melody wanted it. She wanted 'em both, I guess.'

'What was in them?'

'I don't know what the fuck was in Melody's. There were some cufflinks in her old man's – dumb looking, man, to the max. They had like stars or something on 'em. Gross. Hey, why not let me up, O.K.?'

'In a minute. Tell me again about the box getting ripped off last Friday night.'

'Jesus, man! I *told* you. I don't know a fuckin' thing about it. This is the first I've fuckin' heard.'

'Now tell me about your dad, Tony.'

'What about him?'

'Why's he trying to get me killed.'

'I don't know what the fuck you're talking about.'

Posner wrenched his arm. 'Ow. Jesus, man. I swear. You're crazy. I haven't talked to him in like months.'

'How did he and Melody get along?'

'*Mel*ody? He didn't even *know* her. Never even *met* her, asshole.'

Posner almost let go of Tony's arm in surprise, and Tony started to struggle. Posner tightened his grip again and pushed the arm. Tony howled. 'You're lying, Tony.'

'I swear to god, man. Please stop hurting me.'

'Does he know Marty Blittstein?'

'Who the fuck is he?'

'Larry's father.'

'How would he know that dork's father?'

'How 'bout Hawk?' Posner was reeling in confusion, but kept his grip tight on Tony's arm.

'Don't hurt me, O.K.? But you're crazy. My father's never even been to the Space. He doesn't know anybody who goes there, or teaches there, or anything. You've got something all mixed up.'

'Seems that way.' Joe Posner jumped to his feet, releasing Tony. 'Nice talking to you, Tony.'

'Get fucked.' Tony was playing hard again, but Posner didn't feel like bothering with him any more.

'I should be so lucky.' Joe Posner mumbled. Then on the way to the Dart he said it again, to himself.

25. A Streetcar Named Bizarre

Just as he'd expected, Joe Posner saw Tony climb into his van less than five minutes later. It had given him time to warm up the Dart, find the van on the street, and park across from it. Posner couldn't wait to see Tony and Les try to put the blame on each other.

The van took off, leaving rubber, naturally, and Posner followed at a discreet distance. Having little doubt where he was headed, he didn't need to be close. Anyway, Tony seemed the type who didn't have much use for rearview mirrors. Posner was flying on a mixture of amphetamine and anticipation as they sped down the hill. Wanting to stay entirely in the moment, he pushed out of his mind the massive confusion that Tony, Jr had raised regarding Tony, Sr. Judy Williams's boyfriend made a few phantom appearances in his head, but he managed to keep that shit away, too. Getting the upper hand on Les Coniff was all he wanted right then.

At the bottom of the hill, at the intersection with Ramapo Street, Tony went straight instead of right towards Cresskill, but Posner didn't worry, figuring he was probably going to stop for food or cigarettes. When the van kept moving right through the empty business section, Posner started wondering if he'd guessed wrong. Halfway to Ridgefield Park he knew he had.

They were still over a mile from Ridgefield Park, near Bergen Valley High, in fact, when Tony made a left, and a right, and pulled up in front of a modest wood frame house on an old, lower middle income looking block. Posner watched him go in a basement entrance before making the right himself. He parked just off the corner and walked to the house. His shoulders and hips were loose, flexible. His hands were open and steady. Everything inside him was moving fast, but smoothly.

The stairwell was rank with wet, black, rotted leaves. Long, dusty spider webs with clusters of egg sacs stuck to the concrete walls. Posner lowered himself slowly to the bottom, then stood by the door listening. It looked like a do-it-yourself door hanging job, and the sound wasn't bad.

'The motherfucker knows all about the fucking robberies!' Tony shouted. 'What the fuck am I supposed to *do*!? Goddamn fucking Melody.'

The other voice was soft. Too soft for Posner to make out.

'Fucking Les!' Tony answered. 'I can't believe what a fuck he is. He pinned me. I can't be*lieve* it. What a total fuck. It's like so intense.'

Again the other voice.

'I caaan't. My dad'd kill me. I've been like totally on his shit list since he found my fucking roach in his fucking Fleetwood. Asshole. I can't call him now. I haven't like even talked to him in probly like six months or something.' Then after a pause. 'I'm going to my mother's and get some 'ludes. I need to relax, man.'

Posner tried the door. It was open. Tony was leaning his back against a cinder block wall, next to a utility light hanging from the ceiling. Paint cans, tires, suitcases and cardboard boxes took up most of the floor space. In one cleaned area, on a sleeping bag-covered mattress on the concrete floor sat Alice Cabot, her long, thin, unshaven white legs sticking out from under a pink chiffon shorty nightgown. Her eyes showed no expression on seeing Posner but her jaw moved stiffly from side to side.

'Hi Blanche. Hi Stanley,' Posner smirked.

'Get the fuck out of . . . ' Tony started, but Alice silenced him with half closed eyes and a finger over her lips.

'Joposner,' she said flatly. 'I'm glad you found me.' She patted the mattress next to her. 'Have a seat. You look terrible.'

He sat on a blue sleeping bag. It was an expensive one, probably goosedown, and it was well sprinkled with semen stains and burn holes. 'Thanks, Alice. Nice place you have here.'

'Hey, asshole,' Tony started again, pushing himself off the wall, before Alice quieted him again. Posner ignored him.

'It's Cathy Norris's house. We had nowhere else to go. Her mother doesn't mind.'

166

Posner made no comment. He waited, listening to the blood rushing through his body, figuring the silence would weigh heavily on Alice Cabot. It did.

'I wanted to tell you everything last night,' she said, her hands fidgeting with the edge of her sleeping bag.

'Why didn't you?' Posner almost whispered, and wet his lips, drying from the speed, with his tongue. He took another one of his bent Camels from his jacket and stuck it in his mouth. He still didn't have a match.

'I couldn't.' Alice didn't look at him, hanging her head, which emphasized the boniness of her bare collarbone.

'Elvira wouldn't let you?' His voice was dry and gravelly.

'Don't talk to this asshold.' Tony snapped, shaking his head vigorously and stabbing the air with a finger, Jimmy Cagney style.

Posner turned to him slowly and spoke from his diaphragm, for extra weight, cigarette dangling from his dry lips. 'Children should be seen and not fucked – I mean heard.'

Tony sneered, sarcastically, opening his mouth and curling his upper lip.

'Maybe you should leave for a little while, Tony,' Alice said, just like a school teacher. 'Joposner and I have some things to talk about.'

'Uh-uh,' Posner insisted quietly. 'I want him where I can see him.'

'How did you find us, anyway, asshole?'

'You should try looking in your rearview mirror sometime. And if you say anything else, especially if you call me asshole again, I'll break your arm and all your fingers. O.K.?'

Alice didn't give Tony enough time to answer. 'Please, Joposner. Let's just talk.'

'So talk.' Posner took out the unlit cigarette, wet his lips again, and put the cigarette back in his mouth.

'I was going to tell you everything last night. And give you the box.' The cords in her neck rippled with tension.

'But Elvira talked you out of it,' Posner explained for her, comfortingly.

'That's right. She got there right after I called you, and she said I'd get in a lot of trouble and that I didn't deserve it. And I'd get her in a lot of trouble, too.'

'For stealing the box?'

Alice fidgeted with the sleeping bag some more, pulling at it like she was trying to tear it apart. Tears rose in her eyes. 'She was dead when we got home. I swear it. Do you believe me?'

'Tell me more,' Posner said quietly, neither with sympathy nor without it. Tony groaned from his spot on the wall. Posner shot him a warning glance and chewed lightly on the end of his Camel.

'I swear it. I don't know why she came to my place. She told me she didn't want to see me anymore.'

'What about Les?' Posner asked, pretending to know more then he did.

'She had him convinced. Don't you see? He didn't want me anymore, either. It was beautiful with the three of us. Or *I* thought it was. Melody just used me. To get to him. She never really loved me. She just pretended to because I had Les. But I guess she knew that I had this thing for her and . . . she just used it.' Alice was sobbing now, and Posner could barely understand her. 'I loved her. So much.' Tony spat on the floor and shifted his feet.

'Where does Adonis, here, come in?' Posner asked without looking at Tony, who played with an empty coke can with his foot, unaware he was being talked about.

Alice stared down at the mattress. 'We got it on after the party Friday night. He didn't know about my taking the box. I left it in my car. It was just one night, but then, I didn't want to stay with Elvira, so I left there this afternoon and came here. That's all.'

'What about the brooch, Alice?' He asked it gently, resonantly.

'She *gave* it to me,' she practically screamed. 'The last night we got it on, the next morning, I mean, she gave it to me.' Quieting herself, she trailed a finger nail along her pale, furry shin. 'It's so beautiful.'

'And the box?'

'I couldn't stand it. I couldn't stand that I couldn't be with her anymore. Or Les. That's why I left the school. It hurt so terribly. I just wanted something more to remember her by. And get back at her, I guess.' She slid her eyes over in Tony's direction warily, and then back again. 'I was pretty drunk. Her and Les were dancing by the pool. I went into her room and looked around. When I saw the box, and it matched the brooch, it just seemed so perfect. So I took it.'

'There was only one, right?'

'Uh-huh.' Alice was a little confused by the question, but didn't stay with it long. 'I felt so guilty, but I didn't know how to give it back. Then when you came around looking for it . . . that night I was going to give it to you and tell you everything. I swear. Oh, God. I don't know how any of this happened.' She fell over on the mattress and whimpered into her arm. Posner spat out a loose piece of tobacco, licked his lips again, and said nothing. Tony sighed in a display of fidgety boredom.

'Elvira got there right after I called you, like I said. We had a terrible fight. She made me send you away and get out early the next morning. I wanted to tell you. She said I was being stupid. But I made her bring the box to you before we went up there, though. She did, didn't she?'

'Yeah. You didn't finish about the night Melody died. What happened after you found her at your house?'

'We moved her. To the park. I was leaving the next week. It wasn't fair for me to get in a lot of trouble and all the scandal and everything. And I didn't *do* anything. And she had dumped *me*. It didn't seem fair. So we took her to the park. Elvira drove the Firebird. Then I called the police.'

'Tell me about Melody and heroin.' The end of the cigarette was falling apart, and the wet tobacco tasted bitter but good on Posner's parched tongue.

'I don't *know*. I didn't under*stand*. She never *used* any heroin. Not that I knew about. It was all so awful and impossible finding her like that. It didn't make sense. I didn't know what to think.'

'What about her cocaine business?'

'She never discussed it with me. I don't like coke. She used to use it a lot. I tried to get her to stop, but she'd laugh at me and

169

call me an old maid. She never talked about the business side at all. I knew that she was dealing, but that's all I knew. Oh, God, if only she hadn't gotten all involved in drugs . . . ' Alice dissolved again in tears. Tony picked at the mortar between the cinder blocks and spat again. The kid had a lot of snot in him.

'Alice, this is important,' Posner pushed gently, almost apologetically. 'Did Melody have her belt wrapped around her arm when you found her?'

Alice lifted her head from the bed in confusion. 'No. She didn't. People do that when they take heroin, don't they? But she didn't. And she always wore that red belt with the turquoise buckle with that outfit.' Her eyes started streaming again.

'Alice,' Posner slid closer on the mattress, took the cigarette from his mouth and rolled it between his thumb and forefinger. His voice got lower, tenser, even quieter. 'Does anybody have a key to your place?'

'Melody did. That's how she got in.'

'Besides Melody.' He rolled the cigarette back and forth faster, and darted his tongue over his lips.

'Well, Les . . . you don't think . . . ' Her tears stopped, and so did Tony's wall picking. 'When you moved her to the park, did the needle ever come out of her arm?'

'No. I held it in while Elvira carried the . . . body. What are you getting at?'

'I'm not sure myself, really, but I've got a feeling that Melody didn't die in your place at all.'

Alice got all wide-eyed. 'What do you mean?'

'When they found her, there were two punctures in her arm, and when she saw me, she had her belt on. Did she have it on when you saw her, Tony?'

Tony shrugged his shoulders. 'How the fuck should I know?'

Posner turned back to Alice in disgust, still rolling the cigarette nervously between his fingers. 'I think she died somewhere else, and someone moved her body to your place. On the way they lost the belt and the needle fell out. They put it back in her arm, making the second hole.'

'Les? Why would he . . . '

'That asshole!' Tony contributed.

'Did Melody have your key on her that night?'

'I assumed so. I don't know.'

'If she did, it could have been anyone. Anyone who knew she had it. Did anyone but Les know?' Again he increased the speed of the cigarette between his fingers.

'I suppose Tony knew.'

'Hey, I was with Johnny. I can prove it.'

Posner ignored him. 'Anyone else?'

'I don't know. Maybe. It depends who she told. We weren't ashamed of our relationship.'

'It was completely out in the open?'

'Of course not. It was completely confidential. Confidentiality is a basic to a humanistic environment.'

'I see.' He didn't. He bit off the chewed end of the cigarette and spat it on the floor, and stuck the other end between his lips. 'Can you think of any reason why anyone would want to stick you with the problem of Melody's body?'

'*No*. No one. I don't understand it at all.'

'Why the park?'

'The kids always do drugs in the park. It seemed natural. And we didn't think anyone would be out there.'

'What time did you get home and find her?'

'Around nine fifteen.'

Posner got up. 'And what about Tony's father?'

'Tony's father? What's he got to do with this?'

'This guy's crazy,' Tony whined.

'You tell *me*.' Posner replied.

'I don't get what you mean.' Alice was confused again. 'I've never met him.'

Posner stood, grinding his teeth and listening to the blood around his eyeballs for a while. 'I guess I should have another talk with Les, huh?'

'What are you going to do about me?' Alice moaned, her mouth crooked and her lips pulled back across her yellow teeth.

Posner shrugged. 'It depends how this all turns out, I guess . . .'

Alice's contorted grin broke and the tears started up in her eyes again. '*Please* don't get Elvira in trouble. Please? She was just trying to help me.' Her mouth kept moving, but no more words came. Her chest heaved in deep silent sobs.

Joe Posner felt bad. 'Well, so far I haven't told anyone about you *or* Elvira . . . Maybe I won't . . . ' Alice sobbed on, not hearing. Posner didn't need this. 'Good night, Alice. So long, Tony.' Les Coniff did seem to be the man to see.

26. Lonely Woman

Joe Posner felt certain that he and the Dart could beat any Ferrari on the road that night. The streets were empty and his engine was quiet and smooth. The tree branches made perfect tunnels for shooting through. The traffic lights all blinked yellow on the late night cycle. The only thing that kept him down to forty was the thought that it might not be such a good idea to get stopped by the cops just then. Still, Larry had said he hadn't described him, and Posner had never given him his name. It didn't seem likely the cops would make any connections so soon, if ever.

He tried not to think about Alice; it would have depressed him. He made sure not to think about Judy; it would have chewed his guts up. Thinking about Les, he felt eager, intent, determined. And sad. Like tires rolling silently over an empty road.

The wide shopping street in Bergentown was deserted except for a couple of black kids standing outside the closed coffee shop next to the railroad tracks. Posner made his left onto Ramapo and headed north for Cresskill. He reached into the glove compartment, grabbed the salami sandwich, and took a huge bite of it. Speed was supposed to kill your appetite, but it always just made Joe Posner eat faster. Relishing the uncomplicated pleasures of garlic and grease, he polished off almost the first half in three large bites. He was just beginning to feel a lump of it lodging in his chest, when he noticed that the light was on in Hawk Brennan's studio at the Human Learning Space.

Posner parked the Dart diagonally across three parking spaces in the lot, which was empty except for Hawk's Olds. He could hear Ornette Coleman's 'Lonely Woman' playing on the record player. Posner hadn't heard it in a couple of years, and its torchy, alienated melancholy matched his mood enough to give him goosebumps. The clock outside the drive-in teller flashed five minutes to midnight.

Posner called out from the bottom of the stairs, but got no answer. It reminded him of being at Marty Blittstein's house that afternoon, and suddenly, his goosebumps all had babies. Ornette's alto groaned and trembled in pain. Joe Posner didn't want to climb those stairs. He did anyway. He didn't want to find that Hawk Brennan was dead.

He did anyway.

Halfway between a filthy old armchair and the record player, Hawk was lying on his face, his South American cap pulled over to one side. A syringe was on the floor next to him. His belt was on his arm. No pulse. No breath. He was cold. The record changer arm was all the way over, so the record had kept playing. It could have been on all night. Posner followed a telephone cord under a pile of old *Rolling Stones* and found a phone there, dialed the police station, and asked for Sergeant Webster. If they wanted him, they could have him. Enough was enough. After a few seconds, Webster came on the line.

'Webster here.'

'Webster, it's Joe Posner.'

'Look, Posner, I left the message just so's you'd know I hadn't forgotcha, and I was workin' on things.'

'That's not why I'm calling. I haven't been back to my office yet. I'm over at the Human Learning Space, over on Ramapo. There's a dead man here.'

'Holy fucking Moses . . . '

'The music teacher. Looks like an o.d.'

'Don't move. I'll be right over.'

Posner took a look around while he waited, making sure not to change anything. The place was roughly the same mess it had been that morning. That morning. It had been a hell of a day. Next to the armchair a spoon, a candle, and an empty plastic packet lay on a cable spool that had been converted to a coffee table. There was nothing much else to see. He didn't have any great ideas of things to look for. He didn't feel up to it. He went outside to wait for Webster, his face filling with tears and hot blood.

It didn't take Webster long to get there. In less than ten minutes an unmarked car and an ambulance charged into the parking lot as if they weren't too late. Lots of lights. Lots of jumping out of doors. Posner pointed up the stairs and two paramedics and a cop ran up them. Webster took his time, though. He stopped a few feet from Posner.

'Where's the lieutenant?' Posner asked.

'He's busy. What's the story, Posner?' he asked, tight lipped, businesslike.

'Take a look for yourself. Looks like an o.d. Happens every day. Somebody told me that once.'

'Very funny. This is the second o.d. today.' Webster was somber, taking his ranking position seriously.

'No kidding. Who was the other one?'

'Just some nigger kid over in the projects.'

'Oh, no big deal, huh? What was his name?'

'Donnie Taylor. Know him?' He looked at Posner out of the corner of his blue eyes and tugged at the leather strap across his chest.

'Uh-uh. C'mon, let's go up.'

'Let's talk here.' His eyes narrowed. 'How come you happened to find this guy, Posner?'

'Just passing by – on the way to my office – saw the light; wanted to ask him a few questions; came up; called you.'

'Questions about what?'

'Questions I've been trying to get you boys to ask.'

'Don't get cute.' Webster spat on the ground.

'Who me?'

'Who is he?'

'He taught here.'

'Jesus. Now the teachers are doing it, huh? We knew this place was bad news. Fuckin' freaks. What's his name?'

'Brennan. Hawk Brennan. Don't you want to see him?'

'In a minute. Go on.'

'I suppose Hawk is a nickname. He played sax and taught music here and also over at Bergen Valley, from what I hear.'

'Did you know he was using junk?'

'How would I have known that?'

'Why'd you want to talk to him?'

'Melody Gold went to school here. I've been talking to anybody I can find who knew her. Like I said, something you ought to be doing. What's the latest from your lieutenant? Is he interested yet?'

'He's thinking about it.'

'Thinking about it? Jesus Christ, Webster. After what I told you?'

'The lieutenant is thinking about it, Posner. You've done your fucking duty. So take it fucking easy.' Webster flashed his teeth derisively.

'Well, maybe he'll get off his fucking ass after this.'

'He's got a lot of things to think about.'

'I never realized he was such a big thinker. What's he thinking about now?'

'There was a murder today, wiseguy.'

'No shit. Who?'

'Guy named Blittstein. Ever hear of him?'

Posner caught no sign of loading on the question. 'Marty Blittstein?'

'That's him.'

'No kidding. Murdered. Any idea who did it?'

'Not really. His kid was home a few minutes before he was found. Said some guy came by, but couldn't give us anything on a description.'

'Nothing?' Posner asked, trying to keep his voice steady.

'Weird, huh? I think the kid is a little kooky, ya know? Anyway, so far we can't figure a motive for anyone to kill him. No prints. Nothin'. We got a call from someone anonymous who said he found him. Might be the guy the kid saw.'

'Interesting. Marty Blittstein murdered.' Posner wondered if that crime fighting machine known as the Bergentown Police had realized that the boy they had interrogated was a student at the same school as Melody Gold. And whether Hawk's death might finally suggest to them the possibility that they ought to look into Melody's death again.

'Yeah. Strangled,' added Webster, rubbing his eyes with one hand. 'What a fucking day. I've been on since noon.'

'Tell me about it.'

'Yeah. You look like shit.' Webster pulled out a pen and pad. 'Give me a few details and go home. No need to come to the station.'

With unbounded relief Posner gave him the details, and few they were. But he wasn't going home.

27. Minimalism: Les's Mores

Everybody seemed to be in bed in Culloden Crescent. Only one house, the one at the end, had a light on. Walking up the path to Coniff's front door, Joe Posner realized the driveway was empty. After ringing the door bell and getting no answer, he went around to the back and tried the kitchen window again. This time it was locked.

Posner walked back toward the Dart, the gravel on the driveway crunching under his feet. His head buzzed steadily. The dark quivered in imaginary waves of ether. Then, on the spot where Tony's van had been that afternoon, he stopped, and looked up at the loft window. It was still open.

In what seemed like less than a dozen long strides, he was back at the Dart. He started it and backed into the driveway, stopping under the window. There was no reason why Joe Posner should have thought he'd make the window. He was no Marine. But he felt it. In his fingertips, in his calves, in his thighs. He'd make it.

The sounds he made on the roof of the Dart, and then on the logs in the wall were the loudest sounds on Culloden Crescent. To him they were deafening, but he knew they weren't loud enough to rouse any of the snug sleepers in so cosy a parish.

The cracks between the logs seemed twice as large as they had been that afternoon, and though the Dart was a good three feet lower than the van, he had little difficulty going up. Once he got one hand on the window ledge, he was able to pull himself up, like coming out of a swimming pool. Tumbling in the window, he knocked his shin on the ledge, but kept his cursing to himself.

He had to restrain himself from jumping out of the loft, and whispered to himself to stay calm as he came down the ladder.

The desk was closed, but not locked. He opened it and went through the papers. The tickets were gone. He ran into the bedroom. The suitcases were gone, too. Posner sat on the bed hard. Then, from the far end, something moved, fast, under the covers. Toward him. He was off the bed and on the floor before he realized it was only the water in the mattress rebounding from the wave he'd made sitting down. His physical reflexes were O.K., but his head wasn't.

He took the list of stolen antiques out of his pocket and looked at it in the light from the street lights coming in through the window. His hands had started trembling. Vibrato, he grunted to himself. The speed was entering its toxic stage.

Back in the living room, he took as good a look as he could in the dark, but didn't see anything that looked like it was on the list. Then he remembered the locked drawer by the bed.

After rummaging through old paper bags at the bottom of a broom closet in the kitchen, and making more noise than he wanted to, he found a screwdriver and a hammer, and took them into the bedroom.

Thanks to his trembling hands, it took him a few tries to get the screwdriver into the crack between the drawer and the sashing. Then he lifted the handle and gave it a good whack, miraculously right on the head. The drawer came away from the lock cleanly. Posner slid it open and reached inside. A stack of magazines almost filled it. Posner looked at the top two – teenage nude magazines. Groping in the dark, next to the stack of magazines, he felt two small metal things. He held them up to the light, where they glittered: two cufflinks with a star engraved in each. Posner reached into the drawer again and felt something like a coil of leather and grabbed it. It was leather, alright. A red leather belt with a brass and turquoise buckle.

Joe Posner wasn't worried about getting stopped by the cops anymore. Grinding his teeth, beating his thumbs on the steering wheel, and now surrounded in his head by a full orchestral arrangement of Monk's maniacally repetitive 'Epistrophy,' all perfectly synchronized to the rippling of his tires on the pavement – all he cared about was finding Les Coniff before the 10.45 flight to Cartagena, Colombia took off. If worst came to worst, he knew, he could catch him at the airport, but he wanted him then, that night. Guessing that Tony had tipped Coniff off and would know where he was, he headed back to the Norris house near Ridgefield Park, which he made in less than fifteen minutes and just under a hundred and fifty choruses of 'Epistrophy.' Seeing no van in front, and remembering Tony's yen for downers, he headed up the hill to Bagliano's motel-mansion without even slowing down.

The van wasn't parked out front there either, but oddly, Les's old Mercedes was. He pulled up behind it in the semi-circular driveway, hustled to the massive front door, and pressed the bell a few dozen times, syncopating the rings to match the off beats played on Monk's left hand.

Lucille Bagliano's voice came through the door, softly first, 'What in the name of heaven?' then louder, 'Who is it, please?'

'Open up Mrs. Bagliano,' Posner barked. 'It's urgent.'

The huge oak door opened a crack, showing a mascaraed brown eye. 'Oh!' she said, and opened the door more widely. 'The man from the boy scouts. Isn't it sort of late . . . ?'

Posner pushed by her into the foyer, where six suitcases, three of them Coniff's, sat on the floor.

'Hey! What do you think you're doing?' she gasped, pulling a lavender satin dressing gown around a low-cut matching night-gown.

Posner turned back to face her. 'I have to talk to Les Coniff. Now. Where is he?'

'Les Coniff? Why . . . '

'I know he's here. Just tell me where.'

'I'll go up and get him,' she sighed. 'What did you say your name was again?'

'Never mind that shit, lady. Just tell me where he is,' Posner blustered.

'I don't appreciate talk like . . .'

Posner headed up the stairs, taking them two at a time, 'First door on the left at the top,' Mrs. Bagliano called after him. She didn't need to. The first door on the left opened, to reveal Les Coniff in lavender satin jockey shorts, which looked miniscule next to his gargantuan white-fleeced belly and pear shaped thighs. Coniff's jaw dropped; his hand went to his glasses, like he didn't believe his eyes. 'Holy Moses.'

'Evening, Les. So glad I caught you. Let's talk.'

'Posnuh,' Coniff growled in his Brooklyn basso, 'this is totally outrageous. How dare you?'

Posner walked by him into the bedroom. Everything in it was white, except for the sheets, which were also lavender satin. He sat on a while velvet dressing stool in front of a hug round mirror, and motioned to the bed. 'Siddown, Les. Something's come up.'

Coniff remained in the doorway. 'Just speak your mind, Posner. But so help me, if you ever . . .'

'Did Tony come by a little while ago?'

'I just missed him. Why?'

Out in the hallway, on the far side of the mountain, as it were, Mrs. Bagliano appeared.

'Oh, Mrs. Bagliano, I think you better come in, too.'

Mrs. Bagliano nestled close to Coniff, pulling herself in toward the center of her body making herself small. 'What's going on?'

Posner tapped on the underside of the dressing stool. 'Epistrophy' wouldn't quit. Not wanting his hyped up condition to be taken for nervousness, he grabbed the bottom edge and held on tight to stop his drumming. The beat pulsed in his fingers. Then he looked at Les with an expression he hoped would look deadly serious, sympathetic, even. 'Come on in. Sit down, Les. Really.'

At Lucille Bagliano's prompting, they sat on the bed, knees

together, hands held in Coniff's lap.

Posner kept his eyes on Coniff's. 'Three people connected to the Human Learning Space have died in the past seventy-two hours. I now have substantial *conclusive* evidence that you, Les, were involved in at least one of those deaths, that you helped plan several grand larcenies, helped fence stolen property, and in at least one case, received stolen property yourself.'

Lucille Bagliano looked at Coniff in panic, then at Posner. 'So you're not really from the boy scouts?' Posner and Coniff didn't take their eyes off of each other. Coniff's gaze was a mixture of apprehension and suspicion, as if he couldn't decide if Posner was really dangerous or just out of his mind. 'Three deaths?'

Posner kept his face as free of expression as possible. 'Melody Gold. Marty Blittstein. Hawk Brennan.'

Lucille Bagliano gasped. Coniff went pale. 'Marty and Hawk?' he whispered in disbelief. Then he started shaking his head in an irregular rhythm, almost twitching. 'I don't get it. What's going on?' Then, as if he'd suddenly realized something, he clamped his hands on Lucille's lavender satin thigh. 'Lucille, you better let us talk about this in private.' Much to Posner's surprise, she did not argue, but simply got up, taut with determined composure, and left the room.

Coniff's eyes darted around the room, as if he was looking for an answer, a cue, a hiding place.

Joe Posner took the cufflinks and the belt out of his jacket pocket and held them in front of him. 'I talked to Tony tonight. And I talked to Alice, too, Les. Neither of them is keeping any secrets.'

Coniff tried to set his jaw and steady his gaze, but neither would hold. 'Well . . . I . . . This is,' he started three sentences, shrugging nonchalantly as possible, but couldn't finish them.

Posner took over. 'Let's say it looks like this: You and Melody are running a little underworld empire, based on stolen antiques and cocaine. Unbeknownst to Melody, you, Hawk, and Marty are also running a heroin operation. Melody, ever anxious to expand, decides to get into heroin too, but can't. I suppose because you didn't want to split the profits another way. The two of you were going to make a trip to South America, possibly to score some cocaine, but Melody was getting too close to the heroin business – she'd already sussed out Hawk and Marty – so you told her to meet you in Fort Lee, offered to let her in on the heroin deal, got her to take an overdose, and dumped the body at Alice's. Then, since they knew too much, and I was snooping around, you killed Marty and Hawk today. It fits, Coniff. You had the key to Alice's, and the belt . . . the belt, Les.' Posner dangled it from his outstretched hand.

Coniff's head and hands quivered. His mouth had trouble framing words. Finally he got some out. 'No. No. No, no, no, no. It's not . . . it's all wrong. I swear to god. Listen, you've got to believe me. You've got it all wrong.' He looked at Posner beseechingly, with wet eyes.

'Let's hear your version, then,' Posner offered. 'The complete, unexpurgated version.'

'I didn't kill anybody, I swear. I never sold any heroin, either. I came home from a trustees' meeting and found Melody in my place. Dead. With a needle in her arm. I figured it was an accident. She didn't know from heroin. Had no tolerance, I guessed. I didn't know where she got it. I didn't know anything. I mean . . . I knew she'd been trying to get into selling heroin. I was totally *against* it, but what could I do? I gave her plenty of negative feedback on it.'

'You might have tried telling her parents.'

'That would of totally blown any confidentiality between us. As long as she trusted me, I could keep trying to help her, get her head straight. Get her to cut all this drug dealing out. I was *against* it. Even the coke. I swear, I had nothing to do with it. But what could I do? What would her parents have done? They don't understand her . . . ' Coniff slid his fingers under his glasses, wiping the tears that had started rolling down his fat cheeks.

'Keep talking,' Posner said flatly.

'I swear to god. I . . . I didn't want to help with the antiques, either. It was Melody's idea. She and Tony had already pulled the first one without me – they just wanted a buyer. I figured

. . . well, they'd done it. There was no turning back . . . and then . . . I didn't want to sleep with her, either. That was Alice's idea.'

'You're getting harder to believe, Coniff,' Posner warned.

'Oh, sure. It's easy for you. Everything's all black or white, but it's . . . '

'Get back to the story, O.K.? You found her dead at your place. What time was that?'

'Uh . . . about 8, 8.15, I guess.'

'Who knew you'd be at the meeting?'

'I don't know. Anyone. The trustees, the teachers, any of the students who wanted to. Norma.'

'O.K., go on.'

'Well, she told me earlier – ten days or so, I guess – that she'd made this breakthrough on the heroin thing, so I figured she'd scored, got a sample or something, didn't know what she was doing, and o.d.'d. I couldn't believe it. I swear, if I'd of been with her, I would of stopped her.'

'Wouldn't she have snorted it if she was trying it out?'

'How the fuck do I know? She was *there*. It was a needle. What am I going to do, argue with her? Tell her she's not dead? That she should have snorted it?'

'So you found her. Then what?'

'I had to figure something out. I couldn't let her be found at my place. Not for me, but for the school. It would have ruined the school.'

'So you picked Alice's? Why didn't you just leave her in her car on the street somewhere? Why implicate Alice?'

A look of profound wonder and confusion clouded Coniff's face. 'I never . . . thought of that. Not to blame *anyone*. That would of been really creative. I . . . *Some*body had to be blamed . . . I mean . . . I guess I wasn't thinking straight. All I could think of was how Alice got me involved with her. You know Alice was sleeping with her *months* before I was. For all intensive purposes, it ·was her idea. She said it would open things up to bring Melody in. I swear, I did it for her at first. And she was leaving anyway. She was an ex-teacher. I was a current principal. Don't you see? It was best for the school.

182

And she was leaving. Going to another community. It wouldn't of mattered to her.'

'So you put Melody in the Firebird, drove it to Alice's, used your key, dumped her in the living room, and split.'

'Right.' Now that he was telling his story, Coniff's panic seemed to lessen, and the words came painlessly.

'How'd you get home?'

'Cab.'

'And you got home and found that the belt had fallen off her arm, so you slipped it in the drawer. And on the way over the needle fell out, and you put it back in.'

'No.'

'What?'

'The needle didn't fall out,' he shook his head once, confidently.

'Are you sure?'

'Totally. I made sure. I didn't want there to be two punctures.' Coniff started kneading the abundant flesh of his upper arm.

'Are you sure there weren't already two?'

'Well, no . . . I didn't look. It didn't occur to me. Why?'

'How did you know Alice wouldn't be home?'

'I called first.'

'And you weren't meeting Melody in Fort Lee that night?'

'No. I told you. I had a board meeting.'

'What about the trip to Colombia?'

'It was a vacation. Melody's idea. When she told me that she'd made this breakthrough, she said she wanted to get away, and that when we got back, everything would be set up. That's all she told me, but Cartagena sounded good. She wanted to leave then. Before vacation. But I put my foot down. I couldn't leave school a week early. And I didn't want her to miss classes . . .'

'What about the boxes.'

'The boxes?'

'The two antique amethyst and amber boxes. Mrs. Gold gave one to her husband and one to Melody.'

'Oh, that. She was furious. She had a lot of issues to deal with

183

around her parents. That's what I was trying to help her with . . . '

'Stay on the subject.'

'She was real upset when her mother gave a box to her father. She was over my place that night. Totally in hysterics. Her mother had given her one first, and she pawned it right away. Then when the father got one she flipped. She had to have it. Maybe she felt bad about pawning the first one . . . I don't know . . . Anyhow, when she set up the robbery at the house, she had Tony mess up the bedroom so it would look like the burglars were looking for jewels, and she grabbed the box. I tried to talk her out of . . . '

'She set up the robberies?'

'I'm telling you, she set up everything. She came to me with the idea. She needed capital to finance her coke deals. It was crazy. She should of been able to finance them on her profits, but the way she gave coke away . . . there was just no limit. I was trying to help her with that, too.'

'With what?'

'With her insane business practices. Bad business is a form of self-hatred. And if you hate yourself, you can't love anybody else.'

'I never realized that.' Posner rubbed his temples. Vague, blunt corners of ache were starting in his head.

'Sure. So anyway, she wasn't even making a reinvestible profit. Also she was planning an enormous buy. She was saving the money from the antiques to make the big heroin buy and try to corner the local market.'

'What about the cufflinks?'

'I didn't want them. She insisted. So I just stuck them in the drawer.'

'What did you get out of all this?'

'Me? Practically nothing. I was just trying to stay close so I could keep trying to get her to stop.'

'Yeah. And Goering didn't know about the camps.'

'O.K. Maybe a thousand or two. Education isn't a very profitable profession. If I'd of stayed in catering . . . ' He clenched his large, pudgy hands in front of his face, then dropped them into his satin lap. 'Oh, Jesus, Joe. Jesus. You know, I started the Space myself. Almost ten years ago. Kids were miserable. They needed something. A family. Adults who cared. A place to be themselves. I gave it to them. I don't know how this all happened . . . it just got . . . out of hand, I guess. If only Alice hadn't . . . '

'Where's the rest of the stuff, Coniff?' Posner had almost started to feel sorry for him. But Coniff's constant attempts to blame everybody except himself made it impossible. 'Does Anderson have more?'

'Uh-uh. I made sure to spread it around pretty thin. A lot's in Nyack. What they haven't sold. We had to take a few pieces to Boston. About fifteen percent went to the Upper East Side. A little in the Village.'

'Make me a list. I'll be by tomorrow morning for it. Every piece. Every fence.'

'I don't know if I can remember all of it.'

'Do your best. It'll be fine.'

'Hey,' something struck Coniff. 'How did you get into my place?'

'The loft window was open. I climbed the wall.'

'You *did*? And how about the drawer. It was locked.'

'Yeah. I had to break that.'

'You what? That's almost a hundred years old! It cost me a fortune!'

Posner stared at Coniff in utter disbelief. His headache was growing, slowly, as he started down from the peak of his high. After a second, Coniff realized how ludicrous his outrage was and dropped it. 'Are you going to call the police?' Coniff slumped over his belly and stared at the carpet.

'About the antiques? I'm going to give the list to Phyllis Gold and tell her where I got it. The next step is hers. But the other stuff . . . '

'Joe,' Coniff used his Advanced Intimacy voice, 'you don't think I killed her, do you? Not really. I'm an educator. Do I look like a man who could kill a young girl over heroin?'

Joe Posner took a good look at Les Coniff. He saw him with crystalline amphetamine clarity: a blubberous, overgrown baby in a lavender satin diaper on a lavender satin bed in a white velour bedroom. A middle-aged hippy who slept with teenagers and their mothers and called it education. A gangster of good vibes. Did he look like a man who'd kill a girl over heroin? 'Not really, Les. Not really. You may be thoroughly corrupt, but you're not big enough to be evil. I don't think you killed her. I never did.' Then, getting up to leave, he asked, 'But how can I be sure you won't skip out on me?'

'You have my word. Absolutely.'

Posner laughed. 'I'll tell you what. Give my your airline tickets, and your wallet and your passport. I'll give them back tomorrow when I get the list of antiques.'

Coniff sat in a heap, thinking, reflexively resisting a one-way deal, then shrugged. 'Why not? Why the fuck not?' He crossed the room to a white silk upholstered chair, took his blue jeans off the back, emptied the pockets and handed the contents to Posner. 'The tickets are in the wallet.'

'Fine,' Posner clicked his tongue and opened the wallet to check. 'See you tomorrow, Les.'

'See you, Joe.' Coniff answered mildly, too disoriented to react any one way to what had happened.

Posner left him in the bedroom, and shuffled down the steps. Mrs. Bagliano was at her piano. As Posner went out the door, he could hear her singing over the same single block chord.

When ever I think something's so good,
It never turns out like I wish it would.
When ever's a man I think is it,
He always turns out to be a shit.
Oh, sad, sad, sad; sad, sad, sad.
Sad, Sad; sad, sad, sad.
Feel bad; bad, bad, bad.
So sad; sad, sad, sad.

28. The Dream

When Joe Posner got to his office, the speed was still humming between his ears, but he was tired. Plenty tired. It seemed like he hadn't been in the office in months, but it had only been that afternoon. What a fucking day.

He put the basin on his desk and sank into his chair. Sweet Melancholia. He never got depressed on speed, but he always got melancholy. He loved it. It felt noble, or soulful, or something like that. That was just starting to go now, and the toxic crunch was underway. He'd cracked the antique robberies in less than a day. He should have been elated, ecstatic, celebratory. He wasn't.

He leaned over to the flashing answering machine, rewound it, and played it back. The first message was Webster's saying what he'd said it would: he was working on things. The sound of the voice on the second message gave Posner a shudder on the first syllable. When it said 'Joe,' he realized it was Ellen.

'Hello, Joe. It's Ellen. I'm on my way to Washington and I'm just in the city for tonight. My folks are taking me to Lutece and suggested I invite you. If you're interested, call back by eight. Bye.'

A day of murder, depravity, and corruption, and now this. While he had been out humiliating himself over seventeen year olds, finding dead music teachers, cornering principals, and jamming salami sandwiches down his throat, he could have been out with Ellen. Of course she had had to say it was her parents' idea. Heaven forbid she should imply that she wanted to see him. Heaven forbid she should give him 'false encouragement' by saying something nice. By making him feel good. He looked at the clock to see if it was too late to call to say hello. To hear more words spoken by that voice. It was after two o'clock. His headache picked up support from other parts of his body: shoulders, lower back, legs. He could have been out to dinner with Ellen. And her gray eyes. And her great legs. At Lutece. He'd never been there, of course, but he'd read about it every week in the gourmet section. No matter what the category of the week's selection, Lutece was always the top: places for lunch, places for dinner, places for romance, places for dessert, places for seafood, places with gardens. He had never seen the Leonia Deli mentioned. Not even once in any category. It had been awfully nice of Ellen's parents to invite him. As soon as Ellen had broken up with him, he had sky-rocketed in their estimation. He hadn't been sure what to make of that. One thing was for sure: he didn't know anybody else rich enough to take him to Lutece. Maybe in his next life.

He unlocked the drawer of his desk and took out the box. Under the light of his desk lamp, its rich, romantic translucence was even more dramatic than it had been in the afternoon light. He lifted the lid, almost believing there'd be something there this time.

Posner tried to pry the mutilated photograph of Phyllis Gold from inside of the lid. That picture gave him the creeps. It was the hatred, the wild twisted pain of a young girl, that those gouged eyes represented. The picture was stuck on well and his fingers shook like a wino's, but Posner managed to get it off in one piece. There was nothing behind it, and he pushed it back, sticking it with a drop of glue. He turned the box over a few times and put it back in the drawer. Then he put the basin in and took Melody's belt and the cufflinks from his jacket and put them in too. He was almost tired enough to watch some T.V. and try to sleep in his desk chair, but he wouldn't succumb to such abject demoralization. It was time to go home.

To keep from thinking, Posner sang on the way back to his place. Mostly blues – the speed having faded far beyond the bebop tempo. He was gonna lay his head on a lonesome rail-road line, let the 10.19 pacify his trouble in mind. Then he told Betty he'd buy her anything. He was just confessing to not having any loving since Luise been gone, when he rolled up in front of the house he shared with the local branch of the Praise the Lord Club. He dragged himself up the steps. What was the fucking point, he wondered, of living in the suburbs if you still had to walk up these fucking steps everywhere.

He turned on the T.V. and walked into the kitchen to fix himself a drink. Maybe, with his physical fatigue, it would help him sleep. He poured himself a healthy scotch on ice, put it down on top of the T.V., and went into the bedroom. A few Seconal to go with the scotch was what he wanted; to obliterate the memory of Hawk Brennan and/or Marty Blittstein. No to mention Donnie Taylor. Not to mention Willie Whoever. Not to mention Judy. Not to mention Ellen. Not to mention the Lanmore luncheonette. Not to mention Melody Gold. Joe Posner was a guy with a lot to obliterate that night. But twice in one week was too much for that route. Especially on top of the speed. He'd be a junkie himself if he didn't watch it. An aspirin against the headache on its way would have been like wearing a paper hat in an avalanche. Instead, he searched through his sock drawer and found a small tin box in which he'd been keeping a joint of super pot a friend from California had sent him. It might soften the crash. Posner had been saving it for a special occasion, but he was suddenly very tired of waiting. Special occasions didn't exactly seem to be falling like rain lately.

Back in the living room, he flipped around the T.V. dial, looking for something that wouldn't be too insulting to bear. Channel 2 had 'The Jeffersons.' At two o'clock? Posner was perplexed. Johnny Carson was still on 4, too. The only explanation Posner could come up with was that another installment of 'Death Valley Days '81' – another Presidential Address – had pushed everything back. Channel 5 had 'Love American Style'. So far, nothing acceptable. Channel 7 had 'Love Boat.' Out of the question. Channel 9 had a movie. Posner remembered when everybody except NBC had movies from 11.30 on. Now they called a re-run of a sit-com a movie. 'The Monday Night Movie: The Jeffersons.' Talk about the big lie. The movie on Channel 9 looked pretty dumb. It had Robert Wagner in it. A very bad sign. Channel 11 had its sign-off news show. The Mayor of New York was bragging on himself again. Bragging on New York. White New York. The perfect mayor for a bankrupt, brutalized, resentful city.

Posner was ready to switch the channel again when a face

even less appealing than the mayor's, a greasy hack type, filled the screen, smiling a greasy hack smile. State Senator Anthony Bagliano, the announcer's voice-over said. In Washington today to testify for a repeal of export bans on high technology computers. His smile was a crooked twitch lying on a rat-like overbite. His long, thin nose was pitted and looked like it had been broken a long time ago. 'What we're trying to have the committee understand,' his voice was small and scratchy, his tone was a perfect if unlikely composite of unctuousness and condescension, 'is that it's high time we start making distinctions betwen friendly *authoritarian* governments and hostile *totalitarian* regimes. Nobody here is saying we should be selling sensitive technology to the Soviets – of course not. But in today's world we can ill afford to turn our back on valuable friends just because we don't like some of their domestic arrangements. This is what the President has been saying about arms and we simply want to extend that thinking to other spheres, such as computers.'

State.Senator Bagliano had had his time, and as suddenly as he was there, he was gone. Posner had already heard more than he wanted about a retarded six year old's kidney transplant before he realized it was over. So that was State Senator Bagliano. Now Posner had a picture. But not much else. He switched back to the Rober Wagner movie, figuring if he didn't pay much attention to it, it would be O.K. He considered turning off the sound, but he'd resolved to stop doing that since a social worker he'd had a date with told him it was depressive behavior. He collapsed into his armchair, took another pull on the scotch, and lit up the joint. Robert Wagner was driving a sports car on a winding mountain road. It seemed like Robert Wagner always drove sports cars on mountain roads in his pictures.

Posner took two deep hits on the reefer and put it out. He put what was left back in the tin box. Maybe a special occasion would turn up, after all. The stuff had not been overrated. The two hits – on top of the speed and the scotch – had him in orbit. The front of his face buzzed a happy buzz, multicolored rings shivered on the periphery of his vision, and suddenly, old Bob

Wagner seemed like a pretty O.K. actor. Posner watched him run up and down a few sidewalks leading to mountain-top mansions. Though Posner could still feel the electric buzz of the amphetamine, he realized gratefully that he was getting sleepy. He was that tired. Robert Wagner was searching a room. He ran his hand along the side of a fireplace, and a panel in the wall opened up. Robert Wagner walked into a secret chamber. Joe Posner fell asleep.

While he slept, he dreamt. Ellen was wearing a purple and gold Bergen Valley letter jacket and old blue jeans. She kissed him. The kiss was long and wet, and her mouth tasted very sweet. Then she asked him to please come into the locker room. They walked together through the gym of Joe Posner's old high school into the locker room. Ellen held on to him tightly, with desperation. He was happy. Once in the locker room, she wasn't Ellen anymore. She was Judy Williams, and she was wearing Melody Gold's red leotard and denim skirt. But the skirt was very short and showed her fleshy thighs, dappled with light freckles. She lifted the skirt and rubbed her naked crotch against Joe Posner's leg and laughed, 'Isn't it fun?' She kept repeating it between laughs. Then she stopped and said 'Wait. Wait for this.' She climbed into a locker and closed the door. Joe Posner became terrified, and begged her to come out. 'Find me. Please find me, Joe,' she cried from inside. He pulled the door open and the locker was empty. He opened all the doors and all the lockers were empty. He couldn't remember which locker she had gone into. Mr. Leibowitz, the jeweler was in the locker room with him and said, 'They're not protected, you're not protected,' then was gone again. Posner started pacing back and forth until he pressed a button on the side of the row of lockers and the back of one of them swung open, to reveal a shower room with hot steaming sprays of water coming from all directions. Judy was standing in the middle, rubbing a purple and yellow bar of soap over her body and giggling, 'It's secret, Joe. It's secret. It's a secret door.'

Posner awoke to see a knife cutting through a steel chain and hear someone shouting, 'And that's not all!' He turned off the T.V. and shivered all the way to the bathroom, before heading back to the Dart.

29. 'Hi, It's Melody'

Joe Posner drove back to his office only half-knowing why. His guts felt dull and dirty. His face was still asleep. He was running on a dream and wasn't asking himself any questions.

Back in the office, Posner sat forward in his reclining desk chair, staring at the box on his desk. He picked it up and started pushing things – any edge or corner that he could get some leverage on. He tried sliding the bottom. He tried sliding the sides. He tried pushing bulges that might have been buttons. Then he put it back on the desk and stared at it some more. For a minute, or two, or three. The bottom of each of the four sides was a strip of amber edged in lead. He picked the box up again and tried sliding each strip in both directions. Then, almost as if he'd known it would all along, the third one moved, just an eighth of an inch to the right, leaving the corner to its left exposed. The strip on the second side slid easily through the exposed corner leaving an opening about four inches wide and an inch high.

What looked like a piece of blue paper was stuck inside. Posner's pen was too thick to get in the space, but a little fumbling with a bit of cardboard got the paper out. It was a list, in an exaggerated left-handed writing, of telephone numbers and initials. In the margin, in another handwriting, a young girl's, Posner thought, was a phone number and 'Room 24.' Posner dialed the number.

'Williamsburg Inn,' said a bored, but clear man's voice.

'Room 24, please,' Posner asked.

'I'm sorry, sir. There's no one registered in Room 24.'

'When did they check out?' Posner didn't really expect the guy to answer, but he did.

'Let me see . . . day before yesterday that was, but it was only one person: Mr. Nolan.'

'I see. Where are you located?'

'Route 4, sir. Right between the BP and Exxon stations on the eastbound side, two miles before the bridge.'

'Thanks.' Posner hung up. After tossing a vision of the Williamsburg Inn around his imagination, he looked back at the list. The numbers and initials were arranged in three groups. The first group had five numbers, all with exchanges Posner recognized as being in Bergen County. The second had six numbers, all with exchanges Posner didn't recognize. The third group had only two numbers, both in New York and one with the same Washington Heights exchange as Apfelbaum.

Posner knew it was late, but he wasn't worried about being rude. He dialed the first number on the Bergen County list. The initials were 'L.R.' No answer. Posner let it ring. After twenty or so rings Posner gave it up, wondering what kind of number didn't answer at four o'clock in the morning. Next on the list was 'R.A.' at a Leonia number. After two rings, Posner got an answer. 'This is Doctor Raymond Arons' office. The doctor is not in. Please leave your name and number, and we will get back to you as soon as possible. In case of an emergency, call Engelwood Hospital at 927–5854.'

Next on the list was 'B.T.' at a Hackensack number that Posner thought he'd seen somewhere but couldn't remember where. 'B.T.' didn't mean anything to him. It didn't answer. 'M.B.' rang more than ten times before a very tired woman's voice came on the line. 'Out There Press.'

Posner thought quickly. 'Is Marty Blittstein there?' he got in with barely a pause.

There was silence on the other end. 'Listen, I don't know what I'm supposed to say. We're not really open . . . I mean, I don't know if it's supposed to be secret or what, but Marty's dead, man. O.K.?'

Joe Posner hung up the phone without answering. The last local number was a machine telling him that Techtronics was closed till 9am. Posner called the operator and found out that the second batch of numbers were in Newark. He tried all six, but only one answered, again a machine, this one for Sciadelli Construction.

The first New York number answered after only four rings. 'Yeah.' The voice was distinctive enough for the one word to tell Posner that it was a black man and that he was a heavy and that he wasn't sleepy.

'Say,' Posner answered, 'you hear about Marty?'

'Who the fuck is this?' the man challenged. Posner thought the man had an awfully quick temper.

'I'm a friend of Nolan's . . . ' The guy hung up. So much for cleverness. He tried the other number. This one answered, too, only in Spanish.

Posner tried the same line about Marty, and the guy replied in English. 'You must got the wrong number, man,' and hung up. Not really feeling like a master of detection, Posner headed for the Williamsburg Inn.

Route 4 was pretty empty. Even most of the gas stations were closed. The Red Fox Lounge at the Holiday Inn advertised its welcome to the Sink and Drain Assoc. A little closer to the bridge, the Williamsburg Inn didn't appear to welcome anyone at all. Except for the sign offering day and night rates. Set back fifty yards from the road, behind a large BP station and a large lot filled with unattached tractor trailers, it looked to Posner like he imagined a lot of fifties commerical architecture would look in the year 2000. Though little was actually in disrepair, it had the derelict look of a ruin. The only attempt at a motif to justify its name was a pair of square white columns standing outside the door to the office, covered in soot and attached to nothing. Four American made cars stood in the parking lot.

Posner passed through the venerable columns into the office and found a young man sitting behind a counter, watching TV. He rose politely on seeing Posner and smiled diffidently, his dark chocolate skin stretched smoothly over full cheekbones. His natural cut hair was short and neat above a gray and green pinstriped button-down shirt and a thin brown tie. 'Good morning, sir. May I help you?'

Posner wished he had some tongue loosening money. 'I hope so. I just called a while ago about room 24.'

'Yes, sir. I remember.' Posner was getting the idea that the guy's formality was a parody.

'I thought maybe you could tell me something about Mr. Nolan.'

'May I ask your reasons?'

Posner decided to use the front door. 'I'm a detective, and I need to know about him for a case I'm on.'

'No kidding.' The clerk's smile got wry. It was the first expression from him that Posner felt was sincere. 'What d'ya want to know?'

'When he checked in. What address he gave. What he looked like. If he had any visitors. If he made any phone calls. How's that for starters?'

'Isn't this where you're supposed to slip me a couple of double sawbucks; or even a half a C?'

Posner looked at the floor. 'I've only got ten bucks, and I'm almost out of gas. Will five do any good?'

'Keep it,' the guy smiled and shook his head, turning back the pages on the register. 'Here it is. Mr. Nolan. He checked in last Tuesday, and stayed for a week. Gave his address as 220 Hamilton Street, Peoria, Illinois. No zip.' Posner wrote it down, but didn't believe any of it. The clerk went on. 'I don't know what he looked like because I never saw him. He checked in and out on the day shift. I remember he didn't have a car, which is weird. He must have come and gone by cab.'

'Visitors?'

'Yeah. A lot. For this dump, anyway. Nobody gets visitors here. Except for your Mr. Nolan.'

'How'd you know they were visiting him?'

'Does this place look crowded to you? They parked outside his room. And there wasn't anybody next door.'

'You see any of them?'

'Uh-uh, but I saw their cars: an LD from the city was here a couple of times. A real pimpmobile, man. Silver with black trim. I gave it a good look. Then there were a couple of Buicks or Olds, or whatever; but new. And a Mercedes sedan. Money cars, you know? Then two nights ago, I guess that was the night before he checked out, a beat up Olds, maybe '70 or '71. White, or trying to be.'

'When was that? When was it here?'

'Let's see. I noticed it just before the playoff game. I guess around a quarter to eight. Oh yeah, and there was a black Firebird already there.' He shook his head in disapproval. 'Man. Firebirds are so aggressive. And pretentious. Don't you think?'

'I never thought about it much.' Posner said. 'Did you see either car leave?'

'Uh-uh.'

'How 'bout phone calls? Is there a record?'

'Sure thing. Nothing's free at the Williamsburg Inn. Hold on.' He ducked under the counter. where he pulled out a file drawer. and started going through it. While he waited. Posner glanced at the T.V. It was *A Hatful of Rain*. Don Murray was getting pushed around by a couple of hop-head thugs. How appropriate. Posner thought.

The clerk produced a typed charge sheet with dates. times. and phone numbers. There were about twenty-five, and Posner copied them all down on his pad. He wasn't sure about a lot of them. but some of them definitely matched the numbers on the sheet from the box. One that didn't had a 704 area code.

'Thanks.' he said. when he had finished copying. 'You've been too good to be true. Thanks a lot.'

'Man. this is the most interesting thing that's happened to me all month. Thank *you*. What is it, a divorce?'

'No.' Joe Posner smiled from his heart. 'I'm not sure what it is. believe it or not. but it's not a divorce.'

'Whatever you say. Sure there's nothing else I can do?'

'Well . . . you suppose I could look at Room 24?'

The clerk shrugged and tossed him a key from the board. Posner took a look at the room. but there was nothing to see. It was regulation seedy motel; seedier than most. but not as seedy as some. As far as he could see. there weren't any clues there. After returning the key and thanking the clerk again. he spent five of his ten dollars at an open Gulf station and went back to his office.

His adrenalin was really going now. and Joe Posner wasn't bothered by the twenty-one hours. not counting his nap during the Robert Wagner film. he'd been on the move. Or the hangover he'd expected. He took the steps to his office two at a time. then practically threw himself into his chair and took out the list. Every number on the blue list matched a number on the motel list. On the night Melody Gold died, at 8.15, Mr. Nolan had called Marty Blittstein at Out There Press. That afternoon, he'd called the 704 number and, at noon, a local number that wasn't on the blue list. Posner tried the local number first. After a ring and a half a girl's voice came on the line. It hurt Joe Posner more than Ellen's had. It was the voice of Melody Gold.

'Hi, it's Melody. Too bad for both of us I'm not here now. Leave a message or I'll totally hate you forever. Bye.'

'Bye, Melody,' Joe Posner said into the phone. 'Bye, Melody,' he said again after he'd hung up. He'd have to tell Mrs. Gold to turn the machine off in the morning. He wondered if she even knew it existed.

According to the phone book, 704 was western North Carolina. A funny place to call, thought Posner. But cheap before 8am. He dialed it.

'Black Oak Sanitarium,' a wide drawl drawled.

Posner wasn't sure he'd gotten it right. 'Excuse me?'

'Black Oak Sani*tar*ium. Is this an emergency?'

'Yeah. Yeah, it is. It's an emergency.' Posner was trying to think up something quick. He settled for a shot in the dark. 'This is Melody Gold's uncle. I'm calling from New Jersey. Her aunt's been in a car accident and may die before morning. I have to speak with Melody Gold.'

'Melody *Go*wuld? I don't think we've got anyone by that name. Let me check the book. Uhhh . . . Oh. That's funny. She was sup*pos*ed to get here two nights ago, but she *did*n't. It's crossed out.'

'Oh. I see. How horrible. I must find her. Is there anybody or place to call that you might have?'

'Sorry, nothing.'

'Thank you anyway. Good night.'

Suddenly, Joe Posner had a lot of bright ideas. He grabbed the flyer he'd received earlier in the day for the bullet proof vest campaign, and checked the list of sponsors. Then he flipped through his notebook and confirmed where he'd seen the Hackensack number before. He had to check out one more angle, but it was much too early to call Teterboro Airport.

30. Sickness Unto Death

Joe Posner took his last five bucks to the Fort Lee Diner to kill some time and get some relief. The pancakes, syrup, sausages and eggs, and three cups of coffee took some of the sting out of his moral and physical fatigue; the five glasses of ice water helped his raging speed dehydration. The ammonia water that the clean-up man kept sloshing around his feet didn't help anything at all. When he walked out of the place, he had thirty-seven cents in his pocket. The sky was just getting light.

He spent the next two hours on a bench in Fort Lee Park looking at the sun come up over Manhattan and watching a few thousand trucks and cars pour over the bridge into the city. All the way from the park he could hear the elephantine roar of the trucks changing gears and the rumble of their engines reverberating on the roadway and echoing around the steel girders of the lower level. The sun burned a crazy red-orange that cut through the dirty wet air. On the far side of Manhattan, the sky over Astoria glowed in patches of emerald, ionized by pollution. Slowly, the oranges and greens drained from the sky, and the Hudson deepened to a dark, almost metallic blue. Posner watched the birds for a while, then the bridge traffic again. Then he went home.

The hot shower felt like little rivers of life running over his dead flesh. Afterwards, shaven, dressed in fresh corduroys, blue cotton shirt, and an olive tweed jacket, and bolstered by another two cups of coffee, Posner could almost have fooled himself into thinking he wasn't as weak as a dead fish, or as sleepy as a marathon dancer.

At eight o'clock, he called Ben Duberman, his old supervisor at Kennedy Customs, to get a contact at Teterboro. He phoned the contact at eight-fifteen and got exactly the information he'd expected. Then he checked a new idea, comparing the list of phone numbers from the motel with the Space staff and student lists. Everything, or almost everything, was adding up.

He called the Bergentown Police, and, surprisingly, Sgt. Doug Webster was already in. 'You're working too hard, Posner,' was the first thing he said.

'Too true, Webster. Listen. I'm going up to the Golds' place in a few minutes. I don't really expect any trouble, but if you don't hear from me in an hour, do me a favor and look into it, O.K.? 572 Allenby.'

'What the fuck are you up to now, Posner?'

'Please?'

'O.K. An hour.'

'You're a prince, Webster. Thanks.'

The cleaning woman answered the door. Her yellow eyes were as serious as they were uninterested.

'Mrs. Gold's in the kitchen,' she said flatly and walked into the living room, giving Posner just enough of a wave of her charcoal hand to set him in the right direction. He found Phyllis Gold draped in a green and silver caftan, at a formica table. The kitchen smelled of coffee, expensive perfume, and Fantastik Spray Cleaner. Her brown hands clutched a huge ceramic coffee cup, eight inches in diameter. Her hair was tied back in a bun. Fixing immediately on the basin and the box in Posner's hands, she croaked the early morning greeting of a caffeine addict.

'Joe. My God. You work fas'. C'min. Siddown.' Posner did. 'Well?'

'Well?' Posner answered.

'Jees' Chris', Joe. Iss too early for games. Where'd you find 'em?' She put down her cup and reached needily for the antiques.

'Different places. I can probably get you a list later of where everything is.'

'How'n hell . . . ?'

'It was sort of an inside job, Mrs. Gold.'

's'fraida tha'. Who?'

'It was Melody.'

'What?' That woke her up good. She looked like someone had just jabbed an icepick into a bruise, then tried to cover the hurt with a big swallow of coffee. 'I should have known.'

'She got her friend Tony Bagliano to help with his van, but I've checked his story, and it seems to have been her idea. She got their principal, Les Conniff, to help them fence the stuff.'

Phyllis Gold just managed to keep her coffee down. 'That goddamn bastard. I'll kill him. Are you sure? I'll kill him. I'll have him put away for a thousand years. And Tony! That little shit! He had the fucking gall to sit at this table and drink my coffee, and he was *stealing* from me? I'll kill him, too. I'll wring his greasy little neck. Yecchh.' She had no more words for Tony Bagliano or Les Coniff and returned to Melody. 'She must've done it just to hurt me. That's all. God knows she didn't need money.' Phyllis Gold was trying to be hard, but her pain was showing. A lot more than it had the day after Melody's death.

'Well, kids today have a lot of unexpected expenses, Mrs. Gold.'

'Are you holding back on me? I want to know everything.'

'Why?'

'Why?' She was confused by the question. 'Why? Because. That's why.'

'I'm getting you your antiques back. Or rather the insurance company's antiques. Which reminds me: the bill. Should we work something out between us, and you can deal with the insurance people? Or do you want me to talk to them. I'd rather deal with you, if it's O.K. I don't need the red tape, if you know what I mean.'

'I know you're changing the subject, is what I know. What are you hiding?'

'Look, Mrs. Gold, do you want what I'm giving you, or not? I can forget the whole thing now and just go to the insurance people. Of course that way the whole thing might get in the papers and . . .'

'Is this blackmail?'

'Jesus Christ,' Posner was playing it very cool, keeping his voice just above a whisper. 'This is not blackmail. You gave me a list of stolen items. I've found two, and I can find the rest. I've told you all you need to know to be sure the robberies are over. I'd like to be paid, and I don't want to tell you anything I don't want to tell you. It's that simple.'

'You're tougher than you look, Joe Posner.' Posner didn't reply. 'O.K. I'll give you the thousand bucks back and another thousand if your list checks out. How's that?'

'That's swell.' Posner meant it. 'Is Mr. Gold home?'

'He's having his coffee in bed. Why?'

'I'd like to talk to him. Alone. About the box. I can get the check for the thousand dollars from him while I'm at it. He's already written one.'

Phyllis Gold gave him a look of wry scrutiny as if her penetrating stare could either reveal what was on Posner's mind or induce him to tell. He ignored it. 'Sure go on into his study. I'll send him in.' Posner left her the basin and took the box with him.

The drapes in Burton Gold's study were drawn. Faint traces of cigar smoke hung in the dark air. Joe Posner pulled open the drapes letting in the morning sun, then stood for a few minutes, staring at the father-daughter portraits on the wall. Looking at Melody's black hair tumbling over her shoulders and her father's beefy hands, Posner heard the voice on the answering machine in his head. 'Too bad for both of us I'm not here. Leave a message or I'll totally hate you forever. Bye.' He'd forgotten to mention it to Mrs. Gold.

Posner heard the rustling of silk behind him, and he turned to face the Papa. 'Morning, Mr. Gold.'

'Good morning, Joe.' Gold approached him, wrapped in a black silk robe with tiny crimson figures embroidered all over it. Under it, he wore dark green satin pajamas with dark blue piping. His slippers were made of well oiled kid-glove leather, etched in Middle Eastern geometric patterns. Gold held his hand out to shake Posner's, but Posner could have sworn it was aimed at his throat. Gold closed the door behind him with his other hand. 'Phyllis tells me you've done a stupendous job. In one day yet!'

Posner accepted the handshake and turned as Gold slid behind his desk. Gold's eyes swelled as they passed over the box, trying not to show notice. 'Sit down.' Gold's face became grave. 'Are you sure Melody was behind these robberies?'

'Yeah I am. Pretty sure, anyway.'

Gold gritted his teeth in anger. 'I told you. It's that goddamn school. This is the last straw. I'm going to have that place closed down, if its the last goddamn thing I do. I want to see that fat slob Coniff out of business. He has no business with little kids. You tell a kid sex is O.K. You tell a kid drugs is O.K. How in the hell do you expect a kid to know that crime isn't O.K.? You've got to teach kids standards. Dontcha?'

'I'm hardly an expert. There's your box.'

'I see,' Gold smiled. 'Amazingly fast work, Joe. Do you have a card? Maybe my agency could use you sometime.'

'I'll send you one. What does your agency do, Mr. Gold?'

'P.R. and advertising. Big stuff. You see us all the time, but you don't know it. Class stuff.'

'You wouldn't handle anything as small as a construction firm or a computer outfit, would you?'

Gold looked puzzled. 'Not unless they were very big. I handle the government of South Africa,' he said proudly, confident that the government of South Africa was very big. 'And, in the little bit of extra time I have, I help with the Universal Foods account.'

'Aren't you also on the Board of the New Jersey Citizens for Better Law Enforcement?'

'Yes, I am, but that's not business, that's my civic duty. How'd you know that, Joe?'

'They send me stuff. It's listed on their letter head. Do you still have that check you wrote me yesterday?'

'Right here.' Gold plucked the check from the drawer and dropped it on the desk in front of Posner. 'You said you'd earn it, and you did.'

'Why don't you open the box?'

'Are the cufflinks still in it?' Gold lifted the lid. 'They're really not . . . ' His face went dead. 'Did Melody do this to Phyllis's picture?'

'I suppose so.'

Gold shook his head sadly. 'Is that what you wanted me to

see?'

'No, actually. I meant for you to open the secret compartment,' Posner said dryly, laying the cufflinks on the desk.

Gold looked at him like he was crazy. 'Secret compartment?'

'Sure. You know. On the bottom.'

'I really don't know what you're talking about,' Gold said pleasantly.

'No?' Posner took the blue list from his jacket pocket. 'Then how'd this get in there?'

'What's that?'

'A list. Of phone numbers and initials.' Posner unfolded the list and held it up in front of him, showing it to Gold. Then he picked up the check and held it next to it. 'I think you'll agree that the handwritings match.'

Gold's eyebrows rose halfway up his forehead in an attempt to look unconcerned. 'Well?'

'Well?'

'Well, what's this supposed to mean, Joe?'

'It's supposed to mean that you killed your own daughter, Mr. Gold.'

'That's not even a little bit funny. I feel foolish even dignifying that crack with an answer, but I was in South Africa when Melody died. Remember?'

Posner ignored the comment. 'You know, Mr. Gold, it's funny how people with similar interests seem to bump into each other in all sorts of situations. Take a couple of guys like you and Senator Bagliano, for instance. Not only do your kids go to the same school and . . . well, see each other, but you're both on the board of the New Jersey Citizens for Better Law Enforcement. And then there was this other coincidence: I saw him on T.V. last night saying they ought to repeal export bans on high tech computers to something he calls friendly authoritarian countries, and I ask myself, who does he mean by that, and I figure: why, he must mean South Africa, right? And then I remember you do public relations for South Africa. Small world, huh? And then, I happened to notice on this list of phone numbers there's one here for Techtronics. They make high tech computers, don't they? And I think they're right in

203

Senator Bagliano's district, too. So, there I am, sitting in my office, and I start to wonder. What if Mr. Gold and Big Tony Bagliano – that's his private number here where it says B.T. – what if Mr. Gold and Big Tony and somebody from Techtronics have been running computer equipment to South Africa in violation of export bans? And what if a smart guy like Mr. Gold realized that that sort of an operation would provide a great mechanism for a little drug trafficking on the side? You know, getting around customs, maybe even a little government help at either end? Just an occasional extra diplomatic pouch, for instance, could come in real handy. It'd be awfully helpful in getting, say, a kilo or two of heroin in every year. Maybe something comes into Cape Town from Hong Kong and back out again to here . . . the details aren't important. The point is, the wheels have already been greased. And a kilo'd be plenty for you and Marty Blittstein and maybe a few other friends to be running into Bergen County and Northern Manhattan. Just a smallish sort of an operation, but a much surer bet than the stock market, and a nice little hedge on inflation. Might interest quite a few fellows. And maybe they could each contribute a little something. Say a doctor at the hospital. I guess Dr. Arons could probably kick in a few thousand pills for the needle-shy crowd. Marty had distribution contacts and retail outlets, like Hawk Brennan. I know that doesn't cover everybody on the list, but I've only had it for a few hours.'

Through it all, Burton Gold seemed to only get calmer. When Posner finally paused, all he said was, 'Is that all, Joe?' Posner was worried. He needed Gold to get angry. To lose control.

'Not by a long shot, Gold,' Posner tried to sneer. 'Cause there was a problem, wasn't there? Your little coke dealing daughter. Oh, yes, like father, like daughter. Only Melody decides to expand her coke operation and move into the local heroin trade. She gets to Marty and wants to buy in. Marty tells you. Of course, this is hardly the kind of business you want your little bundle of sunshine involved in, so you say no way – keeping your identity well concealed, of course. Complication number two: Melody steals the box. Maybe she wants to get at her mother, or maybe replace the one she had hocked some-where, but she gets more than that. She doesn't realize till she opens the box – having found out about the secret compartment from a book at Coniff's – not till then does she realize that you've been using it to hide your list of distributors and partners. My guess is that she must have tried the numbers till Marty Blittstein came up. She probably bluffed Marty some to stampede him into admitting your involvement. So her next step is to confront you. Either you let her in, or she . . . what? Starts calling your partners and scaring them off? Tells her grandfather what you're using the South Africa account for? Or even goes to the cops? Any one of them would have given you big problems.'

'This is getting to be too much,' Gold interrupted. 'I'm losing my patience, and I'm afraid I'm starting to get a little angry . . .' Not enough to suit Joe Posner. He had to hit a nerve.

'Let me finish. You tell Melody that you'll let her in when you get back from South Africa to give yourself some time. When you get back, you call her up – after a few days, that is – and tell her she's in. She should come meet you. She tells her friend that some guy is back from South Africa. That's you. Only her half-wit schoolboy thinks it's South America. He doesn't know the difference. He's been too busy studying Intimacy and Richard Brautigan. Anyway, to hold up her end of the bargain, Melody needs to hand over the list, which she doesn't have, because, while you were away, somebody stole it. Which is why she hires me. Meanwhile, you've arranged to have Melody shipped off to a sanitarium in North Carolina. To keep her out of the way at least till you can figure something out. Maybe even a little electric shock or chemotherapy might help her forget. Who knows.'

'So then you call Marty, who gives you Hawk's number. The two of them come over to help you shoot Melody up with enough junk to put her out of commission till you can get her into the sanitarium, or maybe to help convince the sanitarium people that she's crazy, if they need any more convincing than your checkbook can do. Anyway, you goof. Or, more probably, Hawk goofs, and she gets too much and dies on you. Figuring, as you would, that Les is really to blame for corrupting your daughter, you dump the body at his place – maybe Hawk could have told you that she'd have the key, and that he'd be at a meeting. On the way over, the needle falls out, though, and you have to re-insert it, leaving two punctures. Then, you and Marty decide to get rid of Hawk, since he knows too much, by giving him some junk so pure that it's enough to kill him and the unsuspecting kid he splits it with. After Marty gives him the junk, you go to his place and kill him. The woman at the Leonia Deli said you bought her strudel over an hour before you got home – ten minutes away. Maybe Marty was getting cold feet; maybe he was trying to blackmail you; maybe you just wanted him out of the way cause he knew too much, too. Personally, I don't think you went there planning to kill him, or you would have used something besides the headphone cord. Anyway, it would have been easy for a guy your size. Even though it must have hurt your hands. You did keep rubbing them when you got home, I noticed.'

'Are you finished,' Gold asked, 'or are there more murders I'm responsible for?'

'Not that I know of. But it's not even ten o'clock yet.' Posner was trying to keep his cool, but Gold's steadiness had him unnerved.

'You keep forgetting that I was in South Africa until the day *after* Melody died.'

'Oh, did I leave that out? You see, you weren't, were you? You came in a week early. I checked it out with Teterboro Airport. The Finkel, Finkel, and LeBarron jet came in last week. The same day a Mr. Nolan checked in at the Williamsburg Inn and started calling phone numbers that match the numbers on that list. The one in your handwriting. I'm sure the day clerk could identify you. The man in room 24, which was written in Melody's handwriting in the margin. The same room Melody's car was outside of the night she died. And when Mrs. Gold called South Africa to tell you about Melody, it wouldn't have been hard to have a secretary with a story ready at the other end, and just call back from Fort Lee, saying you were in South Africa. It must have been a regular routine – coming in early, staying at a motel to do your drug business, then showing up "just back from South Africa." Your secretary probably thinks she's covering up an affair, doesn't she?'

'So your wife tells you that I've been snooping around, and you call Big Tony and tell him there's another little problem. And what d'ya know? Big Tony has just the solution. Nothing as dangerous or expensive as a contract for a little shnook like Posner. Uh-uh. Big Tony happens to know that a Mr. Santangelino is going to have a terrible accident that night, and that anyone else in his immediate vicinity will be equally unlucky. So he calls his occasional errand runner, Al B.Lopes, and has me set up. The same Al B.Lopes he hired to find your box when it first got stolen.' Posner heaved a sigh, almost passing out from the exertion of telling the story.

'Are you finished now?' Gold still seemed calm.

'I think so. It's a lot to remember.'

Gold rubbed his eyes briefly. 'I was never accused of smuggling, murder, and heroin trafficking so early in the morning before.' He smiled warmly at Posner. 'I don't really understand what would make you cook up this silly crap and even more why you'd come here to tell me. If you believe this garbage,' Gold's voice started to pick up anger on the word, 'why not go to the police?'

'Well, I was hoping you wouldn't be so cool about it, frankly. I thought you'd be shrieking in terror and rage about now and ready to go to the police with me to confess. But I guess you know as well as I do that I can't actually *prove* enough of this to really interest the police.'

'That's right, you little shitass creep. You haven't got enough on me to lynch a *schvartze* in Mississippi.' As to punctuate his deft analogy, Gold lifted a .38 from behind his desk and pointed it at Posner's face. 'But too bad for you, my little schmendrick, you know enough to seriously fuck up my business activities. It would be a problem, as you put it, a real problem, if you started nosing around the names on that list. And Big Tony wouldn't like it at all. He might even be cross with *me*.'

Posner suddenly came to the realization that he had made a grievous tactical error. All the evidence bore out Gold's assertion that he was, in fact, a schmendrick. He never should have made his final moves after being up all night. He felt like the guy who studies all night for an exam and spends the whole time on the first question. Only this was a lot worse than flunking out. 'Uh, Mr. Gold. I don't think you need to worry about me, really. I only wanted to know just . . . '

'Forget it, Joe. We're gonna get in your car now, and we're gonna drive to your office, and then, we're gonna kill you. Let's go.'

'Uh, Mr. Gold?' Posner pointed out with utmost deference, 'you're still in your pajamas.'

'That's O.K., Joe,' Gold assured him, 'I'll just put on a long overcoat.'

'But Mr. Gold,' Posner insisted, 'your beautiful slippers . . . they'll get ruined.'

'That's O.K., Joe. I can get more. I know the wholesaler. Let's go.'

When Posner has seen similar situations in movies, he had always thought that the prospective murderee should stand his ground and force the prospective murderer to use the undesirable locale for the murder, rather than comply with his plans. Looking down the barrel of Gold's .38, Posner felt differently about it. 'Sure thing. My office. Good idea. Let's go.'

Gold didn't budge. Then Posner remembered. 'I've contacted Sgt. Webster of the police that I'm here. If I don't call him back in about a half an hour, he'll come running.'

Gold wasn't upset by the information, but he was distracted by something. His eyes seemed to be glazing over. Then, briefly, he snapped out of it. 'Call him now,' Gold said distantly, waving the gun at the phone.

Posner didn't understand, but picked up the phone, dialed the police and asked for Webster.

'Tell him anything you want,' Gold said. 'Really.'

'Posner,' Webster answered on the other end, 'How's it going?'

'Not good. Listen, Webster, I've uncovered a lot of stuff that makes this guy Burton Gold here responsible for these murders – Blittstein and Brennan – and drugs – a lot. And, uh, he's sitting here holding a gun on me . . . '

'Posner, don't be such a smuck,' Webster laughed. 'Mr Gold's a good citizen. The best. He wouldn't do anything like that.'

'Webster,' Posner was getting panicky. 'You don't understand. He's got a gun on me, and he says he's going to kill me.'

'Baloney, Posner, No way. Maybe you're gonna have an accident, though. I told you you've been working too hard. It was bound to happen sooner or later. Look, I gotta go. Uh, by the way, I was just kiddin' about telling the lieutenant all that crazy stuff about the Gold girl. Sorry I couldn't help you.' Webster hung up.

Posner looked back at Gold for an explanation, and saw that Gold was even further gone than he was. His eyes stared out into space and his mouth had a strange crook in the corner. 'Sgt. Webster's been handling things for me and Senator Bagliano on this case. Right along,' he explained, absently, almost mechanically.

If Posner hadn't been too scared to think of it, he would have pissed in his pants.

'You see, Joe, you really do have it wrong,' Gold said, not looking at him. 'She was going away with that fat pervert.' His hands were starting to shake now. Thank God, Posner said to himself. A delayed reaction. Gold was starting to lose it. If it hadn't been for the .38, Posner would have thought he had him. 'I say to her 'Honey, this heroin thing isn't for you. Come with me. Tomorrow. We'll go to Martinique together. For a week. Just us, baby.' But she says no. No to me, her dad who loves her. Why? Cause she's going away with him. With Coniff. That fucking lecherous pig who calls himself a principal. You got him!' he shouted suddenly, eyes shining. 'You got him, Joe! You *proved* he was a crook. A pig! So ugly, with those *glasses*. And that *hair*. Feh! Joe! Hah? Feh!' His neck and cheeks twitched a couple of times, and then his voice dropped. 'She says she's coming back in a week, and she wants her junk ready for her, or she starts calling people on the list. Upsetting them. Is that any way for a daughter to talk to her father? And the cursing! The names she called me. Her father . . . I didn't know how she got the list. I asked, of course, but she wouldn't say. It never dawned on me that she could of been involved in the robberies. I really couldn't figure it out. I mean, I knew the box . . . I knew . . . the robbery was . . . Well,' he said in an explanatory tone, with a flourish of his hand, 'it was really Coniff. Wasn't it? Sure. Coniff. But it wasn't the list or the heroin. We could of gotten over that. Her and me. We were close, you know? It was him. I couldn't let him take her away like that. And you know what else? She told me she'd been . . . ' he coughed once, sharply, bringing a gob of phlegm up to his lips, where he let it remain, ' . . . having sex . . . with him. For months. She showed me the key to his place. That's why I wanted her to go to the sanitarium. To help her. She was a sick little girl. To let him touch her? I ask you, Joe. Sick, no? *Sick.* I had to get her help. So I told her to come back later – this was in the afternoon – and I could give her some stuff right away. Then the accident . . . how could . . . my baby . . . Hawk said ⸱. . . the rest . . . the rest was like you said.' Gold was out to breakfast, lunch and dinner. Posner figured he'd have a fifty-fifty chance of getting the gun away from him if he made a lunge for it. The odds weren't good enough. 'Let's go, Joe.'

Posner led the way out of the room. He was ten feet into the living room when he heard a sharp crack and a loud 'ow' from Gold. Posner turned to see Gold on the floor with blood pouring from his head. He had no idea where he was. Mrs. Gold stood above him, holding a bloody silver chalice, ready to hit him again. Apparently, she'd been hiding behind the door.

'I heard the whole fucking thing, you bastard,' she screamed. 'All her life you kept that girl from me. You made her hate me. You made me hate her. Just so you could keep both of us on a string. No wonder she was such a fucking mess. *You* did it. You were never a *real* father. At least the creeps at the fucking school were there for her every day. Not three times a year, like you, you shit. You were never there to say no. Oh, no. That was for mean bitch mommy. Daddy always said yes. Daddy took her away and bought her presents and left mommy to take care of all the *shit*. And I saw you touching her. When she was just a baby. A girl. I saw you, you filth. But I pretended not to.

To you. To myself. But always, everything was you. Everything was *for* you, you goddamn son of a bitch. Sure, you killed her. You couldn't stand for anyone else to have her, so you killed her.

'If it wasn't for you I could have had a daughter. But no. You stole her. You hid her. You couldn't stand for anyone to have anything except you. And she turned out the same way.'

At first, Posner couldn't tell if Burton Gold had taken any of this in. He was losing a good deal of blood and his eyes were unfocused. But the man had staying power. He sneered back at his wife, 'Why shouldn't I touch her? What should I touch, your dried up prune of a pussy? Would you let me, you cunt? You couldn't be a mother any more than you were a woman . . . '

Phyllis Gold was momentarily stunned by this unexpected counter-attack. Then she mumbled softly, 'I'm gonna kill you, you bastard.'

Joe Posner jumped for her arm just a second too late. The chalice came down hard in the middle of Gold's face. When she raised it again, there was no way to tell whose face it had been.

31. These Times

Although Erica, now the Sensuelle American Beauty, was as thoroughly ludicrous as ever, Joe Posner could barely raise a chuckle; and when Erica wasn't funny, 'All My Children' wasn't worth watching. Posner switched off the office twelve-inch and leaned back in his chair. He'd spent the entire two hours since returning from the police station 'tubing out.' The phone had rung three times, but he'd let the machine do the answering.

He leaned over to the machine, rewound the tape, and played it back. The first call was a guy from Allstate that sometimes gave him subpoenas to deliver. That was good news. Even with a nice fee from Phyllis Gold's insurance company – she was likely to be a bit tied up with legal problems for a while – he could use some work. Sure, it was good news. So how come, he wondered, didn't it make him feel anything but sick?

He wondered what would happen to Coniff and Little Tony. Phyllis Gold would not only be busy, but, Posner guessed, appreciably less vindictive, given her new set of circumstances. Insurance companies, however, were uniformly and humorlessly vindictive in all cases. Posner decided to give them the list he'd get from Coniff without any accompanying information, and let the insurance people try to figure it out. That would give Coniff and Tony a better than even chance. The Human Learning Space, though, was unlikely to withstand the shock. People would find out things. Any one part of this whole mishagass ought to be enough to cause a parent stampede. He hoped the place would hold together till June so Judy could get her diploma.

The second message on the machine was from State Senator Anthony Bagliano, Sr.'s office. It was a woman, stating simply and calmly that any unsubstantiated statements made publicly, to the police, or in court, tending to call into question the integrity of Senator Bagliano, would be answered with the harshest civil actions possible under the law. They'd wasted their dime. He hadn't mentioned Bagliano in his statement to the cops. Nobody had to tell Joe Posner that a state senator with mob connections couldn't be busted by a Jewish private investigator with nothing but a telephone list, a conversation with a dead man, overheard by a crazed murderess, and an uncooperative sleazeball detective. All Joe Posner could get out of trying to make trouble for Big Tony was trouble of his own. Trouble that would have made the 'harshest civil actions possible under the law' look like two weeks all expenses paid in Miami Beach. Similarly, he had nothing on Webster that was likely to prove to anybody that he was any more than routinely corrupt – an accusation that could harm only the accuser. Corrupt alternative schools might fold, but corrupt politicians, businessmen, and cops would go on forever.

The third message was from Judy Williams. 'Hi, Joe. Where'd you go last night? What happend with Tony? Wanna come by the deli and tell me about it? Or call me at home. My number is . . . ' Posner switched off the tape and erased it.

He sat, staring blankly for a few minutes, then opened a day-old copy of the *Bergen Record* to the classified. It was time to look for a new line of work. After about ten seconds of looking, he dropped it in the wastepaper basket and went out for a *Times*. A *New York Times*.